# DELUSION

## G. H. Ephron

St. Martin's Minotaur
New York

www.minotaurbooks.com

Library of Congress Cataloging-in-Publication Data

Ephron, G. H.
    Delusion / G. H. Ephron. — 1st ed.
      p. cm.
    ISBN 0-312-30500-1
    1. Zak, Peter (Fictitious character) — Fiction. 2. Forensic psychiatrists — Fiction.
3. Paranoia — Patients — Fiction. 4. Trials (Murder) — Fiction. 5. Boston (Mass.) — Fiction.
I. Title.

PS3555.P49 D45 2002
813'.6 — dc21

                                                                        2002068351

First Edition: October 2002

10  9  8  7  6  5  4  3  2  1

For Sue and Jerry

# Acknowledgments

We would like to thank Trooper Edward Stanley and Sergeant Detective Herbert L. Spellman for their help with police procedure; Christopher Paretti for his computer game wizardry; Kenneth Parker for game industry background; Kit Ehrman, Ray Hearn, and Shelby Peck for sharing their knowledge of surveillance technology; Greg B. for sharing his experiences; Michael Getz and the folks at Illumina Interactive for nurturing our Web site, www.PeterZak.com; writers Connie Biewald, Maggie Bucholt, Kate Flora, Carolyn Heller, Pat Rathbone, Delia Sherman, Sarah Smith, and Donna Tramontozzi, who don't let us cut corners; Bruce Cohen, M.D., Sumi Verma, M.D., and McLean Hospital for their support; our wonderful editor, Kelley Ragland; and as always, our agent, Louise Quayle, whose efforts make things happen. Any errors are solely our own.

# DELUSION

# 1

I WOKE up craving watermelon. My mouth watered for a bite of a brilliant pink slice. I opened my eyes. I was lying on my stomach, my arm hanging off the edge of the bed. For a moment, I wasn't sure where I was. Numbers glowing radioactive green on a digital clock told me it was two in the morning, but my clock didn't have green numbers. Light and shadows danced against a wallpaper of cabbage roses. This was definitely not my bedroom.

The smell of watermelon was still potent in the air, overlaid now by the heady scent of musk, like a ripe Brie. I inhaled, feeling a delicious languorousness as the sweet, sharp smells worked their way up the back of my nose and filled my head.

I closed my eyes and savored the rush of memory. I was at Annie's. My car was at the mechanic's—a busted timing chain was more than I cared to tackle—so Annie had picked me up at work and driven me to her place for dinner. And no, we hadn't eaten any. A pound and a half of prime aged Angus beef was still sitting on Annie's kitchen counter, alongside a bunch of asparagus with half the bottoms snapped off, a loaf of French bread, and an open bottle of a Ridge Zin.

That sweet smell was Annie. The Brie was us. We'd left behind no dirty dishes, just a trail of discarded clothing starting in the kitchen and ending in Annie's bedroom hallway. I wondered if forensics could lift body prints from walls and carpeting, because there would be several to find, marking our slow progress to the bed.

Why it had taken us nearly a year finally to . . . that was another story. My wife, Kate, would have been horrified that it took so long. She wouldn't have wanted me to entomb that side of me in her grave. But I hadn't been ready, and I hadn't been ready, and then I still hadn't been ready. I tell my patients, Listen to your feelings, listen, and do what you're ready to do when you're ready to do it. Grief takes its own good time.

After so long, I'd seriously wondered if everything still worked. It did — sensationally.

I rolled over. Annie was awake in bed beside me, propped up on her elbow staring at me. Around her face, a halo of reddish-brown curls was backlit by a pair of candles flickering on the bedside table behind her. Golden candlelight poured over her hip, dipped to her waist, and then spread up across her upper arm and shoulder. Her smile radiated contentment.

"You up?" she asked.

I reached out and ran my hand gently over her cheek, down her nose, her lips. She sucked on my fingers. I continued down, over the swell of her breast, tracing a line around her nipple. Annie took in a deep breath and arched her back. I pulled her toward me, ran my hands down her back, and cupped her ass.

"Mmm," she said, "you do seem to be."

It was true. I grinned. I guess when you wait that long, you've got a lot of "up" stored in you.

As I held Annie in my arms, the memory of Kate's body came back to me. Softer, smaller. Kate was spices, cinnamon and clove. I remembered how I could tuck her under my arm while we walked, how I took care as I lay on top of her. I'd had to discover what pleased her, coax her out. She liked me to be the one in control. Annie was another story. She was almost as tall as me, sinewy strong, and as greedy for the lovemaking as I was. There was no doubt about what she wanted, and I delighted in making her swoon. The pleasure of giving and getting merged. I wanted more, and then more after that.

Our lips met and what had started out as a leisurely, gentle kiss turned hard and urgent. I slid over on top of Annie and pressed my body into hers. Her skin was smooth, muscles tensed and strong, and I could feel her rising to meet me. She wrapped her long legs high around my waist.

I wanted to touch and taste every inch of her body. I reminded myself that it was only two in the morning. Plenty more night left. I could take my time, and I did.

I was working my way down her smooth belly, pausing to taste her belly button, when there was a chirping from somewhere across the room, like a cricket trying to get out of a pocket.

"Oh, shit," we said in unison. My beeper or Annie's, who knew?

The sound stopped. Annie locked her arms around me and groaned. I buried my face between Annie's breasts and pretended it would go away. But thirty seconds later the beeper started again, as I knew it would. It was hopeless. Even though it was the weekend, I was on call—I was always on call—and they wouldn't be beeping me unless something or someone on the Neuropsychiatric Unit was out of control.

I rolled off one side of the bed, Annie rolled off the other. I fumbled through the trail of clothing, trying to remember where

I'd shed my pants. I found them in the hall and pulled out the beeper. When I pressed the button, the sound stopped. The number on the readout wasn't the unit. Who the hell else would beep me at this hour?

My stomach lurched. Please, God, not my mother. Mom lives in the other side of my two-family house, and she'd been just fine when I'd last seen her early in the evening as she set out for a date.

I stumbled down the hall. Where had I left my jacket? My cell phone was in the pocket.

In the kitchen, I stubbed my toe on one of Annie's boots. "Damn!" I bellowed and hopped across the linoleum. My jacket was there, on the back of a chair. I pulled out my phone and punched in the number as I limped back to the bedroom, giving Annie's boots a wide berth.

On the first ring, the caller picked up. "Ferguson here."

It felt as if someone had turned a knob, and the outlines of objects in Annie's bedroom morphed from fuzzy to sharp. Chip Ferguson was a former public defender, now in private practice, whom I'd helped out on several cases as an expert witness — when he needed a neuropsychologist who could explain to a jury why a witness's memory might be fallible, for example, or how a young girl's addiction to Ritalin might alter her judgment. We weren't working on a case together at the moment, but I knew Chip wouldn't be calling in the middle of the night unless it was a matter of someone's life or death.

"Chip," I mouthed at Annie, who was back in bed, looking spectacular, lying naked among the tangle of sheets. All that was missing were the rose petals . . . and time.

She raised her eyebrows in surprise. It wouldn't have been unusual for Chip to have beeped Annie in the middle of the night. She'd been his investigator when they both worked for the public defender, and now she'd followed him into private practice. But for him to be beeping me was odd.

I said, "Peter here, and this better be damned good."

Annie slipped off the bed and disappeared into the bathroom.

"Peter, sorry to have to wake you, but I need your help," he said. I wanted to scream, *At two in the morning?* "Someone I've known for years just called. Nick Babikian. He sounded very distraught, barely coherent. He asked me to come over."

"What's that got to do with me?"

"I'm worried about this guy," Chip said. "We were in the chess club together in high school."

"Chess club?" It seemed like a tenuous link. I tried to imagine Chip as a chess-playing kid. It wasn't an easy image to square with his daily three-piece suit and tie, or with the Grateful Dead poster hanging on his office door.

"Actually, I met him my sophomore year of high school. I was probably the closest thing he had to a friend. He's not the type who makes friends easily. A very odd guy. Intense. Owns his own business—invented some computer game that made him a mint. Lives in a fancy part of Weston now with his wife and his mother, who's got Alzheimer's. I've helped him out before with legal advice. I don't know what it is this time exactly, but he's distraught. Barely holding himself together."

"You think he's having a breakdown?"

"Peter, I know when I'm over my head, and I'm over my head with this. I thought about getting him to call a crisis hotline or go to the ER, but he'd never trust a stranger. I don't know what he might do, and I sure as hell don't want to do the wrong thing. You deal with people in crisis all the time."

I knew what was coming next. I thought again about watermelon and rose petals. But the sound of the toilet flushing brought me back to the present. Tonight was over.

"Could you meet me there?" Chip asked.

"Sure," I said reluctantly.

"It's in Weston. Just off Route 117 . . ." I found a pencil on the bedside table and tore a piece of paper from a pad in the drawer. He gave me directions, up a winding road, right at a fork. I knew the area. It was chockablock with mansions hidden in the hillsides. "Number 238."

Chip went on talking. Annie came out of the bathroom. Everything about Annie is long. Long limbs. Long neck. And in between, all wonderful curves. In this light, her shoulders and breasts, stomach and legs were luminous, marred only by an angry red blotch on the side of her thigh. I went over to her and touched it gently.

"Rug burn," she whispered with a smile.

I bent and kissed the scrape. I could so easily have kept going.

". . . over there right away . . ." Chip was saying. He stopped. "Peter, are you with me?"

"Sorry, I was distracted for a minute. What was that?"

"I'm going over there right away. How long do you think you'll be?"

That's when I remembered. I didn't have my car. I put my hand over the receiver. "Can you drive me to Weston?" I whispered.

Annie nodded. From her expression, I realized she'd been expecting this. She disappeared into the bathroom again. A moment later the shower went on.

"Should be about a half hour, maybe a bit more," I told Chip.

After I hung up, I sat there. At least there wouldn't be any traffic. Twenty minutes over, an hour max to determine how much help Nick Babikian was going to need, twenty minutes back, and that still left time for me and Annie to pick up where we'd left off.

I was in the kitchen pulling on my pants when Annie's phone rang. Who'd be calling in the middle of the night? Two rings. Three. Annie was still in the shower. I heard her muffled cry, something, and then ". . . get that!" I picked up.

There was wet breathing. "Annie?" The man's voice was slurred. "Is this Annie the Blowjob Queen?" He laughed. "I'm lookin' for a good time, Annie. Says right here, call Annie." In the background I heard music, voices. "You there, honey?"

I wanted to reach through the phone line and strangle the guy. "Who the fuck are you and what do you think you're fuckin' doing?" I barked.

"Huh?"

"Fuck off!" I shouted.

"Hey, easy buddy. No offense!"

"You call again and I'll rip your head off."

"Oooh, you got me scared shitfaced," the man said, crooning at me. The line went dead.

I slammed down the receiver. My stomach had started to knot up. I couldn't stand the thought of anyone slobbering over Annie.

Annie came into the kitchen, zipping up her jeans. I tried to keep my voice calm. "You just got a very disgusting phone call."

"Why'd you answer it?"

"You told me to."

"I said *don't* get it!"

"Well, that's not what I heard."

"Yeah, well," Annie said, buttoning her pale blue cotton work shirt, "I've been getting some crank phone calls lately."

"Lately?" Now that stomach knot had worked its way up into my throat. "Since when?"

"A week. Maybe more." Annie was avoiding eye contact. "It seems like someone's been posting my name and number in bars."

"Did you notify the police?" I asked.

"The police? Are you kidding?" Annie gave me the eye. Her

look softened. "Peter, don't go all protective on me. I'm a big girl."

Annie straightened the baby doll that was tipped back on a chair by the kitchen door, its legs up in the air. The doll was as incongruous with Annie's I-can-take-care-of-myself image as the cabbage-rose wallpaper.

"Some jerk calling you. I don't like it."

"Well, I don't like it, either. I usually take the phone off the hook at night. Last night I got . . . uhhh . . . distracted. I'm sure you know how that is." She gave me a long, lingering kiss. She radiated the smell of warm soap, and her hair was still damp. We stood there, staring at each other. "And I don't want to have to wait a year for the next installment," she said.

"Can you wait two hours?"

"Barely."

"That makes two of us," I said, staring deep into her gray eyes. "You might have to get used to me hovering over you. It's what I do when I care."

"It makes my teeth itch."

"Tough." I glanced at the clock. "We need to get going."

THAT PART of East Somerville at that hour, without the cars, with only the occasional homeless person huddled in a store-front, feels like a stage set. Building flats waiting for film crews to light, for actors to populate. Wooden triple-deckers like Annie's crowding the sidewalk. A pair of mongrels foraged in overturned trash barrels in front of a dingy brick apartment building.

Annie drove her black Jeep like a seasoned cabbie, weaving around the potholes that bloom each spring on the city streets. I related what little Chip had told me. She'd heard the name before. Nick Babikian. "We helped him out about six months ago," she said. "Right after we opened the new office. He had a disgruntled employee. Theft, some vandalism. Bomb threat too, as I recall. It was one of our first cases in private practice. Felt weird, not working defense."

I smiled. Now that they were no longer in the public defender's office, Annie and Chip had bills to pay. They had to be a whole lot more ecumenical about the cases they took.

"What's he like?" I asked, wondering what we'd be walking into.

"I never actually met the guy. Pays his bills on time, that much I know."

Annie stopped at a red light and waited for no one. She revved the engine, her fingers tapping impatiently on the wheel. I was glad I wasn't driving. I'd probably have run the light, delighting the cop skulking in a shadowy alley alongside the corner building.

The light turned green and Annie peeled off, past a warren of garages and body shops. We approached a Dunkin' Donuts across from a plumbing supply with old sinks and toilets on the front lawn. I could smell the coffee. I tried to suppress a groan. I rationalized. Two minutes here versus being alert there. It was a no-brainer.

"Annie . . ." I started.

"All right, all right," Annie muttered, and she pulled in and rolled up to the take-out window. A minute later, we were on our way again and I was burning my tongue on an extra-large, extra-light.

We continued into East Cambridge where the delis turn from Portuguese to Italian, then down into Central Square. A two-block detour and we could have stopped at my house. Instead, we headed for the entrance to the Pike. We couldn't see the river, but I knew it was there. I could almost smell it. Tonight's full moon would be reflecting off the still water. "So when are you going to let me teach you to row?" I asked.

Annie had just taken a sip of her coffee. She sputtered. "Is that what I've gotten myself into?"

"That's only a piece of what you've gotten yourself into," I said and squeezed her thigh. "Besides, you promised. If I tried roller blading, you said you'd—"

"In-line skating," she corrected me.

"Right."

"Which you didn't like."

"Which I *did*," I protested. "Just not enough to want to run right out and repeat the experience. It took a week for my feet to recover." I'd expected my ankles to be sore, but it had been the balls of my feet that felt like someone stuck them with red-hot pokers.

"We'll see. Maybe."

"No maybes."

Annie had turned off onto 128. We continued up an exit and onto the winding road toward Weston. Gradually the landscape changed from industrial to residential to upscale-residential. In Weston, the houses that lined the road were a mishmash of overgrown Victorian relics, fifties ranch homes, and bloated mansions with columned facades. The occasional one-island gas station still pumped full-service gas and had its own gourmet convenience store.

We turned and started up a narrow road. The houses up here were modern, tucked discreetly into the hillside. Annie slowed so I could read the house numbers painted on the mailboxes. She stopped at the end of a driveway that disappeared into woods.

"Why don't you let me out here," I said.

Just then, Chip rolled by. He parked in front of us.

"Shit," I said. Why hadn't it hit me before now? Any idiot seeing us would realize that Annie and I had spent the night together. And Chip wasn't any idiot. "You okay with this?" I asked too late, reaching for Annie's hand.

Chip got out and walked back, his hand shading his eyes from the Jeep's headlights. "Annie?" He knew her car.

"If I wasn't okay with it, I'd have made you call a cab," Annie said. She rolled down her window. She smiled at Chip and shrugged. "Peter's car is at the garage."

I got out. Chip looked from the Jeep to me and back again. He grinned. I could read his thought: *Well, it's about time.*

"Since you're here anyway, Annie, mind hanging around? Just long enough to see what's what," he said. "Frankly, I'm not sure what the story is, but I have a bad feeling about this."

Annie got out.

Gravel crunched as we walked up the driveway and through a pair of open security gates. When we cleared the trees and emerged from the shadows, a low modern home sprawled before us. It had layers of a flat roof, narrow ribbon windows facing the driveway, walls of steel and stucco that stretched out on land surrounded by trees and bushes. There was a two-car garage connected on one side. Every light in the place seemed to be on.

Chip rang the bell. We waited. A breeze rustled the leaves. Not a sound from inside the house. Chip rang again and knocked.

"Maybe he's changed his mind," Chip said. Just then, the peephole in the door went from light to dark. Someone had been looking out at us.

"Nick, it's me, Chip," Chip called out.

The door opened a crack, a chain fastened across the opening. "Who are these people?" rasped a man's low voice.

"I told you I'd be over with a colleague, someone I work with."

"I see two people," the voice said. The door slammed shut.

Annie and I exchanged looks. I didn't need this. I'd have been just as happy to hang a U-turn and head back to Somerville.

Chip leaned on the bell. He shouted, "Nick, you asshole! We're here to help you. These are the people I work with all the time. I trust them. You can trust them too."

"I'm not letting them in," came from behind the door.

"Open up, you idiot!" Chip hollered, exasperated.

The door pulled open again, this time with the chain un-hooked. Nick Babikian stood peering out at us, still not inviting us in. He was about average height, a wiry build. He had on a white polo shirt and jeans. Dark eyes gleamed from beneath the navy blue brim of a Red Sox cap.

"I asked *you* to come. I don't know who these people are and—"

"Mr. Babikian," I said, cutting him off, "I'm Dr. Peter Zak. I'm a psychologist. I've known Chip for ages, as I gather have you. I work with him and Annie Squires, here, all the time. For the life of me, I don't know why, but he must care about you because he dragged us out in the middle of the night."

His eyes were in shadow. I couldn't see his expression to tell if this was making any impact on him. I went on. "We're here to help. We won't say or do anything you don't want us to."

Nick opened his mouth, closed it. Started to turn, hesitated. He was like a wind-up toy that was running down. He looked at Chip.

"You can trust them. Really, you can," Chip said.

Nick slumped, his chin sinking into his chest, and let the door swing open. He followed us into a large open living area, dragging his feet like a sleepwalker. The place had a hard-edged, antiseptic feel to it—white marble floor, white walls, chrome and black leather chairs, and chrome and glass tables.

I stopped and did a 360. The walls were hung with masks. There was a gaudy lacquered Mardi Gras mask—a laughing white face with features outlined in black, red plumes on top. Beside it leered a primitive, distorted human face with one eye partly closed and a wrinkled forehead carved in wood. Nearby, a brilliantly painted red devil mask with white horns and a green tongue grinned. The masks were sensuous and grotesque at the same time.

There were several masks made from bird feathers. On one,

an obsidian-black bird skull and beak formed the nose; glossy black and iridescent feathers shaped the upper part of a face. It reminded me of one of my Rorschach cards.

I scanned the room again. Regardless of their expressions, the masks seemed emotionless. And despite the empty eye sockets, I had the suffocating sense that I was being watched.

I'd already drawn a tentative conclusion from the obvious. Nick Babikian was paranoid. Masks were an odd decorating choice for a man who was suspicious and distrustful to begin with.

Annie and Chip had followed Nick into the kitchen. I joined them. The three of us sat around a white kitchen table. There were dirty dishes on the table, the remains of a meal of scrambled eggs and toast. A late-late dinner or an early-early breakfast? My stomach rumbled and the smell of bacon made my mouth water. Annie and I hadn't eaten. Nick picked up the two dirty plates.

"Leave it," Chip said. "Tell us what happened."

Nick didn't answer. He stared down at his feet. The boat shoes were splattered with reddish-brown spots. I glanced over at Annie. She'd noticed the same thing.

"Your mother," Chip said. "Is your mother all right? Is she here?"

"She was hungry," Nick said. "I gave her breakfast." He gestured at the dishes. "That's how it is with Alzheimer's."

"Where is she now?"

"I took her"—Nick's eyes darted around the room, as if the words for where he'd taken her would appear in the air—"took her to Oakvale House." I knew the place. It was an assisted-living facility. We'd actually passed it on the way here.

"When?" Chip asked.

"They didn't want to admit her, but I had to leave her there."

"When?" Chip said, louder this time.

"I just got back."

I could imagine the scene. Oakvale was a good retirement community, but it was in no way equipped to handle someone with Alzheimer's. Besides, you couldn't leave an elderly parent on the steps of a nursing home in the middle of the night, any more than you could leave a baby on the steps of a church.

"There isn't anyone here who can take care of her now," Nick added.

"What about your wife?" Chip asked. "Where's Lisa?"

"She's . . ." Nick's voice caught in his throat. "Oh, God, she's dead. He killed her."

The three of us exhaled in unison.

"What do you mean *he* killed her?" Chip asked, his voice going flinty.

"I was working. I always work late. Down in the basement. When I came up, there was blood all over. Everywhere. My mother woke up. She came out and started screaming and screaming and screaming."

Chip stood. "Where's Lisa? Are you sure she's dead?"

Nick gave a haggard stare. "Oh, she's dead all right. She's out there." He pointed a shaking finger toward the back of the house.

We followed him through the living room and into a family room. The room was chilly, its double doors thrown open to the back of the house. I barely registered the leather couch and chairs that softened the space, or the masks on these walls too. Alongside a wrought-iron-and-tile coffee table was an area of dried blood on the blond oak floor.

A trail of red tracked across the room, ending at the doors to the outside. There were reddish footprints everywhere.

"Keep back," Annie said. "It's a crime scene."

Heedless of her words, Nick Babikian drifted over to the outside door. He flipped a switch and the patio sprang to light. The lights in the pool came on. Nick groaned, as if someone had punched him in the gut. Even from where I stood, through a thin layer of mist that coated the pool I could see a woman floating facedown in the near end. Her long blond hair spread out around her in water tinged pink.

I felt queasy, the coffee trying to make its way back up my throat. I leaned against a leather chair and focused on breathing, in and out, trying to keep the floor under me and the mask-laden walls from spinning.

Annie hugged the wall, working her way around the trail of blood. She went out, up to the pool's edge. The body rocked gently in the water, head bumping up against the blue tile at the edge. The bare back, buttocks, and legs were pale and perfect.

Nick Babikian seemed mute with shock. What in God's name had gone on here?

Annie crouched, reached out, and touched the woman's neck. Then she stood and shook her head at us. She came back in, returning as carefully as she'd left. She looked somber and shaken.

"We should all go back into the kitchen," she said. "Try not to muck things up for the investigators."

"Investigators?" Nick said, coming alive.

"Nick, we're going to have to call the police," Chip said.

"Police? No way. Not in my house." Suddenly, he'd come wide awake.

Chip went over to him and put his hand on Nick's shoulder. He put his face close to Nick's and spoke quietly and with intensity. "You called me because your wife was dead. You knew I was someone who could advise you. Well, here's my advice. We have to call the police. And it's better if you're here while they're here."

Nick's face fell. He glanced out toward the pool. "Okay,

okay," he muttered. "I hate it, but okay." He trudged back to the kitchen and we all followed. He sank into one of the chairs. "Go ahead. Call them."

There was a phone on the kitchen wall. Annie picked it up and dialed. She talked quietly, giving them the information they needed. Then she came over to me and slipped her hand into mine. I squeezed back, reminded of how I never again wanted to lose someone like I'd lost Kate, like I'd lost my friend Channing Temple.

Nick was slumped at the table, staring into midair. He seemed almost in a trance. In the hours after Kate was killed, I'd been barely able to talk. I reminded myself that numbness was a normal reaction to a world gone crazy.

I crouched alongside Nick, our faces level. I sought eye contact, but instead of windows in, I found only myself reflected back. At some level, I realized this was an opportunity I'd never had before. Within hours of a murder I was talking with someone likely to be accused of the crime, witnessing the scene firsthand. Usually I didn't get brought in until shortly before trial. The police reports and statements I saw were months old, dry and lifeless on the printed page; crime-scene photographs were framed and focused by a police photographer who'd made conscious and unconscious choices about what to include and what to leave out.

My first question: Was Nick anchored in the present? "Do you know where you are?" I asked him, knowing full well that the question sounded inane.

"I'm in my own home, Doctor." The shadow of a smile crossed his face. "It's Saturday"—he glanced at his watch— "make that Sunday. And my wife . . ." His voice broke and his face twisted in anguish. "My wife is in the pool. She's dead." He struggled to regain control. "He killed her."

"Who's he?" I asked.

Nick's eyes had glazed over. He didn't seem to hear the question.

"Who's he?" I asked, louder this time.

Nick's head jerked. "He?" His eyes darted one way, then the other, then narrowed. "He's always here, watching."

"Is he here now?" I asked.

"Here now?" Nick half rose, as if this possibility were just occurring to him. Nick looked at Chip, then Annie, then me. His hands gripped the edge of the table. "I don't know."

A chill went up my spine. Fear and anxiety that potent could be contagious.

Blue lights pulsed against the trees. Nick went over to the window and looked out. Tendons stood out like cords in his neck as watched the cars park. He gave me a quick, wary glance, then looked away.

Chip stood, tugged his suit jacket. "I'd advise you to say nothing while the police are here," he told Nick.

Nick gave Chip a questioning look. "Won't that make them think I did it?"

"Don't worry about what they think," Chip said. "When they say, 'Anything you say can and will be used against you,' they mean it. Trust no one."

"Trust no one," Nick repeated the words. "I don't."

As I watched Nick sit down at the kitchen table and rest his head in his hands, I wondered. A man finds his wife murdered. He cooks breakfast, washes the pan before packing his mother up and driving her to a nursing home. Then he has the presence of mind to call a friend who happens to be a lawyer? Seemed like an odd arrangement of priorities.

# 3

ANNIE WENT out through the garage to greet the police. A few moments later, four uniformed officers and a pair of plainclothes cops were crowding into the kitchen. Chip talked to one of the guys in plain clothes who seemed to be taking charge. He was a large man, probably in his midthirties, thickset, his dark hair cut close to his head.

Chip gestured toward the swimming pool. The officer lifted his head, looked out in that direction, and seemed to go white. He shuddered. His look hardened as his eyes came to rest on Nick. I found it somehow reassuring that even a detective, for whom violent death isn't a novelty, could still be affected.

Then the officer's glance shifted to me. "What in the hell is going on here?" He glared at Chip. "As an attorney, you should know better . . ." he sputtered.

"We had no idea this was a murder scene until we got here," Chip explained. "We called you right away."

"Well, I sure as hell hope you kept your goddamn size elevens the hell out of . . ."

"I've barely moved from this table," I said.

Annie said, "It's okay, Al. As soon as we realized what had happened, we stayed in the kitchen."

"Yeah, well . . ." It was Annie's assurances, not mine, that seemed to calm him down. She had the pedigree, an investigator from a family of cops, even if she usually worked for the defense. He turned to Nick. "Mr. Babikian."

Nick blinked up at him.

"I'm Detective Albert Boley. I met you before. You had a theft at your office? A bomb threat?"

Nick squinted up at him. He didn't make a move to shake the hand offered. Boley pocketed it. "I don't . . . yes, I do. I do remember you."

I'd expected Boley to say something more, but he just hung there watching, waiting, like he was looking for some kind of reaction from Nick. Finally he said, "I'm very sorry about your loss. Can you tell me what happened?"

Nick opened his mouth, then shut it. Glanced at Chip. He mumbled, "My attorney has advised me not to say anything."

Boley sighed and shook his head. "Figures. If that's the way you want it." He drew himself up. "I need all of you to keep out of our way. Understood?" He turned to one of the officers who'd arrived with him. "Keep them in here. We'll want statements from all of them. Schedule them to come down for prints." Boley glared at us. "And no one's to leave until I say so." Then he stalked off.

The officer wrote our names on his clipboard. After that the four of us sat around the kitchen table, waiting. The refrigerator hummed on, then turned off with a thunk. A cat-shaped wall clock wagged its tail and eyeballs back and forth, marking the seconds. It was nearly four and the sky hadn't yet started to brighten.

More police personnel arrived. We stayed put as investigators swarmed through the house and the backyard. It was painstaking the way they worked their way across every surface, collecting evidence in carefully labeled bags, collecting them and removing them from the house in batches. With police officers hovering over us, observing our every move, I wasn't about to engage Nick in any further conversation.

Feeling restless, I got up. I leaned against the counter. This was nothing like my own cluttered kitchen. Neatly stored dishes were visible through glass cabinet doors. The only signs of disarray were the dirty dishes on the table and the single frying pan sitting in the drying rack alongside the sink, probably the one he'd used to cook the eggs.

Other contrasts struck me. The granite countertops and the black tile floor were incongruous alongside blue and white gingham half curtains. On a little corner of the otherwise bare countertop were a half dozen blue-eyed, pink-cheeked ceramic angels frolicking around a cluster of canisters decorated with mushrooms and elves. On the massive, gleaming stainless steel refrigerator were several rows of small snapshots of fifty or sixty newborns, their crumpled faces oblivious to the camera. A name and date were written on each photo's white border.

Above this rogues' gallery was a photo of Nick with a pretty blond woman, probably in her early thirties. They were dressed up, him in a tux, her in a long pale blue gown. She was looking at him, and he was looking away without expression. I stared at the woman who was now floating in her own swimming pool, dead, undoubtedly the same one who'd hung the blue gingham curtains and carefully placed each baby picture in its own magnetized frame.

A doorway from the kitchen led to a laundry room. Clean

wash was folded neatly on the dryer. There was a faint smell of detergent and bleach. A wall calendar hung on the door. The photograph for the month of May was a pair of cocker spaniel puppies, their fur bunched over their eyes, sitting in a field of daffodils.

I went over to it. Notes were carefully written on each day, each week the same. Monday, laundry. Tuesday, grocery shopping. The only items that weren't obviously chores were on Tuesdays at seven and Fridays at four. In the same careful hand was printed: DR. T. A biweekly doctor's appointment?

As the hours passed, Nick seemed to float in and out of consciousness. He could sit for an hour at the kitchen table, slumped over in his chair, his eyes nearly closed under the brim of his cap. Only his occasionally clenched fists gave a hint that, for some of the time at least, he was alert to the strangers upending his home.

From the window, I watched the investigators working in the backyard. The perimeter had been marked off with crime-scene tape. Detective Boley was very much in charge. He seemed to be everywhere at once, directing efforts, acting as if the body floating in the pool didn't exist.

It was nearly ten when an officer finished skimming debris from the surface of the pool and tapping it out onto a piece of plastic. I shivered. Among the leaves and twigs, there seemed to be bits of human tissue. I wanted to look away, but I couldn't.

I'd witnessed two other murder scenes, but each time the loss had been intensely personal. I'd found Kate, her throat slashed in her ceramics studio in our home. I'd found my friend Channing Temple in her office, dead from what looked like a self-inflicted gunshot wound to the head. At those times, I'd felt pure emotion, my vision warped by rage and loss. It was only in retrospect that I had any kind of detached perspective.

This was different—the murdered woman was someone else's

wife, a friend to strangers. Despite the horror of it and the profound sadness I felt in the face of death, in another part of my brain was a disconnected sense of fascination, putting this crime firmly in the third person. I felt like a motorist who can't help slowing down and gawking as medics pull a stranger from a car that's flipped over and smashed up against a highway median.

I watched as a diver lowered himself into the pool, swam out, dove down, and came up a few moments later holding a fireplace poker. He handed it to an officer at the edge of the pool. Meanwhile, an officer with a grappling hook nudged the body up against the edge.

Nick stood beside me watching, gripping the countertop, his knuckles turning white. One of the police officers came in and asked him if he'd go out and identify the body. He went.

As Nick stood by the side of the pool, they pulled the body from the water and rolled her over. He shuddered and looked away. Lisa Babikian's face was covered by a half mask—the white lacquered face made up like a clown. Intestines that trailed in the water were pulled along. She had been cut open, through the sternum and abdomen, like a carcass of meat. I closed my eyes.

Nick was led back into the house. When he returned, his face was wet with tears. Outside, Detective Bolcy knelt beside the body. Maybe it was the blue of the water reflecting off his face, but Boley seemed pale. One of the medics tried to tell him something, but Boley held up a hand to silence him. He bowed his head for a few moments, then seemed to shake himself out of it. He staggered a few steps when he got up, then stood back while they lifted the body onto a gurney and zipped a dark body bag over her.

• • •

It was nearly noon by the time they let us leave, and then only with the promise that Annie and I would each drop by later in the day to give them fingerprints and hair samples. I was exhausted. The fantasy of returning with Annie to pick up where we'd left off had long since faded. At least it was Sunday, and I didn't have to go to the Pearce.

I needed a shower, something to eat, but most of all I needed sleep. I wondered how long it would be before the image of the young woman's butchered body would wash out of my consciousness.

Chip walked us through the laundry room and to the door to the garage. A step farther and he'd have lost sight of Nick sitting at the kitchen table. Chip lowered his voice. He told me he'd talked to Detective Boley. "They think the cause of death is related to a head trauma. Her skull is pretty well dented."

"The fireplace poker?" I whispered.

"Probably."

Head trauma? If a blow to the head was what killed her, then why butcher her and then drown her? I could already imagine the newspaper headlines: Overkill. There would be interviews with so-called experts pontificating on the psychology of it. They'd probably tell the drooling reporter that overkill wasn't unusual in a "thrill killing" where typically two or more killers gang up on a stranger just for the fun of it. More often you saw it in crimes of passion against a loved one. Then, the violence was intimate — strangling and stabbing as opposed to shooting or poisoning — and the perpetrator was often a man driven by a terror of being abandoned.

Chip held his hand over his mouth. "And they found bloody clothing in the bathroom hamper. Nick's. Looks like he changed his clothes and took a shower before he drove his mother to Oakvale."

I turned my back to the kitchen and said quietly, "If he didn't kill his wife, then how the hell did Nick get blood all over his clothing?"

"I have no idea." Chip's voice was weary. "I'm hoping he'll be able to explain." Chip glanced back at Nick. He was sitting at the table, watching us from under the cap brim. He looked quickly away, got up, and opened the refrigerator.

"Weird," Annie whispered. "I wonder why he didn't change his shoes."

"Shoes?" Chip asked.

Nick took a glass out of the cabinet and ran the water at the sink.

"Looks like they're spattered with blood," I said. "Wouldn't you think someone changing his clothes to cover up his involvement in a murder would change his shoes too?"

"Not much of a cover-up if he leaves his bloody shirt hanging halfway out of the laundry basket in the bathroom," Chip added.

Chip went on to say that he expected Nick to be arrested. He'd request bail, of course, but said he'd be surprised if the judge granted it. "The DA is going to want to get the state's shrink in to interview him," Chip said. "I've already told Nick not to talk to anybody unless I say so. I hope you'll have time to get in there and evaluate him right away."

"Whoa, hold your horses," I said. It came out louder than I'd intended. I was glad that Nick had the water running as he rinsed out the glass.

Were there some crimes so horrific that they rendered the standard arguments for mitigating circumstances—insanity, diminished capacity—irrelevant? And when had we slipped from being concerned friends and friends of a friend to being Nick's attorney and support team? There were plenty of things I could see doing with my time other than defending a man who'd butchered his wife.

"I'm not so sure you're going to want my help on this case.

There're lots of other folks out there who, for the right amount, will do whatever you want them to do and testify accordingly."

Chip did a double take. His eyes widened. "Peter . . ." he started.

I realized that hadn't come out the way I'd intended. "I'm sorry. That sounded like I was questioning your ethics, and I don't. But you can't just assume that I'm going to jump in and help. And I'm not so sure you're going to *want* my help on this case. I've got very strong biases about men who kill women and what should happen to them. You might even say it's a blind spot."

"Peter, we don't know *who* did it. And besides, you always call them the way you see them. This time won't be any different."

"You may not like what I have to say."

"You make your findings. I decide whether to use them."

I glanced back into the kitchen. Nick was slumped at the table again, the brim of his cap shadowing his face. Was this really different from any of the other murder cases where I'd defended an accused? Probably not. But with my nose rubbed in the reality of it, I was finding myself forced to face my own competing impulses. Admit it, I told myself, I was repelled and fascinated at the same time.

Chip rushed on. "Can you do a preliminary evaluation right away? Once he's charged and in custody?"

I gave a mute nod.

Chip returned to the house, and Annie and I walked back to the Jeep. I put my arm around her, as much to reassure myself that she was there as to show her that I cared.

As we neared the end of the driveway, I could see neighbors huddled on the street in tight groups. They gave us the once-over.

A Channel 12 News camera team had floodlights set up in

the street. A perfectly coiffed blonde smiled at the camera and read from notes clutched in her hand. The story would be tomorrow's lead. Most people would hear about it and be shocked by the barbarity of the crime. They'd assume the husband did it. That was usually the case.

I opened the door of the Jeep and reached in for the Dunkin' Donuts cup that was sitting on the dash, opened it, and dumped the cold coffee on the ground.

"Hey, you!" someone yelled. When I looked up, a flashbulb popped in my face.

Annie and I quickly ducked into the car.

"Asshole," Annie muttered. "Jerk. Didn't even ask permission." She had her key out and was trying to jam it into the starter. "Damn. Stupid. Asshole."

I put my hand on her arm. "House key," I said.

"House key?" She stared at me. Then she looked down at the key that was never going to fit into the ignition. "Oh."

She switched keys. The engine started up with a roar. Quickly Annie eased up on the gas pedal. Clearly she wasn't as inured to violent death as she seemed to be.

Annie turned the car around and we headed home.

As we cruised along the main road, I thought about the Babikian home. Physical evidence isn't my thing. I look at behavior, state of mind, not bloody smears across the floor. But what struck me were the contrasts. The fresh smell of laundry detergent against the slightly sour smell that wafted in from the pool. The restrained monochromatic walls, glass and chrome furnishings in the living room with its menacing masks, against a cozy kitchen with its puppy dog calendar, frolicking cherubim, and gallery of newborns. Tabletops with nothing on them—no unopened mail, no piles of newspapers, no magazines or books. No disarray at all. Everything in complete control, chaos squelched. And against that, an excessive crime: a woman bashed in the head, butchered, and drowned—any one of which would have killed her.

I knew someone had mentioned it, but at that moment, I couldn't for the life of me remember the young woman's name. Suddenly, that seemed very important.

"Lisa." Nick Babikian could barely say his wife's name.

Nick sat hunched over the battered table in the examining room of the Middlesex County Jail. Hours after I left the Babikian home, he'd been arrested. They'd been holding him now for two days.

In the unforgiving fluorescent light, his skin looked green against the orange of his baggy prison scrubs. Otherwise, he seemed much the same. Still wired, still suspicious, Nick kept his eyes on me from beneath bushy eyebrows and a tangle of black curly hair. The air vibrated with anxiety.

"She was twenty-six when we met," he said. Six words. This was the richest response he'd given me in the hour since I'd started the evaluation.

For at least the fifth time since he'd come into the bare, windowless cubicle, Nick glanced furtively about. He twisted around and checked the wall and floor behind him. Then he turned back. As he shifted in his seat, the chains from leg irons dragged on the floor.

I'd started off, as I always did with someone I evaluated, by telling him that I was there to help the team prepare his defense. I was reminded, once again, of the unique relationship between forensic psychologist and prisoner. My time is limited and my goals quite specific: to find exculpatory evidence. Typically, defendants are highly motivated to give me what they *think* I want, which often has its own problems.

But Nick seemed oblivious to that script. I'd begun with a mental status exam, hoping to ease his way into answering with the relatively innocuous questions. But even these encountered resistance. From the way he crossed his arms and avoided eye contact, to his terse responses, the message was clear: He didn't trust. I needed him to lower his defenses enough to get our conversation to flow before I took him back through the crime.

As I'd expected, Nick knew exactly where he was and why. He didn't seem suicidal. He also admitted that he didn't feel safe. Under the circumstances, that could be considered normal. There were no frank hallucinations or delusions.

I began to probe his relationship with his wife. "You had a happy marriage?"

"I loved my wife," Nick said. He focused on the oatmeal-colored Formica tabletop. "We had our occasional problems."

"Anything in particular?"

"Like what?"

"You said you were having problems."

"You know, problems. Everybody has problems."

"Sure. I know everyone has problems. How bad were yours?" It felt like pulling teeth.

"We saw someone, couple of times," he said, still evading the question.

"A marriage counselor?" I asked. Nick nodded. "What did you talk to her about?"

"Not her. Him." Nick swallowed and stared off into space. "Do I have to talk about it? Why don't you ask him?"

"May I? I'd like very much to do that," I said.

I wouldn't have been surprised if he'd balked when I took him up on the offer, but he didn't. He said, "Dr. Richard Tei-tlebaum. He's in Newton." The name sounded vaguely familiar. I wondered if this was the DR. T on their kitchen calendar.

I turned to a fresh sheet of paper and quickly wrote a paragraph that would release Dr. Teitlebaum to talk to me, and vice versa. I pivoted it and handed Nick the pen.

"What's this?"

"He'll need to see that you've given him your permission to talk to me."

He read what I'd written, turned the page over and inspected the back. Then he gave me a guarded look and drew a diagonal line across the blank side—ensuring, I suppose, that I couldn't add anything. He turned it back over and signed.

"You ever see anyone else to talk to?" I asked. "On your own?"

"A shrink?" Nick shook his head. "I only went to Teitlebaum because it was important to Lisa."

"And you tried to do the things that your wife wanted you to?"

Nick picked at a curling corner of the Formica top until a little piece broke off. "I loved my wife."

The room had turned stuffy. I took off my jacket and hung it over the back of my chair. Nick's glance fell to my belt. He leaped up, the chair crashing over behind him. "What the hell is that? You're taping this!" He was staring bug-eyed at the pager the guard had given me.

"Whoa, time-out," I said, unhooking the gadget. "It's a panic button, that's all. They give it to visitors whenever they go one-on-one with violent offenders." I held it out to him.

At first Nick reared back as if the thing might be about to explode. Gingerly, he took it and examined it, turning it over. Apparently satisfied, he handed it back to me. Then he righted his chair and eased back in it. "They make security cameras that look a lot like that. Tiny little things with pinhole lenses. I've got them all over my house." It was the longest, unbroken thought I'd gotten out of him. "What I don't get is why the hell the police haven't looked at the security video and arrested the murderer."

I remembered the stark interior of his home. Where could you hide surveillance cameras?

He seemed to read my thoughts. "You didn't see the cameras, did you?" Nick smiled. "What the hell good would that do? They're in the masks."

Now I understood why someone who was paranoid would choose to hang masks on his walls. With video cameras hidden in empty eyeholes, he'd feel like the watcher, not the one being watched. His own vigilance could be extended through an arsenal of pinhole lenses.

"Maybe the police don't realize . . ."

"They know," he said coldly. "Boley does. I had a break-in at my business six months ago. He got the guy because I caught him on camera."

"Boley?"

"That detective. Something about him . . ." Nick shook his head.

"Something what?"

"I don't know. The way he was looking at me. Felt like he knew something that he wasn't letting on."

Nick would probably have attributed dark motives to any cop investigating the case, but there had been something odd about Boley. For one thing, here was a homicide detective who dealt with violent death every week. I wouldn't have expected him to have been so shaken by the crime.

"Why didn't you mention the video cameras when you were arrested?"

For a moment, Nick seemed baffled, as if he were trying to remember: Had he been arrested?

"Did you tell Chip?"

"I . . ." he started. "Honestly, I don't remember."

"I'll pass the information along," I said. I made a note. It wasn't all that surprising. In a crisis, people have lapses about all kinds of basic things. When we'd rushed my father to the hospital after his final heart attack, my mother couldn't remember their home phone number or the name of their insurance company. But she could rattle off the list of the half dozen medications Dad was allergic to.

I said, "Whenever I evaluate someone, I try to get as complete a picture as I can. Maybe you can tell me about yourself. What was it like growing up?" Most people like the opportunity to talk about themselves, and open-ended questions like this one usually get them going. I never knew exactly where it would lead.

Nick did a slow blink, as if he were trying to read between my words and find the hidden intent.

"Sometimes the past helps us to understand the present," I said, trying to reassure him and reaching for an offhand tone. "So what were you like as a kid?"

He stared down at the table, his gaze sliding from there to the floor.

"Look," I said, leaning forward, "if you want me to help you, you're going to have to do what I ask you to do, even though you may not see the point."

For the first time, he gave me a long direct look. I could see him weighing the pros and cons. Then he started. "I grew up in Watertown. Lived with my parents, my grandparents. We owned a bakery on Mt. Auburn Street." I knew the area. It was known for Middle Eastern grocery stores and bakeries that specialized in *lamejun* pizzas and baklava. "My grandparents worked in the bakery. My parents worked in the bakery. I came home and worked in the bakery. That's all I did—I went to school and worked in the bakery."

I was encouraged. Nick was loosening up, no longer spending each word like a precious coin. I waited, hoping he'd keep going. But he didn't.

"You mean you didn't hang out with other kids?"

"Huh? I didn't have time for other kids. And my mother—well, my grandmother actually—was paranoid about letting me out of her sight. From the minute school ended until I got to the bakery, she'd be hanging out the door, waiting for me to get there." He shook his finger, hunched his back, and with a thick accent he muttered, "Terrible things can happen out there!"

"Sounds like she was pretty protective."

"She earned it," he said. "You know about the holocaust?"

"Of course . . ." I started.

"Not 'of course.' I'm talking about the *Armenian* holocaust." His look dared me to confess that I was pitifully ignorant, which I was.

"Not as much as I should."

"At least you admit it. Everyone tiptoes around the Jews, builds memorials. Know what Hitler said before he invaded Poland, as he was telling his high command that it was okay to kill the Jews? 'Who today remembers the Armenian genocide?' That was in 1939, just fifteen years after the Turks annihilated three million people." With a bitter laugh, he went on. "But never mind all that. These days, the Turks are our allies. Israel's allies. The world chooses to get selective amnesia. Of course, Americans could care less. They don't know the difference between a Czech and a Slovak, never mind between an Armenian and an Azeri. Jews, they get." He glared at me. "But not Armenians." He stared down at his hands, clasped together on the table, his fingers pulsing. "My grandmother remembered."

"She was a survivor?" I asked.

"I supposed you could say that," he said, giving me a sideways look. "She lived through it. But she never got past it. Her memories were as vivid as . . ." His voice trailed off. "She told me the stories of how she survived."

"What kind of stories?"

"She'd recite them to me. How they hid. How their neighbors informed on them. How the Turks came to their house." His eyes had glazed over. "How they took her mother . . ." There was a burst of static on the prison's loudspeaker system. Nick shook himself. "She lost her father, her mother, her sister, two brothers. Plus aunts, uncles, cousins. But she had memories."

"You learned about this when you were a kid?"

"My parents never used to talk about it. Not at dinner. Not in church. It was like it never happened. As if all those relatives, all those people never existed. But my grandmother told me, when it was just us. Over and over."

We sat in the quiet for a few moments. I imagined Nick replaying the tapes his grandmother couldn't help replaying over and over and that she'd now bequeathed to him. It began to explain his own paranoia, his distrust of authority, of people in general. I filed the information and moved on.

"Tell me about high school," I said.

"BC High," he said. I must have looked surprised, because he added, "Scholarship. They didn't know quite what to do with me, an Eastern Orthodox kid in the bastion of Catholicism."

"How was it?"

"That's when I realized my grandmother was right. They *were* out to get me. I'd get beaten up all the time. This one kid . . ." Nick shook his head at the memory. "Bastard." He gave me an appraising look. "Your friend Chip. He was my only friend. He was the only kid who wasn't a Turk. He fought the other kids when they beat on me. I never forgot."

"And college?"

"Harvard."

Nick told me his years at Harvard were better. The students ignored him in his quiet separateness. From chess, he got turned on to computer games—first playing them all the time, then creating his own. He'd gotten a part-time job, programming for one of the hot technology companies near MIT. Later, he rented an office and started Cyclops Productions, then more space as his business prospered.

Becoming animated for the first time, Nick told me about *Running Scared*, the first computer game he invented that hit it big time. He took my pad and drew quickly, first strong outlines, then shading with the side of the pencil. He turned the pad and thrust it at me.

The figure looked like an elf, small with well-articulated muscles in his arms and legs. Huge eyes gleamed from under a hood. "Tell me about this guy," I said as I examined the drawing. The creature reminded me of Nick when I'd first met him, his eyes peering out from under the baseball cap.

"He's the Seer. He watches," Nick said. "Players have to learn when to trust him. Sometimes he misleads them. But other times, he holds the key."

I made a note to myself to find out more about Nick's games. I checked my watch. Only twenty minutes before I had to head back to the Pearce. Nick had gradually opened up, his responses less guarded. It was now or never. "I need to ask you about your wife," I said.

Nick tensed and shrank away, like I'd poked at a sensitive spot. I knew these kinds of questions could be a form of torture.

I hated it when well-meaning people asked me about Kate. But this was different. It was my job to ask.

"Your wife worked?"

"Mostly she stayed home. Took care of my mother. Alzheimer's." His voice was a monotone and his body had stiffened, as if his back were broken and the least amount of movement would topple him over.

"Your wife didn't mind doing that?"

Nick shrugged. "She's a nurse," he said, as if that explained it.

We were back to terse responses. "Mmm," I said, taking a note. "Where had she worked as a nurse?"

"Brigham and Women's," he said. "Delivering babies." His jaw clenched and unclenched. "But she didn't want that for herself."

"Want what?"

"Children. We agreed when we got married." He blinked and looked away, holding back tears.

I was surprised by this intimate bit of information, which I hadn't really asked for.

"You were working late Saturday night?"

He nodded. "Like I do most nights, in my basement office. I work best at night. Must've been around one when I came upstairs." Nick stopped, staring into the space between us, like he was walking through this in his head. "I went into the family room to check that the back door was locked."

"What happened?"

"The lights were off."

"Um-hmm."

"I wouldn't have known anything was wrong except that I tripped over something. I fell, and the floor"—Nick closed his eyes and grimaced at the memory—"was wet." He rubbed his palms on his pant legs. "Sticky. I got up and turned on the light.

"First thing I see, blood on my hands, on the wall, on the light switch. There's a floor lamp, knocked over. That's what I tripped over." He quickened his story, rushing to the end. "Next thing I know, I'm outside, washing my hands in the pool water. Lisa is floating in the deep end. I know she's dead."

He stopped as if he'd come to the edge of a cliff and run out of words. I turned over his words in my mind. *Next thing I know . . .* I wondered if he might have slipped into some kind of a dissociative state, temporarily not there. In the kitchen afterward, he had seemed to drift in and out of awareness.

"Do you remember going outside?" I asked, trying to probe.

He sat still, thinking. "No. I remember turning on the light. Next thing I remember, I'm outside."

"What happened after that?"

"My mother. She was standing on the deck, crying. Then babbling. Then she's wailing like a banshee. 'The Turks! The devils are coming,' she's screaming. Exactly what my grandmother used to say all the time."

"You didn't call the police?"

"I was going to. But my mother was screaming and then . . . then . . . I had to find somewhere safe for her to stay. Right away." Nick paused. "She had to eat something. God knows when she was going to get something to eat."

"So you scrambled some eggs?"

Nick nodded. "And while I was washing up, I realized I had blood all over my shirt, my pants. I put mother's favorite video on and took a shower. All I could think was, I had to make sure my mother was safe."

It sounded as if he'd been confused, distracted. In shock. It explained why the frying pan had been washed but the plates and silverware hadn't been. It began to explain the shower, and why he'd changed his clothes but not his shoes.

I'd heard of cases where a killer enters a dissociative, trance-like state after the murder. A Los Angeles man killed his wife and children, then boarded a bus for San Francisco. He was picked up by the police at the San Francisco bus station, still wearing his bloody clothing. I supposed a similar thing could happen to a distraught husband upon discovering his wife's butchered body.

"Do you think it's possible that your mother might have witnessed the murder?" I asked.

Nick swallowed. "Oh, God," he murmured. "It never occurred to me." I found that hard to believe.

With advanced Alzheimer's, even if Mrs. Babikian were able to express herself, it would probably be impossible to interpret her convoluted thoughts, to disentangle her inner world from whatever memories she had of real events. There was no telling what she might say, if and when the police questioned her.

"The police will probably try to interview her," I said. "They may even have already done so."

"Police? They won't get near her," Nick said. "She hates cops. Always has. Anyone in uniform." His look turned worried. "It would upset her very much if they tried."

I didn't see any way of reassuring him. His mother was a potential witness to a murder. The police would have to do their jobs. I said, "I haven't discussed this with Chip yet, but I think it would be a good idea for me to talk to her. It's in your best interest to know what she says."

"I don't want you upsetting her," he said.

"I'll do my best. But she may have seen or heard something. Or thought she did."

Nick gave me an stricken look. "You think I'm trying to cover up."

The door to the room opened and the guard came in. I watched as he shackled Nick's hands. No, I thought. Someone trying to cover up doesn't leave his bloody shirt hanging from the bathroom hamper, and doesn't put bloody shoes back on after he takes a shower. Still, if he were innocent, then as vigilant, perhaps even paranoid as Nick seemed to be, why had he initially assumed that the killer was no longer in the house?

THAT EVENING, I met Chip and Annie at the Inman Lounge. The place had recently had a makeover, like a lot of dives in that neighborhood. The smell of stale beer was just beginning to grow back.

Chip was waiting for me at a table in the back. I sat and ordered a Bass. Chip passed me the newspaper. The Babikian murder was front page, with what looked like high school yearbook pictures of Nick and Lisa. Lisa had been a pretty teenager with long blond hair and a shy smile. I wouldn't have recognized Nick. He wore a suit jacket and tie, and his hair was slicked down. He didn't smile at the camera but he didn't look overly sullen, and he sported a shadowy mustache.

I scanned the story. Even I was shocked by the graphic detail. The media really gets off on mutilation. I noticed there was no mention of the white mask Lisa Babikian had on when they pulled her from the pool. I wondered if that information had been withheld.

I turned to the continuation of the story. There was a picture of me and Annie by Annie's Jeep at the murder scene, along with a sidebar about the defense team. I winced as I read the lead. "Is forensic psychologist Peter Zak revisiting his own wife's tragic murder?" I closed the paper and wondered, not for the first time, if journalists ever think about the effect of their words. And for what? To titillate a public with an appetite for barbarity.

My beer arrived. Annie emerged from the shadowy back of the bar. She stopped and talked to the bartender. Showed him a piece of paper. He shook his head.

"Goddamnit!" she exploded when she reached the table. "This"—she threw the hot pink paper onto the table—"was in the men's room."

Chip and I looked up at her and chimed in unison, "The men's room?"

"I've been having a little problem," she said. The words came out staccato, and her face was tense. "Phone calls. Someone's been sticking these things up in bars, mostly in the men's rooms."

The flyer was an invitation to anyone looking for a good time to call "Annie." There was a graphic description of what was meant by a good time, and then Annie's phone number. Worst of all, there was a picture of Annie looking like a biker's moll in dark glasses, her leather bomber jacket, and jeans.

That explained the crank phone call I'd picked up at her house.

Annie glared at the paper. "Damn. I found these plastered in the men's rooms in two bars in Central Square too."

"Sounds like you pissed someone off good," Chip said. "Have you called the police?"

"That's what I told her," I said. Annie glared at me. "Annie, maybe you should go in and talk to someone."

"Really. It's just a nuisance." Annie crumpled the piece of paper and jammed it into her pocket.

Chip and I exchanged a look. "Sounds like more than a nuisance," Chip said.

"Don't worry about it," she snapped. She must have seen my face and realized I was going to have a hard time doing that. "All right, all right. If it'll make you happy, I'll talk to Mac."

Why couldn't she have just called 911? As recently as a few months ago, Annie and Detective Sergeant Joseph MacRae had been dating. I wasn't sure if he was still a contender or back to being an old friend.

"It'll make *me* happy," Chip said, who was extremely adept at reading silences. "There're all kinds of lunatics out there. At least this one's giving you fair warning."

Annie sat and picked up her beer.

"One of us could go with you," I said.

Annie sipped her beer and looked away. Vulnerability. As she would have said, it made her teeth itch.

Chip sighed. "Peter, how'd your meeting with Nick Babikian go?"

I told them about the two hours I'd spent with Nick, summarizing Nick's version of the murder. "His actions do make a weird kind of sense," I said. "A traumatic shock and the world careens out of control. It's not unusual for people to fixate on something like feeding the dog or watering the plants, just to show themselves that they're in control."

I remembered my mother vacuuming the house for days after my father died. Never mind my own habit of working on my car whenever I woke up at four in the morning and couldn't sleep because I knew my wife's killer would be waiting to taunt me in my dreams.

I went on. "In Nick's case, he fixates on getting his mother breakfast and then tucking her in somewhere safe. Says he doesn't remember going outside."

"Doesn't remember?" Chip asked.

"Sounds awfully convenient," Annie said. "I'm sure the DA will make sure the jurors notice that he was with it enough that the first thing he did was call a lawyer."

"It's unusual for someone with a paranoid personality to zone out like that," I said. "If anything, he'd be the opposite — hyper-vigilant and focused, focused, focused. I think it's more likely that it only seemed to him that one minute he was in the family room, the next he was out at the pool. In reality, he just focused on other things to put off feeling the pain."

I went on. "He's given me permission to talk to the psychiatrist they saw for couples therapy."

"Couples therapy?" Annie said, incredulous. "He hardly seems the type."

I agreed. Nick had said he'd done it for Lisa. I wondered what incentive or threat had been potent enough to drag a paranoid into couples therapy.

"Did Nick tell you about the security cameras he's got all over the house?" I asked.

"Security cameras?" Chip asked, sounding more annoyed than surprised. "I knew he had them at the company, but I had no idea — " This wasn't the kind of thing he wanted to be finding out from me.

"He says the house is full of them. And there's a room in the basement where computers collect the data. Says he's got a similar setup at his company, and the police knew about it. He gave them video footage that helped them catch a burglar awhile back."

Annie said, "I'll see what I can find out. I'm pretty sure they didn't find a surveillance setup."

"One other thing. His mother," I said. "Nick has given permission for me to talk to her."

"I got her admitted to Westbrook Farms," Chip said.

I knew the place. It was one of the best-run residential eldercare facilities in the area, and they had a special unit for Alzheimer's. "You were lucky to get a room on such short notice," I said.

"With cash up front, it's amazing how doors open," Chip said. "I'll set things up. What's your take on Nick so far?"

I knocked back the last of my beer and thought about the insular life Nick Babikian had maintained. His life was work and family in a world populated by sinister strangers. "He thinks everyone is out to get him."

"Paranoid." Chip sounded pleased. At least it might be a line of defense.

There were plenty of diagnoses that involved paranoia. Paranoid personality. Or paranoid tendencies. If Chip was going to argue that Nick *didn't* kill his wife, then one of those diagnoses could make his odd actions after finding his wife's body plausible to a jury. If Chip was going to argue that Nick *did* kill his wife but there were mitigating circumstances, then a diagnosis of paranoid delusions was better, and Nick's preoccupation with the Armenian holocaust was promising. But was that a core issue for Nick, so much so he saw the world about him as hostile, and all of his actions were based on the delusion that he was the "Armenian" in a world of "Turks"? Or had he simply taken the tale as metaphor: Yeah, the world's a tough place and you have to watch out for yourself. At this point, I didn't know.

What I did know was that Nick was some flavor of paranoid and definitely smart. It was a combination that could be lethal.

Annie and I lingered at the bar, ate a couple of greasy burgers and fat french fries. Reluctantly we went our separate ways. We both had work the next day.

· · ·

When I got home, it was after eleven. I unlocked my front door and turned off the porch light. Just then, my mother's door opened and she poked her head out. "Petey? That you?" I hate it when she calls me that. She peered out into the dark.

"Pizza delivery," I said.

She flipped the porch light back on and looked out anxiously, like she was afraid there was an incendiary pizza lurking in the shadows. She was holding a baseball bat, the one she keeps in the umbrella stand. I'd hit a home run with it to end the final game of the season in Prospect Park when I was eleven years old.

"Just kidding," I said.

"Don't make jokes." My mother was in her pink quilted bathrobe. Wispy white curls escaped from the scarf she had wrapped around her head and knotted over her forehead. She set down the bat. "If I wanted to not laugh, I could be watching Johnny Carson."

"Johnny's retired."

"My son," she muttered to no one in particular, "thinks I was born yesterday." Then after a pause, "Have a nice evening?"

I knew that wasn't what she'd come out here to ask about, and she'd long ago stopped waiting up for me. "You saw the paper?" I asked.

Even before Kate was murdered by a man I'd helped defend, my mother wasn't thrilled with the idea that I work with accused killers. "Mitzvah, schmitzvah," she'd say when I tried to explain why I considered it a good deed — most people who get accused of crimes are poor schnooks, in the wrong place at the wrong time, who rarely get an adequate defense.

"It would be nice if you occasionally told me these things, so

I wouldn't have to hear from Minnie Sadowsky what my son is doing."

I didn't like where this was going. Minnie Sadowsky was my mother's friend, and her son was a neurosurgeon who'd given his mother the ultimate in one-upmanship: grandchildren.

"You alone?" she asked, squinting into the shadows at the edge of the porch.

"Nothing up this sleeve." I held up an arm.

"Always the comedian." She started to close her door, then stopped. "What kind of a man cuts up his wife like that?" she asked. She pursed her lips, like she'd taken a whiff of sour milk.

"We don't know for sure that he did," I said.

"Be careful," she said and closed her door.

I went inside. The *Boston Globe* was on my kitchen counter where I'd left it unopened. I turned to the articles about the murder that I'd skimmed at the bar. I reread the news story. Then I started on a three-column feature article: "For Lisa Babikian, Dream Turned Deadly."

It was one of those sicky-sweet pieces that turn victims into saints. There were interviews with Lisa's family, her childhood friends and neighbors, colleagues from the hospital. "She had such a cute way, a funny way of looking at things," it quoted a nurse who had worked with her.

Even at the storybook wedding, after a courtship in which Nick had swept her off her feet, one of her bridesmaids claimed she knew something was amiss. "She looked great. But when I hugged her, it was like there was nobody there." Amazing how prescient friends become after the fact.

They all recalled Lisa becoming more reclusive after her marriage. She no longer had her hair done or her nails sculpted, stopped wearing fashionable clothes. One friend had been shocked by the message on their answering machine. It was Nick's voice: "I can't talk to you right now . . ." As if he were the only one in the house that mattered, she said. The article told how Nick kept the bank records, stock purchases, their car, all in his name only. And on it went.

A quote from Lisa's mother ended the article. "We hope she is remembered as someone who was as beautiful on the inside as she was on the outside."

I put down the paper, took off my glasses, and rubbed the bridge of my nose. Newspapers managed to reduce the most horrendous of tragedies to cliché.

I was exhausted but not ready for sleep. The bottle of wine on the counter had only a thimbleful left in it. I went down to the basement and got a fresh bottle and brought it up. I wiped away the dust and uncorked it. A Ravenswood Zin. It had been Kate's favorite.

I poured a glass and carried it and the newspaper into the living room. I sat in my cushioned morris chair and sank back. Surely the brothers Stickley, who'd popularized these simple, wood-framed chairs with adjustable backs, had been tall. This was one of the few chairs in the universe that are perfect for me. My mother won't sit in it. Her feet dangle in midair.

I swirled the wine in the glass, inhaled, and took a sip. I closed my eyes. The smell of currants, leather, and earth seemed to fill my brain.

I wished Annie had come home with me and we'd both said to hell with work. I could call her, but it was already pretty late. Months ago, when I was home alone, late like this, I'd go out and work on my old BMW. It occupied my mind. But I'd banged out all the fenders that needed banging, painted and buffed all the rough spots.

Kate and I used to sit up late at night like this. She'd be lying on the sofa opposite me reading, her legs drawn up under a crocheted afghan. Even the afghan was gone now. I'd taken it to the cleaners and forgotten to pick it up.

I picked up my glass and stood. I climbed two flights and pushed open the door to Kate's ceramics studio. The large, high-ceilinged room with windows around three sides was dark. But it was easy to see the outlines of the pots on shelves spanning the windows. I put my wine down on Kate's workbench and made my way around the perimeter. I could tell by feel which ones were Kate's, and which pots were made by the Arts-and-Crafts masters we collected. Kate's were smooth, like polished glass, incised with bold designs. I was glad Annie liked them too. The first time I'd brought her up here, she'd run her hands over the pots, as if she knew that feel was as important as appearance.

A tile was leaning on the window frame. I took it down. I'd forgotten it was there. It was a glazed tile Kate's mother had saved. On it was a handprint, Kate's hand from when she was in kindergarten. I felt the imprint, traced the thumb, then each finger. Even then, Kate's hands had been strong, the fingers stubby. I remembered how the pads on her fingers were always callused. I could still feel their roughness as she stroked my chest.

I got my wine and sat on the small settee that Kate kept off in a corner but that I'd moved to the center of the room. I took a sip and leaned back. Annie was becoming more a part of my life. But it calmed me, gave me my center, knowing Kate was still here.

I CALLED Dr. Teitlebaum the next morning and left a message.
He called back a minute later. He sounded surprised when he
heard Nick had given him permission to talk to me. The guy
seemed pretty freaked. Who wouldn't be, picking up the morning paper to discover one of your patients murdered and another
one arrested for the crime? He wanted me to come over and
talk with him right away. I told him I had a day full of appointments and meetings.

It wasn't until after six that I left the Pearce and headed over
there. Shrink City, otherwise known as West Newton Hill, was
a twenty-minute drive from Cambridge. But it might as well
have been another planet. The suburban blocks were crowded
with oversized Victorian homes fenced off from one another.
Front porches with wicker furniture and swings welcomed
neighbors and friends, while signs from security companies conveyed the equally clear message to outsiders: Keep out.

Dr. Teitlebaum's house was yellow clapboard and white trim,

with a wraparound porch and a corner turret. I drove up the driveway and followed a discreet PARKING sign to a paved area. A silver Volvo was parked by the open garage.

There were lights on at the front and at the office entrance on the side. A pair of rhododendron plants, their roots balled in burlap, leaned against the house next to a pitchfork and a shovel. The earth had been turned over in a three-foot border on either side of the entrance. Two tall yews were already planted at either end. I stepped over the trail of dirt that ran across the driveway.

Green rubber gardening shoes with whitish treads stood by the door. I was impressed. Not too many homeowners in this neck of the woods did their own yard work. I'd never planted a bush in my life, never wanted to. Kate had been the bush planter, though with a bit of bribery she did manage to get me out in the fall to rake.

The door opened before I could ring the bell. When I extended my hand to shake his, he reeled me inside and slammed the door. "Sorry," he said, peering out through the window. "I keep expecting to find reporters camped out."

"But they haven't mentioned you in the media."

"Just a matter of time," he said, his mouth set in a grim line. "You can be sure of that."

I don't know what I expected—maybe someone balding, rotund, and fiftyish. Teitlebaum was none of the above. He was maybe forty, tall and lean. He had dark curly hair and startling blue eyes. He looked pale and tired, as if he hadn't slept, and his jaw was covered with light stubble. He gave off an odor of salty sweat and overworn gym socks. I'd come to recognize it as the distinctive scent of anxiety.

From the salmon-colored cashmere sweater and the cordovan tasseled loafers, I'd have expected smooth hands, maybe even a manicure. But the hand I shook was rough and callused, the stiff arm keeping me at a distance.

Despite the unusual circumstances, we did the usual do-you-know-so-and-so dance. He knew quite a few of my colleagues at the Pearce—he had gone to Brown Medical School and then did a residency at the Pearce before moving back to Rhode Island. Turned out he'd even been to my house—came with mutual friends to a New Year's Day party Kate and I threw eight years earlier.

He ushered me into his office and I waited while he photocopied Nick's release. It was a comfortable room with photographs of sailing yachts, a fainting couch with an oriental remnant protecting the foot end and a napkin-covered pillow at the head end. An impressive array of diplomas and awards lined the wall behind the desk. A nearly floor-to-ceiling mahogany bookcase spanned one wall of the office. On its shelves were all the classics in his field, from Freud to Kohut. The meeting program for next week's American Psychiatric Association meeting in DC was on his desk. It would give him a good excuse to get out of town and let any media attention die down.

He put the photocopy into a manila file folder already on his desk, gave me back the original, and then settled into a generous leather-cushioned chair. He pushed aside the matching ottoman and sat forward, his arms resting on his thighs. His eyes were bright, and I had the impression that he had his hands clasped together to keep them still. "What in God's name happened?" he asked.

I took the leather sling-back chair opposite him. "If you read the papers"—Teitlebaum nodded—"then you know pretty much what there is to know. You were surprised?"

He waited a beat before answering, his face somber. "You don't have to be a psychiatrist to know that husbands kill wives."

I'd once heard a colleague present a paper at a meeting on just that topic. The numbers were so overwhelming, they'd stuck in my mind. She said as much as seventy percent of the women killed in the United States each year died at the hands of a man who was or had been an intimate partner. A piddling five percent of men killed were done in by wives, ex-wives, or girlfriends.

He went on. "No one can predict who's going to go over the edge." He bit his lip. "I've been wrong before."

It was one of the hardest things about working with troubled individuals. Anyone who tells you he can predict which ones are going to go berserk has his head up his ass.

"Have the police contacted you?" I asked.

"Not yet. They will. I'm sure they will. They like you to twist in the wind first."

The intensity of his tone suggested firsthand experience. His answers were a beat off, as if something turbulent going on inside his head were competing for attention.

"You were counseling Nick and Lisa Babikian?" I asked.

"I knew I should have referred them to someone else."

I waited for him to explain. He swallowed. "I moved to this area a little over a year ago." I wondered why the move, but he rushed on before I could ask. "It was hard to leave the practice I'd been building for years." A vein pulsed in his forehead. "I admit it, I needed the business. So when this couple comes in, no referring doc, they give a false name neither one of them can remember from the beginning to the end of the session, I tell myself: No big deal." He grunted a laugh. "He pays cash. Wouldn't that tell you something? Looked under the desk, ran his hand across all the books. Checked that out"—Teitlebaum indicated a mirror set into one wall—"like he thought it was one-way glass. Wasn't until the third session that I found out their real names. And that was by mistake. She spilled it. I should've said forget about it."

"When did they start seeing you?"

"Back in the fall." Teitlebaum reached for the file folder and paged through it. "October fourth. Lisa, Mrs. Babikian had quit her job to take care of Mr. Babikian's mother. She was having a hard time making the adjustment. She chafed—that would be a mild way of putting it. He's a very controlling man, but that doesn't seem to have bothered her as long as she had the outlet of work and friends.

"When she quit her job, it bothered her. The more unhappy she became, the more he withdrew. Spent more and more time working. They were having problems with intimacy as well. It made him uncomfortable, having sexual relations with his wife while his mother was in the house. And she was always there. He was effectively impotent. He could do it only when they both wore masks. Creeped her out."

Teitlebaum tossed off this bit of information as if it were of no great significance. It gave me one more piece to explain why, as paranoid as Nick was, he willingly surrounded himself with masks. Once the masks became intertwined with the sex act, having them on the wall would be a reminder that *he* was in control.

I wondered how many other people knew about this particular kink in Lisa and Nick Babikian's life together. The killer must have known that putting a mask on Lisa's body would implicate Nick.

"Usually that's a sure sign of stress and disorganization," Teitlebaum went on. "Ritualization of what should be a pleasurable act. He fetishized it by adding accoutrements in order to engage." Teitlebaum's face had gone neutral. The language of psychiatry had a wonderful way of leaching emotion.

He glanced through the file, pausing to read some of the entries.

"He was breaking down?" I asked.

"The marriage was breaking down."

"Did you feel they made any progress?"

He thought about that. "A little. He agreed to enroll his mother in a day center a few mornings a week so Lisa could work part-time. She was going to start out by helping at his company while she looked for something at the hospital. It was a start."

"But overall, sounds like you weren't too optimistic."

"No," he said flatly. "Mr. Babikian has an overwhelming need to control. It was clear to me that he was driving the pathology for the couple. Lisa Babikian, on the other hand, was compliant, moldable. Of course, that's why he married her."

"Pathology?"

"Under that controlled facade, he was doing a slow burn. I thought that his paranoia bordered on the delusional. He believed he could control everything in his life, and for the most part, he could. His mother's dementia was upsetting to him. And then his wife's unhappiness added to his feeling that his life was getting out of control. Of course, the more unhappy she got, the more he tightened the reins, the more unhappy she got—you know the cycle."

"Did he ever act out his anger?" I'd slipped into psychiatric-speak too. I could as easily have asked: Did he beat his wife?

"Not as far as I was aware." It was a hedge.

I must have looked surprised. People who kill their wives usually work their way up to it. Bruises and broken bones along with a broken spirit lay the groundwork for the final act.

"It wouldn't have surprised me. He didn't trust her. At one point, he even accused her of having an affair with me." Teitlebaum stared at his case notes. "No physical abuse." He grunted and shook his head. "That's what I kept telling myself. That's probably why I took the case. But that doesn't mean he didn't scare the shit out of me. Of course, I recommended individual therapy to him. And medication. I wanted to put him on something to calm him down, help him control his anxiety. He'd have none of it. He was more afraid of losing control than he was of losing his wife."

"Were you aware of Mr. Babikian experiencing any fuguelike episodes?" I asked.

Teitlebaum looked skeptical.

"There seems to be a period of time he can't recall on the night of the murder," I explained.

"He's not trying to convince you that he's got some kind of dissociative identity disorder, is he?"

From his tone, I could tell he thought this highly unlikely. I agreed. Multiple personality had been quite the vogue back in the seventies, but in reality it was extremely rare.

Teitlebaum rubbed his chin. "On the other hand, if it did happen, he'd be the kind of guy who'd have trouble admitting to any loss of control."

"How long did they continue to come to you?" I asked.

"Maybe a half dozen"—Teitlebaum paged through the file—"no, seven sessions. Then they just stopped."

The folder looked a lot thicker than notes from seven sessions warranted. I waited. He blinked back at me.

"Lisa Babikian continued seeing you?"

Teitlebaum's eyebrows went up a micron.

"Her kitchen calendar. She's got appointments with 'Dr. T' written on it."

He stared at the file. We both knew he was walking a line. With Nick's permission, he was free to tell me about what had happened in the couples therapy. But that didn't extend to his one-on-one treatment of Lisa. Doctor-patient privilege survives death.

"She called a couple of months after they stopped coming as a couple. Wanted to come alone."

"Sounds like you were surprised."

He didn't answer.

"Look, I run the Neuropsych Unit at the Pearce," I told him. "I'm well aware of the stress that taking care of a person with dementia can cause both to a relationship and to an individual."

Teitlebaum seemed to come to terms with his conscience. "No. I wasn't surprised. She'd started somatizing. Headaches, chronic colds, insomnia. Her husband had become even more distant, withholding. The more upset she got, the more he tightened the screws.

"The only thing that surprised me was that he *let* her come." He looked me in the eye. "I'm even more surprised that he signed a release allowing me to talk to you. He didn't trust me." He closed his eyes and rubbed the back of his neck. "On the other hand, he's a guy who covers his bases."

Teitlebaum kept rubbing the back of his neck. I had the impression he was deciding what to do next.

"Let me show you something," he said. He put the file on the desk and opened the top drawer and rummaged through it. If the contents of a man's desk mirror his own consciousness, then Teitlebaum had an exceptionally orderly mind. Little plastic boxes corralled his paper clips and rubber bands, his calculator was placed into the drawer so it fit perfectly alongside a checkbook and a stack of zip disks.

"Where the hell," he muttered. "I know I put it somewhere." He pulled open the next equally tidy drawer, reached his hand in back, and felt around. He drew out a small, black, rectangular object and handed it to me. It was made of metal and heavier than it looked. On one side was bolted a faceplate with a sort of bull's-eye with a hole in the center. It was attached to a small metal stand.

Nick's words came back to me. *They've got security cameras the size of a quarter these days.* "Surveillance camera?" I asked.

"How'd you know?"

"Just a guess. Where'd you find it?"

He paused. I wondered if he was about to cross that invisible line again. "When Lisa called me, she was frantic. They'd just had a break-in at the office, and she found out that her husband had security cameras all over the place, tiny ones, like this. She'd had no idea."

He went on. "She's actually the one who spotted this thing. It was up there"—he indicated the top of the bookcase—"and it may have been there awhile."

I stared at a spot on the top shelf where Nick Babikian might have tucked the little black box alongside the vase, or perhaps between the books. I felt the shadow of the profound sense of violation that Teitlebaum must have felt when he realized he was being watched. The privacy of the therapy room is nearly sacred, and here it had been deliberately and systematically profaned.

"It had a pack of about a dozen batteries wired to it. Apparently, he had gizmos like this all over the place at his company, hardwired into the electrical system. That's one of the things that pushed Lisa over the edge. She found out he could watch her while she worked. He could watch everyone. With those surveillance cameras, he went a step too far. At first she was frightened. Then angry. And from that anger she drew strength."

He took the little camera from me and dropped it back in the drawer.

"Did she know he had surveillance cameras all over their home as well?" I asked.

He didn't seem surprised. "That's really sick. Well, I don't need to tell *you* that."

"Did you see any changes in Lisa Babikian before her murder?" I asked.

"The changes were all for the good," Teitlebaum said, kneading his hands together. "When I first saw them together, she was pale, listless. Her clothes hung on her. She was the kind of person you looked right through. Over the last few months, she'd become much less transparent. She wore pinks, bright blues, much less of the olive drab. She was taking care of herself, wearing a little makeup. Wearing her hair down. She might even have gained some weight.

"Of course that was just a reflection of what was going on inside. When she married him, she'd shut herself down. But she wasn't going to any longer. I encouraged her, of course. She was trying to disentangle her identity from his, to become fully her own person. It was heroic.

"For him to cut her down, just when . . ." His voice broke. "Just when . . ." He shuddered and sat back. "I should have protected her." His voice turned derisive. "I was a fool. It was pure hubris on my part. I wanted to save her. She came to me, and I failed her."

*I wanted to save her.* His words jumped out at me. Here was emotion more intense than the kind of countertransference I would have expected from a relationship that had lasted six months, even if he had been seeing her twice a week. It made me wonder. It had been awfully easy for Teitlebaum to skate over the border of patient-therapist confidentiality. Why not skate over the intimacy boundary as well? Or was Nick Babikian's paranoia rubbing off on me?

Despite the sympathy I felt for Teitlebaum, for his apparently sincere concern and anguish over what had happened, I pulled away. I wanted to come right out and ask, *Were you having an affair with your patient?*

Instead I asked, "Did you think she was going to leave her husband?"

"She didn't say so," he said, looking away. It felt like an evasion.

"Did you think she was having an affair?" I asked, pressing the point.

The look he gave me said I'd crossed the line. "I can't answer that," he said and closed up. This line of questioning had come to a dead end, but why? He'd readily violated other boundaries.

"She liked nursing?" I asked, moving to safer ground.

He answered this readily. "Loved it. The first time I saw her get truly animated about anything was when she talked about delivering babies."

I remembered the rows of just-born snapshots on Lisa Babikian's refrigerator. "And yet they had no children of their own?"

"*His* choice."

"Nick says Lisa didn't want children either."

He gave me a look that said, *and you swallowed that?* "She went along with it. Just like she went along with pretty much whatever he wanted. She was afraid to argue, to express herself."

"You think Nick Babikian was capable of killing his wife?" I asked.

Teitlebaum's face collapsed. "God help me." He stared down at his clenched fists. "His progressive preoccupation with his wife's whereabouts, the loosening links between his thoughts and reality—I didn't admit it to myself, but I knew."

THE NEXT day was a gorgeous New England spring day, a blip between the freeze-dry of winter and the hot-steam of summer. If you blinked, you'd miss it.

The grass on the rolling grounds of the Pearce Psychiatric Institute was threadbare. The road through was still gritty with sand as it wound past the brick buildings, some with Dutch gables, others with ornate French flourishes, still others encrusted with Victorian gingerbread. Even back at the turn of the century, design must have been by committee. A splash of red and yellow tulips at the back of the Neuropsychiatric Unit was a reassuring sign that months of drear had indeed ended.

I let myself in and hurried down the hall past our conference room. No one was there yet. I had time to pour myself coffee and check my mail.

My colleague and best friend, Dr. Kwan Liu, was blocking the entrance to the tiny room behind the nurses' station. Gloria Alspag, the nurse who really runs the place, was inside peering at a clipping someone had tacked up on the bulletin board. I should have expected it. Someone, probably Kwan, had pinned up the article and picture of me from the newspaper.

As she read, Gloria pulled a few dead leaves from Audrey, the philodendron she'd nurtured from a sprout. It had wound its way around the bulletin board and was reaching for the window.

Gloria was one of those people who look unimposing—not too tall, glasses, short straight hair that she's always running her fingers through but never tossing. But unimposing she was not. She had the persistence of a terrier and the power of a pit bull.

"Good morning," I said.

"Great picture," Kwan said. It was *his* cologne that was competing with the coffee smell in the small space. Gloria wasn't a perfume person. "Especially if what you were striving for is the Johnny Cochrane, just-rolled-out-of-bed look."

The rumpled look was anathema to Kwan. He had a standing appointment to get his dark hair trimmed every two weeks, and the cut of his three-piece suit was impeccable.

"You do look a bit scruffy," Gloria said, standing on tiptoe. "Probably hadn't had time for coffee. No, wait, look there." She pointed to the Dunkin' Donuts cup I was holding in the photograph. "It's our Peter."

"Give me a break," I said. "And clear the way. I haven't had my morning quota."

Gloria squinted at me and stepped aside. "You sure you're ready for this?"

I poured myself some coffee and kept my head down. I should have been grateful. Gloria was worried about my getting involved in another murder. But instead I felt a flicker of annoyance. I had a mother who did that. I didn't need it from friends.

I checked my watch. "Shouldn't we get going?"

As we walked down the corridor, I asked Kwan, "You ever heard of a psychiatrist, Dr. Richard Teitlebaum?"

"I can't say the name rings a bell. Why?"

"This case I'm working on. He was the victim's therapist. I'm just curious to know if he's got any kind of a reputation, one way or another. He did his residency here about eight years ago. Then moved to Rhode Island. Moved back about a year ago."

"Richard Teitlebaum," Kwan said, turning over the name.

"Sounds like he's well connected." I mentioned a few of the doctors at the Pearce that Teitlebaum said he knew.

"I'll ask around," Kwan offered.

By the time we got to the conference room for rounds, the others were waiting. Our social worker, physical therapist, and lead mental health worker were at the table. A young psych postdoc, Roger Burnaby, was sitting in a chair against the wall, writing in a notebook. He looked up and nodded when we arrived. Then he pulled his chair up to the table.

The tall, narrow room, with its glorious but now defunct marble fireplace, was looking a bit spiffier than usual. The holes in the plaster had been repaired, and the formerly pink walls were now a tasteful eggshell. It had been only a month or so since the hospital's chief financial officer had departed rather than face an investigation of his personal financial ties to pharmaceutical companies. The place was becoming more humane with him gone. One thing hadn't changed. Spring or no spring, the all-or-nothing heating system was going full-blast.

Kwan went over to open the window. He pulled and strained, but it wouldn't budge. Apparently it was painted shut. "Move over, Schwarzenegger," I said.

I took a crack at it with no results beyond a spasm in my lower back.

"Men," Gloria snorted as she sized up the problem. She systematically whacked the window frame all the way around with the heel of her hand, gave a yank on each of the window ropes, blew into each of her open palms, and effortlessly raised the window.

"I guess it takes brains *and* beauty," Kwan said.

"Finesse," Gloria said as she took a little bow. "Always works better than brute force." The message wasn't lost on either of us: Women do heavy lifting better than men. I didn't disagree.

We turned our attention to the white board and the list of eighteen patients we had on the unit. There was only one new admission. Elizabeth Smetz.

Kwan said, "She thinks she's the Virgin Mary, and she's here to give birth to the Messiah."

Gloria took up the tale. "She was trying to build a manger in her garage, screaming at her husband that the innkeeper wouldn't give them a room. Mr. Smetz was frantic. Brought her in to the emergency room at the Carney. They shipped her to us."

I took the file from the rack and opened it. "Seventy-five years old." I scanned the admitting report. "No psych history," I said, noting that she'd never been treated for mental illness.

"Gradual decline?" Kwan asked. That's what you'd expect if it were dementia.

"Not that I can see." I offered him the file.

He flipped through it. "Odd, the sudden onset. The admitting doc put her on an antipsychotic, Zyprexa. That may make a difference. Has it?" He looked to Gloria.

"No. She's driving staff crazy—asking where the manger is. She's not redirectable or cooperative."

Roger, the postdoc, spoke up. "We just sent off her labs."

"An intriguing puzzle," Kwan said.

After the meeting, we visited Mrs. Smetz during walk-rounds. She was a stout woman with a plain face the color of a burlap bag. Her hair was dyed red. We found her pacing up and back in her room, leading with her right shoulder and muttering to herself.

"Mrs. Smetz?" I said as we entered the room. "I'm Dr. . . . ."

She lurched to a halt. Her face lit up. "At last!" She clasped her hands together. "The wise men are here. And one of you is a woman!" She beamed at Gloria. "How delightful."

I went along. "We're here to see how you're doing." She smiled at me. "I hope it's all right if I ask you a few questions."

"But you're the ones who have all the answers," she said.

"Even the wise can learn. You're not at the inn?" I asked.

"No. I'm in a hospital." That was unexpected.

"Do you know why?"

"The innkeeper won't give us a room. So we had to come here. My husband . . ." She glanced about the room, momentarily confused. "Oh, yes, he went to get me some apple juice." She lowered her voice, "You mustn't tell him"—she patted her stomach—"about this."

A tired-looking older man in a blue plaid shirt and a zippered jacket came into the room carrying a paper cup. He smelled faintly of tobacco. "Joseph!" Mrs. Smetz said.

He handed her the cup and gave us a weary look. "Bill," he told us. "My name's Bill Smetz. Been married fifty-three years, and all of a sudden she can't remember my name." He harrumphed. "Thinks she's Mary, mother of God." He seemed to be making light of it, but his eyes told another story as he searched us for an explanation, looking for words that could make it all go away.

I explained that we were there to give his wife a mental status exam, and that he could stay if he wanted. He took a seat. I invited our postdoc to take over.

Roger began by talking to her informally, putting her at ease. That was good. A mental status exam needn't feel like an interrogation. Then he asked her if she knew the date.

"May"—she thought for a moment—"eleventh." Close enough. It was actually the twelfth. Then she gave the correct year.

He asked her to repeat numbers. She had no problem. Then words and phrases. Again, no difficulty. She was able to spell words forward and backward. And she remembered three items after five minutes. Attention, concentration, immediate and short-term memory—all seemed unimpaired.

When he got to, "Do you feel safe here?" a guarded look dropped over her face. She gave an anxious glance toward her husband. "Oh, no," she said. "The innkeeper doesn't like us, and the soldiers are looking for us."

"Mrs. Smetz . . ." Roger began.

"You can call me Mary," she said.

"Mary?" Roger looked at me.

Mrs. Smetz scratched her forearm.

Roger said, "You're in a hospital. We're doctors and nurses who will be helping you get well."

The information did nothing to ruffle her surface calm. "Of course, my dear. But you know," she lowered her voice and confided, "being with child is perfectly normal."

When we were out in the hallway, Roger said, "She seems so lucid. Knows the date, where she is. Then she goes down the rabbit hole. Wouldn't it be possible to talk her out of it, to sort of reeducate her?"

"You could try," I said.

"Until the cows come home," Kwan added. "She's delusional."

"Generally speaking," I said, "delusions are immune to reality. We could show her on her own birth certificate that her name isn't Mary. And she might humor us. But she'd come up with an explanation. All the logical arguments you can make won't yield anything, because the delusional logic makes complete sense to her. And furthermore, the truth of the delusion is *felt*, it's not just cerebral. That's its power."

"Not quite the same thing as hallucinations, then, is it?" Roger asked.

"Not at all the same," Kwan said. "With hallucinations you can often appeal to a person's observing sense of self. In essence you sometimes *can* talk them out of it."

"With delusions, there is no observing sense of self," I added. "For example, you see it in someone who's anorexic. No amount of logic can convince that person that she's already bone thin. Or someone who's paranoid—you can't make the fear go away by pointing out that it's irrational."

Building a manger was relatively innocuous. What worried us were the potentially destructive behaviors that made complete sense to a delusional mind. Anorexics could starve themselves to death. And paranoids could become hermits, their fear and anger building until they exploded, like the Unabomber.

"But why is this happening to Mrs. Smetz," Kwan said, "and why now? No history of mental illness. No prior symptoms. Normal neuro exam so no stroke. All of a sudden, bam, she wakes up Mary, mother of God. For now, all we can do is keep an eye on her and continue with the Zyprexa."

• • •

That afternoon, Annie beeped me while I was working with a patient.

"Why is it so hard to talk men into doing the logical thing?" she asked when I finally got back to her.

"Me?" I asked. "I'm easy. And for you? Anything."

"I know *you* will," Annie said. "I'm talking about Al Boley, the detective in charge of the Babikian case. I don't know about that guy. I told him about the video surveillance setup, and it was like he didn't want to know. Said they already had all the evidence they needed. I felt like reminding him that it wasn't his job to find enough evidence to incriminate the obvious suspect, his job was to find *all* the evidence there was to find."

"I'm sure you were very persuasive."

"I pointed out that maybe—just maybe—what was on the security video could poke holes in his airtight case."

"And?"

"He still didn't want to hear about it. Told me he *knows* who did it."

"But he went back anyway?"

"Went back. Found the cameras. Found the basement office. Receivers are down there, and it all feeds into a computer."

"So why was Boley surprised? I thought Nick had a break-in earlier, and the police identified the guy from the video surveillance tape."

"Wouldn't be tape. High-tech stuff. Some kind of electronic media. And that break-in was at Cyclops Productions. Boley claims that without a blueprint of the house, you wouldn't know the basement office was there. That's why they missed it. Only one problem."

"What's that?"

"The data's gone."

"Gone?"

"Gone-gone," Annie said. "The hard drive's been removed."

"What does Chip say?"

" 'Shit.' "

I couldn't have put it better myself. "Is it possible that Nick removed the hard drive himself?"

"I'm sure that's what the DA will argue," Annie said. "If it counts for anything, Chip thought Nick was completely stunned when he heard about the missing hard drive. Took a while before he could even say anything." There was a pause. Then Annie said what I'd been thinking. "Sure does narrow the field.

If it wasn't Nick, it had to be someone who knew about the setup. Have you reached the shrink?"

You could get whiplash talking to Annie, the way she veered from one subject to another. Or maybe there was a connection.

"I talked to him last night," I told her. "He did know about the surveillance setup. Says Nick even tried to bug his office. He showed me a little video camera. Lisa Babikian spotted it."

"What did you think of him?"

What did I think of Dr. Richard Teitlebaum? "I feel for him. He seems broken. Maybe it's losing this particular patient in this particular way. Or maybe there's more to it than that."

THERE WERE a couple of messages waiting for me when I got home that night. Annie had called to say she'd be working late and would catch up with me tomorrow. I played her message a second time, just to listen to her voice.

Chip had called, too, to let me know that Nick Babikian had been arraigned. They'd transferred him to Bridgewater State Hospital for a twenty-day evaluation. He'd instructed Nick to continue to refuse to talk to the state's psychiatrist until I'd finished with him.

In typical Chip fashion, he just assumed that I'd go beyond the preliminary evaluation I'd agreed to do. Atypical for me, I didn't even think twice about it. I'd gone beyond curious. Was Nick Babikian a psychopath, or did he have a conscience? Would he abandon his need to control, even in a crisis, and enter a dissociative state? I reminded myself not to underestimate him. After all, he'd bugged his own psychiatrist's office, presumably breaking in without leaving a trace.

Between patients, meetings, my regular duties on the unit, and a promised weekend drive to Brooklyn to visit relatives with my mother, I didn't get to Bridgewater until the following Tuesday.

That morning, I took out my rolling suitcase. I packed it with the test materials I needed. The IQ and the memory tests were standard. Then I pulled out the Thematic Apperception Test—the TAT. There were about forty cards depicting scenes, each one pulling for a different theme. I'd be asking Nick to tell me the story that each picture told. The images on the cards are like searchlights, and personalities cast distinct shadows.

I flipped through. The one with the schoolgirl in the meadow would be an innocuous one to begin with. I clipped together a few others that I thought would be useful in getting at what I wanted to tease out.

It was overcast when I left the Pearce. I was heading south on 128 when the skies opened up in a downpour. I slowed the car and turned the defrost up to a roar.

By the time I turned off the highway, the rain had stopped and the sky was clearing. There was the small sign for the turnoff for the prison hospital. Then, it's about a half mile down a rural road until you're dumped out onto a huge field of asphalt. Bleak, multistory concrete prisons stand surrounded by steel fencing topped with razor wire. I drove to the low single-story hospital for the criminally insane. I parked the car and got out. I pulled the suitcase out of the trunk.

Anyone seeing me might have thought I was getting ready to check into a hotel for the weekend. But this was the last place I'd want to spend a day, never mind a weekend. Last time I'd come here, it had been to interview Stuart Jackson, a man accused of shooting his ex-wife in the head and killing her boyfriend. I remembered how hard it had been for me even to get out of the car. I'd sat in the parking lot, my heart pounding, reliving the interview I'd had here with Ralston Bridges, the man who would pay me back for suggesting he was insane by murdering my wife.

Today I pulled out the suitcase handle and started across the parking lot. I glanced over at the barred windows that punctuated the hospital facade. I knew that behind them, inmates were probably watching me approach. I imagined Bridges—whose fair hair, sleepy blue eyes, and soft features could convince a jury that he wasn't a killer—staring down at me. I told myself Bridges was locked up in the maximum security of Cedar Junction, more than ten miles away, but still I wanted to turn around and head home. Squinting into the sun, I felt like the yellow bull's-eye at the center of a target.

Was it ever going to be easy and automatic, the way it had once been, to drive to this place, haul my ass out of the car, and walk into the hospital thinking only about the present, what I had to do, and where I'd be going next?

I pressed the buzzer at the gate and looked at the video camera. "Dr. Peter Zak, here to evaluate Nick Babikian." The gate clicked open and I passed into a small holding pen. The gate behind me closed and the lock clanged shut. I waited. I knew I was being checked out. That was the routine.

The door buzzed and clicked. I pushed it open. I stepped across a threshold into a barren lobby, a room with cinderblock walls painted yellow. It was furnished with about a half dozen folding chairs and pay phones. Along the far wall was a large tinted window. The shadows of two figures hovered on the other side. They could see me, but I couldn't see them. This business of nearly one-way glass gave every visitor a clear message: We're in control and you're not.

I approached the window and waved my letter of authorization and driver's license. A steel drawer slid out from beneath the window. I put the documents in and the drawer closed.

A few minutes later, a stout officer whose cap seemed a bit small for his round head pushed open a door alongside the window and ushered me into a small room. This room also had a tinted window bordering the guards' station.

I knew the drill. I put my suitcase on the table in the corner, stood back, and relaxed. This could take awhile, depending on how bored the guard was that day. This one took everything out and then went through every sheet of paper. When he got to the TAT cards, he flipped through them and gave me a look like I was some kind of pervert. Then he removed the paper clip and held it up as if he'd discovered a concealed weapon. "You can pick this up on your way out," he said, handing me a claim check.

I reassembled the test materials and zipped the bag. The guard signaled to his partner through the glass. There was a heavy thunk as the next door unlocked. The guard pushed it open and ushered me into another vestibule. The only occupant was a metal detector. I took off anything that might set it off, including my suit jacket and shoes, and stepped through. It didn't make a peep.

I put myself back together, and a shape shifted behind the darkened glass as the guard in the control booth unlocked another door. I followed him down the hall to an examining room. I wondered whose idea it had been to paint everything in the prison yellow or orange.

The small room had a table and a couple of straight-back chairs. I opened my suitcase and started to arrange the test materials in the order I planned to use them. At least I knew this room wasn't bugged. Privacy here was a prisoner's right, and they'd endanger every single conviction if that got violated.

I thought I heard the door opening behind me. I turned and caught a glimpse of someone in the little window in the door.

I had the impression of blond hair, a baby face. It couldn't be. I gave an involuntary shiver.

I crossed the room and opened the door. The hallway was empty.

I went back to work, trying to ignore the tension that had built up in my chest and back. I was ready when the door opened. It was Nick, accompanied by a prison guard.

Nick cautiously eyed the walls and ceiling before easing himself into one of the chairs. Then his eyes came to rest on the materials I'd arranged on the table. The guard removed his wrist shackles.

"More tests?" he asked. I nodded. He looked at me appraisingly. "I've been reading up on you. You're the shrink whose wife was killed, aren't you?"

The pen I was holding dropped to the floor. I took my time picking it up, giving myself a few moments to respond. Maybe he thought my wife's murder gave us some kind of bond.

"I'm a psychologist," I said.

"I know. Like I said, I've been reading up on you."

I tried to keep my face neutral. I grabbed the test materials for the IQ battery and sat across from him.

"I bet you've interviewed a lot of people here," Nick said.

It struck me how Nick's attitude toward me had changed. He seemed relaxed, trusting even. I wondered why. "You're the first one in a while," I said.

"Hmm." There was a pause. Then, "You talk to Teitlebaum yet?"

"Last night. He seems like a nice man," I said blandly.

"My wife certainly thought so." He didn't say this as if it were a ringing endorsement.

"He seemed quite upset about your wife's death," I said.

"More than you'd expect?" he said.

We'd all had to deal with losing patients. Suicide. Illness.

Fortunately, it was rarely murder. I'd have been pretty upset, too, if Lisa Babikian had been my patient. "You sound like you think Dr. Teitlebaum had more than a doctor-patient relationship with your wife."

"What did you think, Doctor?" he asked, behind a knowing look.

I let it go. I was here to evaluate, not to play mind games.

The IQ test went quickly. Nick's verbal IQ was high at 135; his performance IQ was even higher. Then I did a memory test. Sometimes people who dissociate have trouble remembering.

I set out a card with eight yellow circles arrayed randomly on it. I pointed to two and asked him to point to the same two, in the same order. Then three, then four, and so on. This is a difficult test, and the average person maxes out at five. Nick could do a sequence of eight. Then I showed him a similar card with eight purple dots. I pointed to the dots again, and this time I asked him to point to the same dots but in reverse order. Most people can do three or four. Nick could do seven and made only one error on eight.

Then I took out the TAT cards, selecting the ones I'd set aside before the guard mixed them up and confiscated my paper clip.

"I've got some cards to show you," I told Nick. "Each one has a picture on it. What I want you to do is to make up a story to go with the picture. The story should include what's happening in the picture, what led up to it, and what will happen in the future. Also tell me what the people in the picture are feeling."

We started with a fairly neutral card—a girl dressed in what looks like parochial school clothing, standing in a field of wheat. Nick started off with a fairly neutral interpretation. "There's a girl, going off to school. Her family wants her to work at the farm, but she has dreams. Maybe she wants to be a ballet dancer."

"What happens to her?"

Nick stared at the card and smiled. "She meets someone at school, gets married, and they return to the farm to live happily ever after."

Was this Nick's fairytale version of his wife's life? I noted his response and showed him the next card—a drawing of a woman huddled by an open door, her back to the viewer. Something that resembles a rifle was leaning up against a wall at the edge of the picture.

Nick crossed his arms over his chest and stared at the image. This one wasn't going to be so easy. "A story."

"Whatever your impression is of what's happening here."

"Maybe she's sad. Something bad has happened." He chewed on his lower lip. "She's hiding something. They're going to come and take her away. I don't know what it is, maybe she's stolen something."

"Who's going to take her away?"

He eyed me suspiciously. "You tell me."

"It's your story. Who's she hiding them from?"

"I don't know. The police." He thrust the card back at me.

This wasn't the kind of story most people tell. The card pulls for depression. Nick's story, thin as it was, expressed foreboding instead. I wasn't surprised. I also noted that he hadn't commented on the gun. People often gloss over it. Some don't even see it. But it wasn't the kind of detail I'd expected Nick to miss. What I didn't know was whether it was a deliberate oversight, or a function of his pathology. Personality tests are informed as much by what people don't say as by what they do.

The next card was a drawing of a man reaching for a bag that was resting on a table. The man looks over his shoulder at someone's arms reaching in from behind him. Some people say it's a guy being helped with a bag of groceries. To others, it looks as if someone is sneaking up behind him, trying to steal his parcel. I was pretty sure which way Nick would go.

"This guy's scared," Nick said. "He knows they're there. They're grabbing his stuff."

"They?"

He thought for a moment. "Bookies. He owes a lot of money and he knows they're out to get him. See, he's almost smiling. He's relieved that they're finally here."

Odd, though, that for the gambler, getting caught brought relief. As I was about to ask him to tell me more, I caught a blur of movement in the window in the door—something blocked the glass, then disappeared. Adrenaline shot through me as I leaped up and yanked the door open. There was condensation on the outside of the glass.

I stepped out into the corridor. "Someone's been out here in the hall. Looking in through the glass." The hallway was empty.

Nick got up and stepped to the door. He looked up the hall and down. "Maybe it was someone going by."

"It was someone looking in through the glass," I said. "Look, there's even moisture—" Of course, by then it had dried up.

Nick gave me a long look. "This isn't part of some test, is it?"

"Test?" I gaped at him. Then I reminded myself—being paranoid, by definition, meant being egocentric. Whatever happened, he'd assume it was about him. "Never mind," I said and closed the door.

"Maybe *you* should tell *me* what you think of the next picture," he said as I joined him at the table again. It took me aback. I hadn't credited him with a sense of humor. Then he leaned toward me and added, "If it's making you nervous, don't sit with your back to a door." He didn't say this like he was kidding. "I never do."

Even as I took his advice, angling my chair so I could work

with Nick and see the door at the same time, I told myself that the whole thing was crazy.

I jotted a few notes on my pad, then showed Nick the next picture. It was a drawing of two men holding a lantern over the figure of a man swathed in a white sheet, his chest bare. One of the standing figures holds a knife. A young man in overalls stands in the background.

Nick turned pale and pushed the picture away. "You gotta be kidding," he said. "What the hell am I supposed to say to that?"

I slid the picture back toward him. "It's up to you. I know this isn't easy."

"You're manipulating me."

In a sense, he was right. That's what personality tests do. They're like Velcro. If a person has issues that a card speaks to, then he's going to be bothered by the image and his response is going to pick that up, consciously or unconsciously.

"Give it a try. We're almost finished. There's only one more after this one."

He stared at the picture. "The boy . . ." Nick started. He licked his lips. "He's just a schoolkid. Maybe he's just read a book, or seen a movie. And he's remembering some kind of violent scene in the movie. Someone getting cut. He doesn't want to remember, but he can't help himself."

Nick seemed relieved when I put away the card.

I gave him the final picture. It was of a bearded man looking out a window, the room dark behind him. The man's elbows were resting on the window ledge, and his fists were clenched.

"He's scheming. Watching," Nick said. "He likes to stand there because as long as he's there watching, nothing bad can happen."

There was a sound at the door. I glanced up. This time there was no doubt about it. Someone had his face pressed to the glass, nose splayed, mouth open in a Halloween-mask grin.

I leaped to my feet, knocking over my chair. By the time I got out into the hallway, I caught just a glimpse of a man with blond hair running through the door at the far end of the corridor. I raced down the hall, through the door, down another corridor. When I turned the corner, I ran smack into the guard charging at me from the opposite direction. "Did you see him?" I asked.

"Him who?"

"Ralston Bridges." The guard gave me a blank look. "Medium height. Blond. He was out here. He must have gone right past you."

The guard narrowed his eyes. "No one goes right past me without me seeing them. You got that?"

"I wasn't implying . . . but I saw him—"

"I don't know what you saw, or thought you saw. What I do know is you're making a commotion. We don't tolerate—"

"You've got a murderer, wandering around loose . . ."

"We've got lots of murderers here. It's what we do." He put his face in my face. "Bridgewater State Hospital for the *Criminally Insane*."

"But I saw him, I tell you. He was right outside—"

"Sir, enough is enough," the guard snarled. He put a heavy hand on my shoulder and pressed his fingers into the muscle. "I think it's time for you to go."

The condescending bastard. I tried to get past him but he grabbed my arm, bent it behind my back, and propelled me up the corridor.

"I already told you, sir. It's time to leave," he said.

When we got to the examining room, he ushered me in. "Pack up. You're done."

"I'm not finished. I've got another test." I planted my feet and folded my arms across my chest. I ignored the throbbing in my shoulder, aware instead of the bemused way Nick was watching this little drama. "I want to speak to the captain in charge."

The guard picked up the pen from the table and wrote on my yellow pad. "That's his name. You'll have to call him and make an appointment."

"I've got permission from the court to evaluate Mr. Babikian," I tried. "This evaluation is vital to his defense. And besides, the longer it takes for me to finish, the longer it will be before Mr. Babikian agrees to talk to the state's psychiatrist."

The guard blinked at me calmly. "Then I hope Mr. Babikian likes it here. He's in for a nice long stay." The guard hooked his thumbs around his belt. "I don't care who you are, or how many diplomas you got, you're disrupting the routine, you disobeyed my instructions, now you'll have to come back another time, sir."

Furious, I started to jam the test materials back into the suitcase. A second guard came to take Nick back to his cell. As he passed me, Nick whispered, "I saw him too."

THAT EVENING, I went to meet Annie at Johnny D's. It was early and only the bar side of the club was populated, with about a dozen regulars sitting in the shifting half-light of a large TV. Annie was huddled at the bar with a group of men. The only one I recognized was Detective Sergeant Joseph MacRae. Mac was sitting right next to Annie.

I wasn't completely comfortable with the guy. Though after working opposite him on a couple of cases, I'd developed a grudging respect, which I hoped was mutual. Still, I didn't like him up close and personal with her.

Mac saw me before Annie did. He got to his feet and shot out a hand. He was stocky and solid, with a jaw like a piece of carved granite. His red hair was cut so short you couldn't even tell it was red. The handshake had equal parts warmth and wariness.

Annie turned around. She gave me an unambiguous smile

and an easy hug. I wondered if Mac thought Annie and I were "just friends" too.

Annie introduced me to four other fellows, also detectives.

Mac started. "Annie's been telling us . . ." His back hunched and he coughed, a wet phlegmy cough, into the fist of the same hand I'd shaken. "Sorry, rotten cold. Said she's been getting harassing phone calls. Suggestive ads in men's rooms." He coughed again.

"You don't think she's in any danger, do you?" I asked.

"Hey, *she* is standing right here," Annie said. "Do I look like I'm in danger? I just want to find out who's behind this shit."

"We'll spread the word," Mac promised. "See if we can't catch someone posting them."

"I'd appreciate it," Annie said.

"Watch your back," one of Mac's pals told Annie.

"Thanks, guys," she replied. "Let me know if anything turns up."

Mac watched as Annie went over and settled in a corner booth. I got two Bass Ales from the bartender and joined her.

"Tuesday Night Club," Annie told me, jerking her head in the direction of the police officers who were now thumping a newcomer on the back and greeting him with, "Hey buddy, where you been" and "Long time no see." I recognized the addition to the group. It was Detective Boley, who'd been in charge of the investigation at the Babikian murder scene.

Annie went on, "The guys have been coming here for years, once a week. They have a few beers, go off to one of their houses for an all-night poker game. No women allowed." She smiled. "Otherwise none of them would win a red cent."

We sat in companionable silence. After about half a beer, my back started to unkink. Probably the strain of my visit to Bridgewater. "You think paranoia can be catching?" I asked her.

Annie looked over as the door to the bar opened and a couple entered. "You're the expert on that one. But in my amateur opinion? Yes, most definitely. Also hunger." She gazed at me and squeezed my knee under the table. "Lust, too. Very contagious."

"You hungry?" I asked.

"No." Annie exhaled the word slowly, as her foot went slowly up and down my leg. Her lips parted, and she ran her tongue across her lower lip. I watched, mesmerized.

Just then, from across the room, MacRae coughed loudly and blew his nose. "Why?" Annie asked. "You catching something?"

"I hope not. But this morning, when I was interviewing Nick Babikian at Bridgewater, I thought I saw Ralston Bridges."

Annie's eyes widened. She'd been the chief investigator when Chip had defended Bridges against charges that Bridges had murdered a woman who'd made the fatal mistake of spurning his advances. "A dangerous wacko," had been Annie's take on him.

I told Annie about seeing a face pressed up against the window of the examining room, grimacing at me. And about the guard who thought I was nuts. "He tells me, 'You're done, sir.' I hate that *sir* thing that they do. Oh so polite. Then the bastard throws me out." I was huffing with indignation.

Annie had her hand over her mouth.

"Told me to put my complaint in writing," I added. "Barely gave me time to pack up my tests."

Now Annie was shaking with laughter.

"I gather you find this amusing," I said, unwilling to admit that it was starting to sound pretty funny, even to me. "They didn't even return my paper clip."

Annie gave up trying to contain herself. "How many people do you know," she said between yelps of laughter, "who've gotten themselves thrown out of a hospital for the criminally insane? You must have seemed completely bonkers."

I had to smile.

"You have to agree. It does sound just a teensy bit paranoid. On the other hand . . ." Annie's look turned sober. She thought for a few moments. "Nah," she said, dismissing the possibility.

"Babikian saw him too."

"I'm sure you found *that* reassuring," Annie said with a wry smile.

"You bet. Sort of like getting a hypochondriac to confirm my phantom pains."

"Or getting an anorexic to tell you that you need to lose weight. Or getting a psychopath . . ." Annie paused. That wasn't so funny. If we'd ever met a true psychopath, it had been Ralston Bridges.

"Bridges *could* have gotten himself transferred from Cedar Junction," I said. "Bridgewater's where they send you if you flip out."

"But what's he doing wandering around in the corridors? Don't they keep an eye on prisoners over there?" Annie asked.

"Depends on what you're in there for. They keep prisoners they don't consider dangerous on a pretty loose chain."

"They let them wander around in the halls, unguarded?"

"They do."

"Too bad no one asked me," Annie said. "I consider him dangerous."

"Me too. And besides, how would he know I was going to be down there?"

Annie thought a minute. "It was in the paper. That article about the defense team. Then when Babikian got sent to Bridgewater for evaluation, he could easily have put two and two together."

"And here I thought you were going to reassure me that it was only my imagination."

Annie's gaze shifted up and over my shoulder. MacRae's

cough was getting closer. He was standing beside us. "Sorry to interrupt," he said to me. "There's someone here who wants to have a word with you." He indicated his friends. Boley was staring back at me. He picked up his beer and moved away from his buddies to a separate spot at the bar.

I went over and joined him. "Detective Boley?" I said.

"Al," he said, offering his hand.

I looked at it. "This official business?"

"Unofficial. Don't worry."

I shook his hand and rested my behind against a bar stool.

He looked as if he wasn't sure what to say next. Finally he came out with, "Mac says you're okay."

"I appreciate the vote of confidence." I glanced back. Annie and MacRae were now a cozy twosome, with MacRae having slid into the booth alongside her. "You two poker buddies?"

It was an innocuous enough remark on my part, but I could feel Boley's radar go up. "Yeah, well, we've been getting together for years. A little beer. Cards. Takes the edge off."

Despite the careless tone, Boley was gripping the handle of the beer mug. I followed my instincts. "I guess no matter how much experience you have with investigating crime, it doesn't do much to prepare you for a case like this one."

Boley's eyes widened. Then they narrowed as he sized me up. "Yeah, well, you don't see a lot of crimes as horrendous as this one. It can get to you." That seemed fair enough. Police were people too.

"You talked to Dr. Teitlebaum?" he asked.

It wasn't a secret. I nodded.

"Mmm," Boley said. "Just wanted to remind you, if you come across anything that the police should know about, any evidence we might have overlooked . . ." He smiled at me, nodding his head like one of those pottery dogs you put in the back of your car.

"I'd be obligated to let you know. Of course," I said. "But I'm investigating Mr. Babikian's state of mind. It's not likely that I'll trip over a bloody glove."

He reached into his pocket and pulled out a business card. "Hey, you never know. Just in case you do, I'd like to be the first to know. Want to be sure we've got the right guy for this."

"You bet," I said and slid the card into my wallet.

"Glad we had a chance to chat." He strode back to his buddies.

I returned to the table where Annie and Mac were still sitting. "What was that all about?" Annie asked.

"Nothing much. Asked me to let him know if I discover any evidence he should know about. Wants to be sure they've got the right guy."

Annie and MacRae exchanged a look.

"What?" I asked.

"Nothin'," MacRae muttered. Then he gave Annie a hard look, like he was daring her to contradict him. He heaved himself out of the booth. "Annie told me about Ralston Bridges," he said, his tone sympathetic. "Want me to find out if he got transferred to Bridgewater?"

The last thing I wanted was to owe MacRae. "Hey, I appreciate it, but that's not necessary," I said, letting my ego get the better of my common sense.

"Peter . . ." Annie started.

"It's really no trouble," MacRae said.

"Forget about it," I said.

MacRae held up his hands to fend off my words, which had come out harder and louder than I'd intended. "Hey, suit yourself. Just thought I'd offer," he said and sauntered back to his buddies.

"What was that about?" Annie asked.

"Listen, he's a nice guy. I just don't want him in my business," I said.

I didn't return Annie's look.

"In *your* business?" Annie asked. "Don't you mean in *my* business?"

"That, too," I said.

Annie gave me a pitying look. "Me and Mac, we go way back," she said, reminding me that she and Mac had grown up together, their families had been close. Mac's dad had been a cop; so had Annie's uncles. "Now we're just friends."

I knew that, but it felt good to hear Annie say so.

Changing the subject, I said, "When I told you and Mac about Boley, you seemed surprised."

Annie shrugged. "Seemed out of character is all. Mac thought so too, though he's too loyal to say so. Boley likes to rack up those notches on his belt. The quicker the better. Rumor has it, sometimes too quick. That's how he got to lieutenant so fast. Now he's looking for captain. And this is the kind of case that gets noticed.

"So him *asking* you to call him if you tripped over any evidence he should know about? That's not his usual line, especially since he's got plenty of forensic evidence to nail Babikian. Why invite more suspects to the party? Much more up his alley to argue with me about whether or not they'd go back to the Babikian home to find the surveillance setup. After all, why go looking for evidence that may not square with his foregone conclusion?"

Annie squinted toward the bar. "Maybe he's developing a work ethic. Or a conscience."

A young, dark-haired woman in jeans and a midriff-baring T-shirt had joined the detectives. They were all laughing, and Boley had his arm around her waist. His hand drifted down to her ass. She froze, grabbed his wrist, and confronted him. I couldn't hear what she said, or what he said back, but he was holding his palms up like he was apologizing. She took a step toward him and he lowered his hands to protect his equipment. MacRae stepped between them.

"Wouldn't hurt if he developed a little finesse," Annie added.

• • •

When I got back to my house, the porch lights were off. That usually meant that my mother had gone out in the afternoon and hadn't come back.

I opened my door and turned on the outside lights for her. I noticed a package sitting to the side of my door. It was the size and shape of a shoe box.

Just then, Mom came up the walk. She was with her steady friend Mr. Kuppel. He was a few inches taller than her and rotund, and he wore a khaki cap and matching windbreaker.

"Hi there," I said.

My mother's eyes were locked on that package as if it were a live grenade.

"This came for me," I said.

"Throw it away," she said.

I eyed the package. It had my name and address. It was wrapped in brown paper and tied with twine. I picked it up. The box was heavy, and the contents shifted when I turned it over. I gave it a shake. "Sounds like whatever's inside got broken. It rattles."

"You want it should sing too?" my mother asked. "Throw it out! We need it like a hole in the head." Her voice was strident.

Mr. Kuppel stood behind her, supporting her with one arm around her waist and his other hand on her shoulder. "Pearl, don't upset yourself," Mr. Kuppel said, his voice soothing.

My mother does not panic for nothing. When my brother came home, his pinky finger hanging by a thread, she'd barely batted an eye. She'd wrapped the hand in a clean dishtowel and bundled him out of the house. "Try not to get the blood on your new shirt," she'd said as she flagged down a cab to the hospital.

"Do you want to tell me what's going on?" I looked back and forth from Mr. Kuppel to my mother. He was staring at her, and she was tight-lipped. "Have you gotten a package like this before?"

"One isn't enough?" my mother asked.

"Someone sent your mother a package," Mr. Kuppel said. I waited for them to tell me more.

"It had stones in it," my mother said, "and a picture of your father's gravestone with a swastika painted on it."

"What?" I was horrified at the thought of my father's grave being defaced, even more at the agony that would have caused my mother.

"I called the cemetery. They'd already cleaned the gravestone. I burned the photograph, of course. And the stones, I brought back to the cemetery."

My father had been laid to rest in the left side of a double plot, the space alongside him waiting for my mother. It was the way they slept. Him on the left, her on the right. He'd been dead five years. The last time I'd visited, I added another small stone to the dozens already on top of my father's headstone. It was a Jewish custom.

"When did this happen?"

"The other day," my mother said with a wave of her hand, signaling clearly that she didn't want to talk about it anymore.

So this was why my lame attempt at humor the other night, saying I was making a pizza delivery, had upset her. "This one could be legitimate," I said.

"And I might be Miss America."

I looked at the package and back at my mother's terrified face.

I knew next to nothing about the subject, but it seemed to me that the shake I'd given it would have set the thing off if it were a bomb. "Tell you what. I'll take it inside, check it out. Carefully. If it's something terrible, I'll call the police. Seems like we ought to figure out who's doing this and get it to stop."

My mother eyed the package. "You should throw it away. It's probably garbage."

"Why would anyone be sending me garbage?"

"Why would anyone be sending me rocks?"

She would have made a great lawyer. "Good night," I said. "I'll take care of it."

"He'll take care of it," my mother muttered. "He couldn't just throw it away?" She rummaged in her pocketbook for her keys. "Stubborn, just like his brother."

I let myself in, took the package into the kitchen, and set it on the counter. I poured myself a glass of wine and contemplated what to do next.

The address was written in block letters. "Dr. Peter Zak." Return address Boston. No postmark. A bunch of postage stamps with images of flags. I sniffed at the paper. Nothing more than brown-paper smell. It was tied with standard-issue hairy twine.

It would be easy enough to open. Or should I call the police and let them do it? I shook the box again. The rattling didn't sound dangerous.

I went to the hall closet and pulled a pair of leather gloves from the pocket of my winter jacket. I took the package out to the back porch and turned on the light. I set it down on the wood floor and put on the gloves. Then I eased off the twine and loosened the taped edges. Inside was a shoe box from a pair of size-twelve Nikes.

Cautiously, I lifted the lid an inch. Nothing jumped out. No ticking. No white powder. I took the lid off the rest of the way. It had sounded like what it was. Shards of pottery. I brought the box back into the kitchen and put some of the pieces on the table. They were pale gray with a high glaze and deep lines incised.

My gut seized up. They looked like pieces of something Kate might have made. I dumped the rest of the thirty or so pieces on the table and found a few that fit together. I recognized the piece. It was an early work, a large round pot into which Kate had tooled the figure of a woman in outline with generous breasts and swollen belly. It had been one of my favorites.

A red fury boiled out of me, and I hurled my arm across the table, sending the pieces crashing to the floor. I howled with anger. How dare someone . . . Then I stopped. How the hell had someone gotten hold of this pot when it was up in Kate's studio?

I took the stairs two at a time. The door to the third-floor studio was ajar. Inside it was dark. I closed my eyes. Please, God, don't take this from me too.

I pushed the door open. It was still as a tomb, the light from the not quite full moon streaming in through the windows.

The shadowy outlines of the pots on shelves across the windows confirmed that they hadn't all been destroyed. I found the switch and turned on the lights. The collection of pots was there. All except the one piece. I stared at the empty spot on a shelf.

How had he gotten in? I looked back at the doorway, around at the windows. I felt violated, suddenly unsafe in my own home. How had he known where to go, and what would inflict the deepest, most painful wound?

I called Annie and she drove right over. By midnight, the police had come and gone. They'd searched upstairs and down. The intruder had broken in through a back basement window. I had no idea when it had happened. I didn't venture into that corner of the basement very often. And the last time I was up in Kate's studio, I hadn't turned on the lights.

I had them search my mother's side of the house too, just to be on the safe side. She didn't protest.

Next time a suspicious package arrived, an officer told us, "Don't touch it. Double-bag it in plastic." I wasn't sure how I could manage to not touch it *and* bag it, but I got the picture. To my mother, he added, "And don't throw it away, either! Just call us immediately."

After they left, Annie and I sat at my kitchen table drinking coffee. "Looks as if you pissed someone off good too."

"Ralston Bridges," I said, convinced that this had to be his handiwork.

"What makes you so sure? You've worked on lots of cases, Peter. Who knows who's nursing a grudge? Why assume it's Bridges? After all, he's not Houdini."

I agreed. It was one thing to get yourself into Bridgewater for observation, quite another to get yourself to Central Square and back before lockdown. "He doesn't have to be," I said. "All he needs is someone on the outside who'll do his bidding."

"An accomplice?" Annie sounded skeptical.

My coffee was black but I stirred it anyway. I fingered one of the pottery shards I'd swept up and deposited on a sheet of newspaper on the table. I pressed my thumb against the sharp edge until it almost cut through.

Annie stood behind me and rubbed my shoulders. She ran her hands up and down, over my back. "You're all knotted up," she said as she worked her thumbs around my shoulder blades, down my spine.

I tried to relax and feel her touch. It was more than my muscles that were tight. My stomach was tied in knots too.

"How about a hot shower to help you relax?" Annie asked.

I stood, turned to face her, and took her in my arms. Her smile barely masked her concern. "Only if you'll take it with me," I said.

"Mmm." Annie pressed her hips into mine, and I could feel myself getting hard. "Sounds good. You're feeling more relaxed already."

"Only parts of me."

I followed Annie up the stairs. I took off my clothes while Annie started the shower. But even as I did it I was scanning my room, wondering whether the intruder had been in here, gone through my things.

"Ready!" Annie called out.

The bathroom was filled with steam. I stepped in behind Annie. She had her face full into the stream of water. I took the soap and sudsed Annie's back. Her skin was soft and smooth. I put my arms around her and ran the soap over her breasts, her belly, between her thighs. She turned to face me and we kissed, long and deep.

I wanted to lose myself to the sound of the water beating against the porcelain tub, to the water's heat. I wanted to fill my lungs with steam and to abandon myself to Annie's touch as she took the soap from me and ran it all over my body.

We dried each other and left the towels on the bathroom floor. Such a promising start. But in bed, my mind wouldn't turn off. All I could think about was how devastating it would have been if the intruder had smashed all of Kate's pots. Or hurt my mother. And whether there was a video surveillance camera hidden at the top of my bookshelf.

Finally, Annie rolled me off her and rested her head in my armpit while she stroked my chest. I kissed the top of her head and held her, wondering whether I'd recognize Ralston Bridges's accomplice if I met him in a dark alley. An adversary with a face you could recognize was one thing. Vigilance could protect you. A proxy was another thing entirely. It could be anyone.

THE NEXT morning, I felt as if it were me that had been smashed and broken into pieces. I'd slept fitfully, dreaming about not being able to get home in time to save Kate. The feelings of desperation, of helplessness that haunted me in the two dark years after her death returned full force. Not being able to perform the way I'd wanted to with Annie only made me feel worse.

Over coffee, Annie said what did I expect, anyway? After all, I'd had the house broken into, Kate's pot smashed. Someone had defaced my father's gravestone. "I'd be more worried about you if you'd been able to brush it off and perform like Casanova."

Then she opened up the Yellow Pages and looked up security companies. She put check marks by several that she said she'd heard of. That was Annie. She wasn't one to spend more than five minutes in morbid self-reflection. Pick yourself up, dust yourself off, and take action.

I called one of them. Sniffing an easy sell, they'd sent a sales-person right over. I signed the contract for an alarm system for both sides of the house and paid extra to have it installed within the week.

Then I called in and checked my messages. Nothing that couldn't wait. By eleven, I was on my way to Westbrook Farms, the nursing home where Nick Babikian's mother was staying. It was another of those rare, perfect spring days, but I drove in a fog, my stomach again in knots.

Westbrook Farms was a low, modern, two-story brick building set back from the main road on a rise. By the time I turned into the parking lot, I'd reassured myself that this was a temporary setback with Annie and that the house would be a fortress with the new security system. Still, I could feel the hard, sharp edge of the pottery shard from Kate's destroyed pot pressing against my thumb. I looked at my hand. It had left no visible mark.

Double glass doors opened onto a pleasant, spacious lobby lined with comfortable chairs and sofas. Most of the seats were filled with elderly ladies, a few of them asleep. A man slowly pushed a walker across the carpeted floor toward me. I held the door open for him. The place had a slight musty, plastic slip-cover smell, like my Aunt Gertie's apartment when she wasn't cooking. It was the smell of old age.

As I crossed to the desk, one of the women chirped, "Who's he?" Another one said, "Isn't he handsome?" A third added, "Who's the lucky one, I wonder?"

I waggled my fingers at them. They tittered and nodded back at me. I checked in and took the elevator to the Alzheimer's Unit on the second floor.

The differences between the Alzheimer's Unit at Westbrook Farms and your standard elder-care unit were subtle. Ambient light levels were brighter and more natural. The music on the sound system — soft classical alternating with thirties and forties big band—would be familiar and soothing to patients. Alzheimer's distorts how the brain interprets what the eyes see, and reflections and patterns can be confusing, so the plain linoleum floor had a dull finish instead of high-gloss.

I recognized the middle-aged nurse with gray streaks through her dark hair who was busy at a U-shaped work area just opposite the elevator. Dottie Grebow had worked at the Pearce for many years. She'd been a head nurse there on the one-time Reintegration Unit, a unit that had been allowed to atrophy under the reign of former CFO Arnold Destler. When services weren't financially viable, Destler systematically reduced their budgets and reassigned staff until those remaining couldn't stand it any longer and jumped ship.

"Peter!" she said, greeting me with a wide smile.

"Long time no see." I gave Dottie a self-conscious hug. The half dozen patients sitting around the nurses' station watching made me feel like a circus act.

"I heard they gave Destler the old heave-ho. Sorry I missed his going-away bash," Dottie said with a wry smile.

"We all missed it, I'm afraid. Though Gloria celebrated by dancing the fandango on the press release announcing his resignation."

Dottie laughed. "I'd liked to have seen that." Then she turned serious. "So, what brings you here?"

"You have a resident? Mrs. Babikian?" A look of concern washed over Dottie's face. "How's she doing?" I asked.

"Better."

"Were you here when she was admitted?"

"I wasn't on. But I heard all about it. I guess her son tried to leave her on the doorstep at Oakvale. They transferred her to us. When I got in that morning, she was still getting settled. We'd just get her calmed down, and then she'd erupt. Agitated, screaming. Took us a while to figure out what was setting her off. Turned out she was getting upset every time she saw a man in any kind of uniform. We've had to disguise our maintenance staff when they go into her room."

Dottie pulled a chart off the rack and handed it to me. I realized she thought I was Mrs. Babikian's doctor and would be authorized to see it. "Dottie, I'm here because I'm working with the team defending her son. She was at the house the night her daughter-in-law was killed. I have her son's permission to speak with her, and her son is the legal guardian."

Dottie pulled back Mrs. Babikian's chart. "But she's in no condition . . ."

"I know that. But the police *will* interview her, condition or no. She may have seen something."

"It's taken us two days to calm her down," Dottie said.

"I'll try not to undo."

Dottie gave me an appraising look. She looked down at the chart but didn't hand it to me. Instead, she opened it, scanned it quickly, and closed it again. "She's seventy years old. On a small dose of Risperdal"—that would be to calm her and try to mitigate the delusions—"plus some trazodone to help her sleep. She's suspicious, isolative. Takes her meals alone and refuses to leave her room. She has to be coaxed into taking her medication. Always mumbling under her breath. And her clock's a bit off." Dottie smiled. "At three in the morning, she decides it's breakfast."

"What do you do?"

"We get her a bowl of cereal, of course," Dottie said as she hung up the chart, "just like you taught us when you gave those lectures."

"Sounds like a challenge."

"Thank goodness she's connected with one of the nursing staff."

"Maybe I should talk to her before I try to see Mrs. Babikian?"

"Yes. Actually, I'd like her to accompany you," she said. I was grateful, though I knew for Dottie it was damage control. "Here she comes now."

The plump, energetic young woman seemed to bounce along on the balls of her sneakered feet. She had long blond hair pulled back with a barrette at the nape of her neck. The large, block-printed name tag on her pocket said CAROLE.

"Carole, this is Dr. Peter Zak. Here to see Mrs. Babikian," Dottie told her.

I offered my hand. She gave me a firm shake. "You're a relative?" She sounded delighted.

"Mrs. Babikian doesn't know me."

Carole did a deep inhale, then exhale. I knew she was afraid I was about to upset all the work she'd done to stabilize her patient.

"It's okay," Dottie said. "He works with patients like ours every day of the week."

Carole looked me up and down. "Why don't you take off your jacket and tie and leave them here." I did as she suggested. "And roll up your shirtsleeves. She has an aversion to anyone who looks official."

Carole led me down the hall. In the middle of the corridor, an elderly woman was asleep in her wheelchair, slumped over an open, upside-down *New York Times*. Carole gently pushed the wheelchair to one side.

We passed patient rooms, singles and doubles. On each of the doors hung a clear plastic pouch containing a photograph of the room's occupant and a yellow card with the name printed in large block letters. Some of the doors were open. The rooms were painted in pleasant pastels, and I could see touches of home alongside the institutional beds—a rocking chair in one room, a Victorian dresser topped with a lace table scarf and photographs in another.

The place was color-coded. Each bathroom door was purple with a picture of a toilet painted on it. The activity room walls were painted in bright primary colors to distinguish them from other rooms and to help patients remain alert.

We paused in front of Mrs. Babikian's room. The Polaroid hanging on the door showed a wide-eyed, startled face. "How is she?" I asked.

"She's adjusting. It seems like I'm the only person she trusts, although everybody here is like me."

"I know," I said. Westbrook Farms was as good as it got when it came to overall patient care and staff morale. Of course, it was private, and patients paid for the care they got.

"Maybe you should go in first," I said.

Carole pushed the door open. In this room, there were no personal touches—only institutional furniture. Mrs. Babikian whipped around as Carole entered the room. She'd been standing, looking out the window. Her pale green house dress hung from her narrow shoulders, and skin hung in pale crepey folds around her neck. Her head was surrounded by a frizz of thick dark hair, salted with white. She seemed older than her seventy years. Dark, intense eyes strafed us.

"Home," she told Carole. "I want to go home."

Mrs. Babikian picked up a battered black vinyl pocketbook and a pale blue terrycloth bathrobe from the end of the bed, clutched them to her chest, and started marching to the door. When she saw me, she stopped short, as if she'd run into a pole. She opened her mouth, mute at first, and then a howl started to grow from somewhere in her stomach. Quickly it turned to a muttered growl. "Brrgrr, brrgrr . . ." She made the sound over and over, her eyes riveted on me.

"It's all right, Mrs. Babikian," Carole said, coming between us. The muttering faltered. "This is Dr. Zak. He's come to talk with you."

"I'm a friend of Nick's," I said.

Like a faucet being turned off, the growling stopped. Mrs. Babikian approached me, her head tilted to one side, her eyes bright. "I have to get home to Nicky. Mama's at the bakery and Nicky's due home from school. He'll be waiting for his milk and cookies." She walked past me and stepped into the doorway, peering up and down the hall, as if she were getting ready to cross a busy street. "Where's Nicky?"

"I just saw Nicky," I said, entering her fantasy. Mrs. Babikian turned and blinked at me. "He's not home yet. But he's on his way. I saw him at the candy store buying some gum."

Mrs. Babikian smiled and clucked. "He knows gum is bad. He'll get mouth holes."

"Sugarless gum," I said.

Mrs. Babikian's arms relaxed and her pocketbook and robe dropped to the floor. I picked them up and put them in a chair, noting as I did that the hem of the robe had a faded brown stain around the bottom edge. I wondered if it had been soaked with Lisa Babikian's blood, and the efficient staff at Westbrook Farms had laundered it.

"Why don't you sit down," Carole said and gently led Mrs. Babikian to a chair.

"Can I get anything for you?" I asked. "Are you thirsty?"

Mrs. Babikian ran her tongue over her thin, dry lips. "Juice would be nice."

Carole caught my eye as I headed off to find some. "Can of juice. Unopened. Bring a straw."

I returned with a can of tomato juice and offered it to Mrs. Babikian. She looked to Carole for reassurance before taking it. She carefully wiped the top with the hem of her dress, then opened the can. Carole dropped the straw into the opening. Mrs. Babikian took a long drink. Then she gave a quiet sigh.

I pulled a chair up alongside her. "Have you had a good rest?" I asked.

Mrs. Babikian nodded and took another sip. Then she set the can on the floor. "I want to sleep in my own bed," she announced.

"I can bring you something from home. Would you like me to do that?" I asked.

She thought about that. "Nicky?"

"When was the last time you saw Nicky?" I asked.

"This morning. I sent him off to that school where he always gets beaten up." Lines of anxiety etched her forehead. "He was supposed to come work at the bakery but he didn't get there. I have to get home. I hope he didn't get into another fight." She started to rise out of her chair, knocking over the tomato juice. Then sank back down. Juice spilled from the can, forming a puddle on the floor.

"What about before this morning?" I asked. "Did you see Nicky and Lisa?"

Carole pulled some towels out of a dispenser in the corner of the room. She crouched alongside Mrs. Babikian and started to mop the spill.

"Lisa?" Mrs. Babikian said. Her eyes widened. She looked down at Carole. "But Lisa's right here." She placed her thin hand on Carole's head and smiled. Then her brow clouded. "But she shouldn't be right here. She couldn't be . . ." Mrs. Babikian looked down at the wad of paper towel Carole held, now saturated with the tomato juice. Her mouth fell open. She rose to her feet, touched her hand to her chest, and started to scream. "Lee-ssa! Lee-ssa!" She screamed the name over and over, staring at the red toweling.

An orderly appeared in the open door, and Mrs. Babikian's screaming intensified. Now the words were indecipherable gibberish, rich with guttural sounds—perhaps another language—

settling into a muttered "Brrgrr, brrgrr, brrgrr," as she shook her head from side to side. I snatched the paper towels away from Carole and reached over and stuffed them into the garbage can.

When I turned back, Mrs. Babikian had closed one hand over Carole's forearm. With her other hand, she stroked Carole's hair. Recognizable words started to emerge.

"Erzurum," she said. Her fingers were like talons grasping Carole's arm. "My family came from Erzurum." Her tone was urgent, like this was something Carole had to understand.

Carole looked up at her and smiled.

"The Turks came to the house," Mrs. Babikian went on, her voice now a singsong. Her face had turned calm. Wrinkles seemed to smooth themselves away and a decade of age dropped away as she spoke. "Soldiers' empty eyes. Their faces were masks. Took my mother. Tied them together with ropes. It was snowing." She smiled, almost as if this were a bedtime story she was telling to a child. "The mothers. They couldn't carry their babies. So they left them, the babies, crawling all over the sides. Crying and crawling all over the dirt road." Her hand loosened its grip on Carole and dropped to her side "They walked and walked. The River Euphrates was red with blood. Clothing floating in the water. Corpses. Bound together. The river was red with Armenian blood." Mrs. Babikian's voice grew raspy, as if the words hurt to say. "My mother drank. What could she do? She had to quench her thirst."

Carole jerked her head toward the door, indicating that I should go.

I stood in the hall and listened. I could barely hear Mrs. Babikian's voice, now quiet, like she was crooning a lullaby. "They walked for days . . ."

Then I heard Carole's soothing voice. And finally, silence.

Then, "Home." A moment later, "Where's Nicky?"

# 11

ANNIE MET me in front of the MIT Boathouse late Saturday afternoon. The grass and pathway between Memorial Drive and the river were teeming with people. Skaters and bicyclists were zooming around joggers and stroller-pushing couples. Annie was waiting, talking to a pair of bladers. With their shoulder-to-knee matte black Lycra, streamlined silver helmets, and seriously padded joints, they looked like something out of *Mad Max*.

Annie waved when she saw me approaching. The couple took off, muscles pulsing.

"Hey, you," I said. I was trying for nonchalant, but the residue from the last time we were together made me feel awkward, off-center.

"Hey, yourself," Annie said.

I wrapped my arms around her and felt the tension flow out of my back and shoulders as anxiety released itself. I inhaled and filled myself with Annie's sweetness. I resisted the urge to run my hands all the way up and down her backside.

Annie pivoted to face the river. It was a gorgeous day. Two-person sailboats glided past, while motorboats — like the bladers on the shore — slalomed around them.

"It's a good thing we're just using the tank," I said. "We'd be getting waked every two minutes. You want tranquility when you row."

"What I want when I row," she said, pulling away from me and looking longingly at the skaters streaking past, "is dry land. No problem blading today."

For me, the pleasure of rowing was on a par with a Turley Zin or a Toscanini's French vanilla. I'd dreamed of being out on the river at dusk with Annie, slicing through the water, our bodies synchronized perfectly. I was convinced once I got her out there, she'd be hooked too.

"You getting cold feet?" I asked.

"Moi?" Annie asked. "No way." She gave the boathouse a sideways glance. Built in the sixties, it resembled a packing crate someone dropped into the river. "Though you know, I really don't like boats."

This wasn't news. "You won't be in a boat. And the water's only four feet deep," I said, using my best coaxing bedside manner.

Annie didn't seem impressed. "After all the unpleasant things that have happened to you in boathouses, I'm surprised you still row."

The last time she and I had been together at a boathouse, I'd just had my boat destroyed, and MacRae and I got into a pissing contest. He'd ended up in the Charles and I'd ended up face-down in duck shit. I'd say it was a draw.

"That was at the old BU Boathouse. It's been torn down." With its hundred-year-old rotting timbers, the old Boston University Boathouse had looked like a condemned hunting lodge.

I propelled Annie across the gangplank and inside. The boathouse was nearly empty. A pair of young women, probably varsity rowers, were working out with free weights. An older man, lean, with thinning gray hair, was hard at work at the rowing machine, the ergonometer—the erg, for short. I had no doubt this instrument of torture had earned the nickname because of the sound you can't help making while using it.

Erging requires great strength and endurance but very little skill. I can't stand the thing. My mind goes numb and my brain starts screaming *Get me out of here* when I reach the four-minute mark. I'd rather be out all afternoon on the river in a cold rain than spend thirty seconds on the erg.

The man slowed and stopped. Then he checked his watch and took his pulse. His black sleeveless sweatshirt had an inkblot of sweat going up and down his spinal column. I wondered if he competed in the CRASH-Bs, Charles River All Star Has-Beens, the olympiad for indoor rowers held every winter for years when more than a thousand rowers from all over the world packed into MIT's Rockwell Cage.

In the grand tradition of irreverent MIT, CRASH-B winners get hammers instead of medals. A "hammer" is what they call an oarsman who's long on power but short on finesse.

I went downstairs to get some oars. The massive doors, which would have been flung open to the river on any weekday, were shut. When I came back up, Annie was gazing into the long, narrow room that held a tank that was a bit longer than a racing eight. The two outside walls were mirrored to the halfway point. Above that, horizontal windows stretched across.

The tank itself was divided the long way down the middle by a two-foot-wide concrete divider. Eight fiberglass seats slid on rails that were bolted to the top of the divider, with a pair of oarlocks flanking each one.

"Pee-yew," Annie said.

I'd gotten used to the smell. The three S's: sewage, seawater, and sweat. "It'll grow on you," I told her.

"That's what I'm afraid of." Annie approached the edge of the tank and peered in. It was the way my mother approached something in the refrigerator that's turned green.

"You're not going to fall in," I told her.

"I know what I was going to tell you . . ." Annie started.

"You're stalling."

Annie grinned at me. "Maybe. But you're going to want to hear this." Her look turned serious. "Autopsy results."

I set the oars against the wall.

"Lisa Babikian died of massive head trauma. Multiple blows. After she was killed, she was cut open and thrown into the swimming pool. They're unclear on the time of death. The pool was heated." No surprise, so far. I waited. "She was pregnant."

"Christ." I sighed and shook my head. Teitlebaum said she'd been looking radiant. Had gained some weight. "How far along was she?"

"They can't tell. Best guess is seven to twelve weeks."

"Why can't they be more precise?"

"There wasn't any fetus. No uterus. Whoever butchered her took part of her away."

I leaned against the wall. I felt a heavy weight on my chest as I thought about the young woman who'd bled out into the pool and the new life that had been torn from her.

"Hey," Annie said, giving my arm a squeeze. "Sorry, I didn't mean to put it so crudely. You okay?"

I nodded, unable to speak. Finally I said, "Nick told me his wife didn't want children."

"Women have been known to change their minds on that particular topic," Annie observed.

Teitlebaum had said the couple's sex life had become dysfunctional. How dysfunctional, I wondered, and for how long?

Could Nick be the baby's father, and so what if he was? Did it make it any harder to murder your wife if she was carrying your child?

"How was your visit to his mother? Useful?" Annie asked.

"Marginally. That's par for the course with dementia. It's hard to attribute actions to particular thoughts. But she seems to have been fond of her daughter-in-law. And I'll bet she saw something. She got very upset when the nurse mopped up a tomato-juice spill with some paper towels. Could be she associated that with the blood at the murder scene. And I think there were bloodstains on the hem of her bathrobe. But we already know she was there. As a witness, however, she's useless to either side."

"I'm hoping you're going to tell me you don't think Nick Babikian did it," Annie said. "I'm not too thrilled about working for a guy who'd do this to his wife."

Test results plus my own observations usually provide clarity. But in this case, I didn't trust either. Was I getting good data, or just Nick's vigilance reflected back at me? I even distrusted the empathy I felt for the guy. Was I responding to something genuine, or to my own countertransference since I'd lost my wife too?

"I honestly don't know," I said. "He's smart. Very smart. The tests confirm, more or less, what you'd suspect just from knowing about the masks and the surveillance cameras in the home. Paranoia. Problem is, paranoids are very hard to test because they're so very guarded and suspicious. They let out only what they want to let out. I don't feel like I'm getting a complete picture. I wish I could talk to someone who knows Nick, who's interacted with him on a daily basis."

"Chip knew him, didn't he?"

"I don't think he and Chip were that close," I said. "Someone who worked with Nick would be ideal. He would have had to let his guard down eventually."

"I tried talking to a couple of his employees," Annie said. "They're closemouthed."

"Probably afraid of losing their jobs."

"What about that former employee of Nick's who broke into his office?" Annie suggested. "He worked for Nick for four years. You'll just have to take what he says with a grain of salt. He's probably more than a little angry at Nick."

"Sounds perfect, if he'll talk to me."

"I'll ask him."

"Has Chip told Nick about the autopsy results yet?"

"Not yet."

"I'd like to be there with him when he does. I'm curious to see how he reacts."

"I'll let Chip know." When Annie concentrated, her eyebrows came together and her nose wrinkled up. "What else . . ." Her eyes widened. "What about getting a look at one of his computer games?"

Of course. Many people left the imprint of their character on their work. The paintings of Edvard Munch and the writings of Sylvia Plath were indelibly marked by their disturbing obsession with alienation. Maybe the narrative and the visual images in the computer games would shed some light on Nick's inner self.

"You're brilliant," I told Annie, giving her a hug.

"And you're knock-down-dead gorgeous," Annie shot back at me.

I doubled over, cracking up.

When I recovered, Annie was poised to step onto the wall that divided the tank. "God, it stinks in here. Can we get this over with already?"

"Sit in the third seat," I told her.

She picked her way around the other seats. I took a pair of oars, went to the opposite end of the tank, and walked across to meet her.

"Put your feet here," I said, indicating slots in the foot stretcher, "and I'll fasten them in."

I set the oars across the tank and Velcroed Annie's feet in place. I resisted the urge to caress her calves and ankles, to run my hands along the shiny Lycra that clung to her thighs like a second skin.

"No shackles? Locks?"

"Stop complaining. At least you don't have to learn how to fall down, like I did."

I fastened the oars in place and coached Annie through a few strokes from the catch, the legs working first, pushing out, sliding the seat backward on the rails. Then the upper body engaging. Then the layback as the arms pull in completely to the finish. Finally the recovery, where you pull the oar out of the water and slide back into position for the next stroke.

"This isn't so bad," Annie admitted.

"You sure you haven't done this before?"

"I told you. Just a dinghy when I was a kid. Which was nothing like this."

"I thought you said you hate boats."

"A dinghy isn't a boat. And I was in three feet of water in a fishpond. Damn near killed all the goldfish."

I opened the gates at the ends of the tank. It wasn't much of a flow, but the steady current made stroking a lot more challenging than still water.

I went back and crouched in front of Annie, watching her stroke. She was a natural. "It's a great full-body workout, but especially for the legs and quads. Not that there's anything wrong with your legs and quads." I put a hand on each of her thighs. I'd never thought of the tank as a place for a sexual fantasy, but my mind was coming up with some interesting possibilities.

Later, we sat on a bench along the river and watched the sun set. "Way cool," Annie said, pointing across the river to the Hancock Tower. The gouge running vertically down the near side of the skyscraper was catching the setting sun, so there was a single strip of fiery light in the dark mirrored surface. The effect was startling.

"You getting any more calls?" I asked.

Annie didn't answer.

"Shit. You are, aren't you?"

"I'm going to catch him. I've got every cop from here to Arlington checking the bars." Annie took my hand. "Which reminds me, why don't you let Mac find out about Bridges for you. If he *was* at Bridgewater—"

"So what if he was there?" I said. "I could drive myself crazy obsessing. It's time to move on." I looked around warily. A car horn blasted behind us on Mem Drive at the same time that a motorcycle backfired. There are so many trees along the river, so many places where people could watch from without being seen. It was as easy as adjusting the color on a TV, turning the world from benign to treacherous. "If I let it get to me, then I'd just be doing what he wants me to."

# 12

SUNDAY MORNING I met Chip at Bridgewater. When we were inside, Chip conferred with the guard, who fortunately didn't seem to recognize me. We went to the examining room. I put my chair where I could keep an eye on the door.

When Nick arrived and saw us both waiting for him, he stopped short, but he didn't ask why we were there.

Before he sat, he asked me, "How's my mother? I call but there's no phone in her room."

"She's in a good place," I said. "Westbrook Farms is tops. And she's made a good connection with one of the nurses there."

He sat down opposite us. His eyes scanned the room. If anything, his stay in prison seemed to have had a palliative effect. His movements were more fluid, and he wasn't radiating agitation. "She say anything, about the . . . about what happened?"

"She wanted to find you to give you milk and cookies."

Nick chuckled. "That's Mom."

"And she asked about Lisa. I had the impression she knew something bad had happened to her."

Nick's gaze sharpened, but he didn't say anything. He seemed to be straining to hold himself steady. I reminded myself that innocent or guilty, he still wouldn't want his mother constantly reliving what she might have seen.

"Considering how very difficult it is for Alzheimer's patients to adjust to new environments, I'd say she's doing well," I told him. "And it's not uncommon for them to get stuck in the past. Their older memories are still there. For the most part, they don't take in new memories, unless it's something that's emotionally charged."

"Do you think she —?" Nick started.

"She got very upset about a tomato-juice spill. That suggests she remembers something. And the hem of her robe looked like it was stained with blood."

Nick's eyes slid away from me. "So they're taking good care of her."

"I'd say so."

"They taking good care of you?" Chip asked.

Nick shrugged. "The guards. They've been watching me. Through the video cameras." His eyes darted from one corner of the ceiling to another. I wondered what he was talking about. I didn't think they were allowed to videotape prisoners in their rooms. Still, this didn't seem as bizarre as it might have a few weeks ago. It wasn't so many days ago that I'd lain in my own bed and wondered if I was being spied on.

Nick sat up, as if he suddenly remembered where he was, who we were, and that there were two of us. "What is it?"

"Autopsy results," Chip said.

Nick slouched in the seat, like a fighter protecting his vulnerable spots.

"Your wife was killed by blows to the head," Chip told him.

I was watching Nick to see how he'd react. So far, nothing. "Then she was eviscerated. The killer removed the baby she was carrying."

Nick's eyes widened and he went pale. "She was pregnant?"

"You didn't know?"

He stared at his hands gripped together on the tabletop. "Find the father," he said through clenched teeth. "That's who did it."

"You're sure it's not your child?" Chip asked.

"I don't want children." Nick's words bounced off the cinderblock walls. "I've never wanted children. I've had a vasectomy."

"Still, it's been known to happen," Chip said.

"I . . . can't . . . have . . . children," Nick insisted, his eyes drilling holes into mine. "Find the father."

I'd hoped to administer a couple more tests while I was there, but given Nick's level of agitation, I wasn't sure I'd be able to. But he seemed to recover his equilibrium as Chip walked him through some of the legal paperwork that had to be filed. By the time Chip left, Nick seemed to have calmed down.

I got out the cards for the sequencing test. "I'm going to show you some pictures," I said, laying out the first series of five cartoonlike drawings.

"I'm supposed to tell you what order they go in," Nick said.

"That's right. Then I'll take them away and you'll tell me what story they tell. You've taken the test before?"

"No. But I can see how it works. It's pretty obvious."

"Good."

I didn't tell Nick that the test was a good one for picking up on paranoia. People who are paranoid tend to sequence the cards based on a microanalysis of details and without factoring in a broader understanding of human nature. In addition, the test takes concentration, sustained attention. You can see when someone has little lapses and floats in and out of consciousness.

Nick glanced over at the window in the door. I couldn't help myself. I whipped around to see if Bridges was there. When I turned back, Nick was giving me a knowing half smile. "Don't worry," he said, "he's not here anymore."

I didn't like it one bit, Nick sitting there smug, sure that he knew exactly what I was going through. I was supposed to be the one holding all the cards, and instead I was being manipulated.

"I went looking for him," Nick said. "Scary bastard. Know what he said?"

I didn't respond, but Nick continued anyway. "He was laughing. Said you wouldn't be much help to me because you'd be too preoccupied dealing with your special-delivery packages."

"Special-delivery packages." I repeated the words slowly. Bridges had to brag about it. Had to let me know how clever he was.

"Frankly, after meeting that crazy, I was relieved when they transferred him out of here." Nick paused and gave a shudder. "Something about that dead stare and maniacal grin." I'd never seen Ralston Bridges smile. "He's like a blond Chuckie doll. Good thing my grandmother never met him. He'd have confirmed every nightmare she ever had." There was a pause. He cleared his throat. "He's the one who killed your wife, isn't he?" His tone was gentle, like a finger probing under a Band-Aid.

I didn't deny it.

Nick went on. "Seemed like he wanted you to know. About the packages. That he was the one."

I looked up sharply again, thinking I heard a sound at the door.

"Really, he's gone," Nick said. "They sent him back to Cedar Junction yesterday."

"He mention anything else?" I asked.

"I wasn't eager to prolong the conversation. With a guy like that, you never know what you might say that'll piss him off."

It was a very perceptive remark.

"What was it he sent you, anyway?" Nick asked.

"Just something that belonged to me."

"Must've been something you cared a lot about."

I didn't answer.

"Bastard like that," Nick said, "knows just where to stick it and how to twist it."

I straightened the test cards and picked up my pencil.

"You got a good security system?" Nick asked. I didn't respond. "I'm an expert, you know."

"We should get on with the testing," I said.

"What company you using?"

I gave him a bored look.

"I can tell you if you got a good one or not. Some of them out there are nothing but hacks."

In spite of myself, I found myself telling him the name of the company I'd called. He shrugged. "They're okay," he said. "They installed an alarm?" I nodded. "Keypad?" I nodded again. "You got wireless? Secured all the access points?"

The installer had gone over the house inch by inch, identifying every possible point of access, including the window through which the intruder had gained entry.

"Motion sensors inside?" he asked.

My mother hadn't been happy about that. She'd muttered something about having to live under a radio transmission tower.

"Sounds like you got the basics. Still, bypassing that system? Piece of cake. Take a pro a couple of minutes." Nick sounded supremely confident. It was frightening. Anyone who wanted to invade your life just needed ingenuity and persistence.

"How about CCTV cameras?" he asked.

"Isn't that going a little overboard?"

"You think that's the end of your special deliveries? Believe me, you want to know what's going on when you're not there. Thermal infrared cameras see in the dark."

In spite of myself, I was listening. Jotting notes on the test protocol. He continued, giving me detailed specifications of what he thought I needed.

"They can rig it up so the security folks alert you the moment there's an intrusion. They can hook it up to the Internet. Transmit images to you, no matter where you are. You can even get the alarm relayed to your cell phone. You carry around a beeper, don't you? They can alert you that way too. And they'll call the police."

"Who will maybe get there in time."

"If he's psychic and bolts, at least you'll know what he looks like. You'll maybe even recognize him when you meet him on the street. You can bet Chuckie's got people on the outside helping him."

I stopped writing.

"You want to stay safe, you got to have eyes everywhere," he said, looking warily around the room. "Eyes every-fuckin-where."

Nick gave me the name of a security company. He wrote down their phone number on a corner of the test protocol. He knew it by heart. "Tell them I suggested you call. They're the only company I know that's anywhere near as thorough as I am. Maybe if you'd had a good security system installed a few years ago, your wife would still be here."

I felt my face go hot. The worst part was, I'd had that thought myself. After a rash of robberies in the neighborhood, we'd talked about getting the house alarmed. Kate had been the one who'd resisted. She didn't want to live that way, she'd said, in an armed fortress. Besides, our most valuable possessions were our pottery, and the average burglar didn't know an Overbeck from his ass. I should have insisted. I knew the pots weren't what I cared most about.

I had my eyes locked on the test cards. Would an alarm system have made a difference? Don't go there, I told myself.

I looked at Nick, suppressing the urge to punch his self-satisfied face. "You have a security system in your house, don't you? How come you didn't know someone broke in?"

His eyes burned with intensity. "That's the point," he said. "Now you begin to get it. It had to be someone who knows a lot about me and about security systems."

"Don't you have video monitors down in that office of yours, showing you who's coming in and out of the house? Couldn't you see what was happening?"

"I was working. Besides, it was the middle of the night. I didn't need to watch because I knew they'd be asleep."

I wondered, were his wife and mother the threats Nick was monitoring?

# 13

JEFF GRATZENBERG was the employee who'd been caught in January breaking into Cyclops Productions, Babikian's company. Without any prior run-ins with the law, he'd gotten probation. That evening, I met him at a diner in Brighton, a cramped, old-style greasy spoon with tabletop jukeboxes. I got there first and took a booth.

He'd readily agreed to talk with me. He was furious about being arrested. Delighted with Nick's misfortune. Eager to do anything he could to help nail the bastard. I'd been a little vague about which side I was working for. I reminded myself to take whatever he had to say with a grain of salt.

The place smelled great—coffee and bacon. A short-order cook with a dishtowel wrapped around his waist was hard at work at the grill, flipping burgers and frying up a steak and cheese sub. I checked out the menu while I waited for Gratzenberg to show. The section labeled "Deep Fried Foods" confirmed that this place was caught in a time warp.

The waitress was a brunette who reminded me of a girl I'd dated in college, an impression that disappeared the minute she leaned against the counter and shouted to the cook, "Ovah heah! Ovah heah!" The coffee she brought me was fresh brewed.

A dark-haired young man wearing a loose-necked T-shirt under an open, zippered green sweatshirt came into the diner. That's what Gratzenberg had said he'd be wearing. I waved at him, and he came over to the table.

"Dr. Zak?" he said.

"That's me." I stood and offered my hand. His fingers felt cool and liquid, as if there were no bones in them at all.

He slid into the booth. He couldn't have been older than twenty-five, moon-faced, his thin dark eyebrows meeting over his nose. He had hair so short that light glinted off his skull. His skin was pale, like the underbelly of a flounder. Your average computer programmer preferred to work all night and sleep all day.

"Order whatever you want," I told him.

The waitress immediately plunked a cup in front of him and poured. "Thanks, Vick," he said. "Could I get a cheeseburger and fries?"

"Shuah," she answered, giving him a wink. He seemed to be a regular.

"Just coffee for me," I said.

The waitress sashayed off.

Jeff told me he'd had to move back in with his mother since his trial. "It's humiliating. I thought I was finished living at home. Even when the economy goes south, there's a billion jobs out there for people with skills like mine. But now I can't get any real companies to look at me, not with a criminal record. The bastard's fixed me good." He added some cream and a pack of sugar to his coffee, picked up a spoon with long, thin fingers, and stirred. He took a sip, grimaced, and added another sugar pack. "What he says I did? I didn't."

"I thought they got you on videotape?"

"I worked there! He had tapes of me going in and out of the place every day of the week. And I worked late, sometimes all night. Not such a big deal, you know, to alter a date stamp."

I must have looked baffled because he explained. "On the surveillance footage. It's not a difficult thing to alter. Tedious and time-consuming, but doable. And Nick Babikian is one patient son of a bitch."

"So he framed you?"

"Yeah."

"Why not just fire you if he wanted to get rid of you?"

"Just fire me? A clean kill?" He gave a bitter smile. "Not Nick. He's into vengeance. You don't want to get on his shit list, that's for sure."

"Why was he so angry at you?"

"Professional jealousy?" Jeff suggested and laughed. "Not."

The waitress brought the food. Jeff smothered his burger with ketchup and took a bite. He picked at the metal dispenser on the table until a napkin came loose and wiped ketchup from the corner of his mouth.

"How long did you work for him?"

He finished chewing, swallowed, and said, "Four years."

"That's a long time."

"Uh-huh. Yeah, well, at first he liked my work. *Really* liked it. Nick's a genius, you know. His games are fuckin' amazing. And he's always been a step ahead of the competition."

Jeff took another bite. "It was cool, working there on a new game. Felt like we were planning in a war. Everything had to be top secret. He's built his reputation on surprising his competition. Building on their ideas and going one better. I think it's fair to say, they all hate him. Admire what he can do, all right, but can't stand his guts."

"You liked working there?"

"I grew up on computer games. Getting a job at Cyclops was like a dream come true. You know, a chance to work with the guy who wrote the book on first-person shooter."

"First what?"

"First-person shooter." He put down what was left of the burger. "*Doom? Quake?*" He raised his eyebrows at me, as if the names should be familiar. I put up my hands, helpless. His eyes flicked over me, and I could feel him reassessing my age upward. "It's a type of game where the player has the perspective of the gunman. It's like you're looking out of his eyes. Great concept. I used to be addicted to them."

"There's a lot of, uh, first-person shooter games out there?"

Jeff tucked the last bit of the hamburger into his mouth, picked up a fry and gestured with it. "Sure. But he took it to a whole new level. Awesome 3-D. First-person action. Stealth. *Running Scared* was pretty revolutionary. He made you keep moving, keep moving." Jeff pulsed his upper body back and forth, like he was on a basketball court in his head. "It was the only way to survive. You could play it a bunch of different ways. Anyway"—he shrugged—"his games don't get old. I can play for hours without getting bored, and I know where all the tricks are."

"Do you have a copy of the game?"

"Sure. On my computer at home."

The games I'd played, Pong and Pac-Man, would have seemed like silent movies to this guy. "Any chance you'd take me on a guided tour? I understand it takes years to get really good."

"Sure. And I've got the beta version of the new . . ." His voice died.

"Hey, you were working on it. Right?" I asked.

He nodded, grateful for the out.

"When did Babikian stop liking your work?"

For the first time, he looked uncomfortable. "Around the time his wife started working at the office. November, maybe." His eyes shifted to scan the room. "Ask anyone. That's when a lot of things changed."

"Like what kind of things?"

"Like he had to control your every move. You had to sign out and sign in, so he'd know where you were all the time. He started keeping the bathroom key in his pocket. You had to ask him if you had to go. It was degrading. And the fridge? He started keeping it locked too."

Jeff shook his head. "Can you believe, he actually used to go through the trash. He once confronted me about some notes I'd written and then tossed about a game character I was animating. A real baddie." Jeff smirked. "He thought I was writing about *him*. I should have guessed the place was wired."

"And you say these changes started around the time his wife began coming to work?"

"Not *around* anything. From the minute Lisa starts, he gets crazy. He didn't like anyone even talking to her. It was like he had a sixth sense about it. You'd say a few words, shoot the shit, and shazam! He'd like, materialize."

"Did you talk to Lisa?"

"Sure I did. Why not? She was nice." He paused a few beats. "Lonely."

"You were friends?"

"I guess."

"You saw her alone?"

"When? She only went two places. Work and home. And I was never at the guy's house."

"Never?"

"Well . . ." He pushed away the plate with its wilted lettuce, anemic tomato slice, and three french fries. "I was there once. To bring Lisa something she'd left at the office." He stared at his plate. "Actually, that wasn't too long before the shit hit the fan."

"Did you know the Babikian home was bugged too? He had surveillance cameras all over the place."

He didn't look surprised. "Figures it wouldn't just be his office. The guy's a weirdie."

"So Lisa starts work and Nick starts giving you a hard time?"

"All of a sudden like my work sucks. I thought I was going to be fired. Surprised the hell out of me when the cops show up."

"Couldn't you prove that the surveillance tapes were tampered with?"

"That wasn't the only thing he cooked. The police found E-mail on my computer. Supposedly me offering to sell beta code to a competitor."

"You think Nick planted that too?"

Jeff looked at me. A smile grew on his face. Then he started to laugh. "God, I sound as paranoid as Nick. That's what happens when you hang around that guy." His look turned sober. "Sure he planted it. Would've been easy." Jeff rolled a french fry around, drawing curlicues in the ketchup. "Thing is, I didn't do it. That's not the way I deal with my problems."

"YOU'RE BEHAVING oddly," Gloria said when I arrived at the Pearce just in time for the morning meeting.

"Odd how?"

"Well, number one, you didn't rush right in and pour yourself a cup of coffee." It was true. I hadn't needed an extra jolt to wake myself up.

"And number two"—she tilted her head and appraised me—"number two, you look entirely too relaxed for a Monday morning."

"What can I tell you? I had a nice weekend." It had been a lovely weekend. Annie and I had spent Saturday night at her place, Sunday night at mine. By Monday, I *was* feeling extremely relaxed.

"He had a good weekend," Gloria told Kwan when he arrived.

"He did, did he?" Kwan looked interested. "It's none of my business, of course, but—"

"That's right. It's none of your business," I said.

"My dear Peter, you know I always have only your very best interests at heart. Just ask and ye shall receive. Which reminds me. I asked around about that psychiatrist, Dr. Teitlebaum. Did a residency here maybe ten years ago. He's pretty well respected." From the way Kwan was rocking forward on his toes, I knew there was more to tell. "Left Rhode Island not long after he testified in a murder case."

"No shit?" I said, stunned.

"The Ely case."

Even though the Ely murder had taken place in small-town Rhode Island, the story had saturated the Boston media two, maybe three summers ago when the murder took place, then again for the trial. Every semiconscious soul in New England knew the gruesome details. A man beat his wife, then cut her open and impaled her heart on a stake in the backyard. They arrested the guy at an ice cream stand, his infant daughter sound asleep in the car.

I didn't remember much about the trial, but I did remember the one thing that convinced the jury that Ely was not insane: the prosecutor's argument that the crazy confusion of the crime scene was staged by a diabolical killer who knew exactly what he was doing and planned from the outset to plead NGI. State of mind is a critical factor in an insanity defense. Ely's lawyers tried to argue that he couldn't "form intent" — a fancy way of saying he wasn't in the driver's seat when he killed his wife. The jury didn't buy it. Ely was doing life.

I wondered, had Teitlebaum been a witness for the defense or the prosecution? Why hadn't he mentioned that he'd done forensic work?

I was about to ask Kwan how he'd found this out, when a shout came from down the hall. Then, "Stop her!" Followed by a man's voice, "You can't take that!"

Gloria took off first. We hurried past the living area where a woman in a wheelchair sat watching TV, undisturbed by the commotion. On past several patient rooms. A hooded figure, cloaked in a bedsheet, ran into us. Close on its heels was one of our patients, Mrs. Brownmiller, in a flannel bathrobe.

"Make her give it back," Mrs. Brownmiller demanded. I was surprised. Mrs. Brownmiller was an extremely timid person who suffered bouts of depression associated with a head injury she'd received more than a decade ago. She held out a thin, trembling hand.

Another patient joined us. "Those are mine," Mr. Higgins said, indignant.

From underneath the bedsheet, Mrs. Smetz looked out at us, her face flushed. "Oh, here you are again," she said, eyes wide with delight. "See?" She held out what she was carrying in her arms. There were about a half dozen gladiolus stems, some carnations, a few handfuls of dry Spanish moss. There was most of an artificial rubber plant minus its pot, which I thought I'd last seen alongside the piano in the living area. Mrs. Smetz dropped some greenery.

"Oh, dear. If it isn't Audrey," Gloria said. Gloria bent to pick up the three-foot length of philodendron that lay on the floor.

Mrs. Smetz lay her hand gently on top of Gloria's head and said, "God bless you, my child." She took back the philodendron. "Won't be long now."

We followed Mrs. Smetz back to her room. There, in the closet, she had already accumulated a pile of dead flowers, what looked like rotting salad greens, and more Spanish moss. To this she added the rest of what she'd collected.

While Mrs. Smetz explained to me the fine points of constructing a manger, Gloria liberated the gladioli and carnations and went off, presumably to return them to their owners.

Mr. Smetz snorted from behind a newspaper in the chair in

the corner. He'd probably reached the end of his tether.

Gloria returned. "This has been going on for a few days," she said. "And she's got a terrible rash. Wouldn't surprise me if carting around all this vegetation is making it worse." Gloria coaxed Mrs. Smetz out of her sheet. "See?" she said, extending one of Mrs. Smetz's arms. There were the remains of a red scaly rash.

"Looks like poison ivy," Kwan said.

"She got that a couple of weeks ago," Mr. Smetz offered.

"I was building the manger," Mrs. Smetz said.

"Was not. She was gardening and got into some poison ivy," Mr. Smetz shot back, slapping his paper down on the bed. "Didn't realize it at the time—it hadn't even leafed out. Got really bad. Spread up to her armpits and to her legs too. Thought we had it under control—"

Kwan pounced. "Has she been taking anything for it?"

Mr. Smetz fished a small plastic container of tiny white pills from his pocket. "I been giving her these. Got it last time I got into poison ivy bad myself."

Kwan took it from him. Read the label. Then he held it up, triumphant. "Prednisone!"

"Of course," I said. I took the container. It was dated three years earlier, but it was obviously still potent.

"Why didn't you tell us about this when your wife was admitted?" Gloria asked, an accusatory edge to her voice.

"I didn't think . . . It didn't seem . . ." Mr. Smetz stammered. "It's just for poison ivy! Did I do something wrong?"

"You should have told us," Kwan said, putting a hand on his shoulder. "Prednisone is a steroid. And of course, you're right. It's a standard treatment for severe poison ivy. Sixty milligrams is fine for your average patient. But metabolism changes as you get older. You never know what it will do to someone your wife's age. When did she start taking this?"

"Let's see, beginning of the month." That was two weeks earlier.

"And she started talking about a manger a few days after that?" Kwan asked.

Mr. Smetz nodded. "Weekend before last."

"Looks like Prednisone psychosis," Kwan said. "The drugs are causing the delusion. Her labs, even a tox screen wouldn't have picked it up. We'll need to taper her off gradually. In the meanwhile, we'll continue to treat her with Zyprexa. Give her something else for the itching. In all likelihood, your wife will be back to normal in a few weeks."

"You mean Elizabeth's not crazy?" Mr. Smetz asked.

"No. At least, I don't think so," Kwan said. "She's having a drug reaction. Okay if I hang onto this?" Kwan held out the pill container and Mr. Smetz stared at it, shell-shocked.

Prednisone tablets were no bigger than a freckle. I could see why Mr. Smetz hadn't thought it was important to mention them.

• • •

When I got up to my office, tucked into the eaves under the roof, I checked my messages.

The first was a long, rambling message from a woman I didn't know. Kelly something or another. I doodled on a pad as she talked. "I'm a writer for the *Globe*," she said. "I'm putting together an article about obsessions, and the compulsive, repetitive behaviors people use to neutralize them." From the way she used the words, I could tell she'd been prepped by at least one mental health professional. "I understand you run one of the units at the Pearce . . ."

I stood and stared out the window as she finished her pitch, repeated her name, and recited her phone number. I get calls like this all the time, ever since I'd let the *Globe* do a feature article on me as a memory expert. At the time I'd been flattered. But since then, every time I'd let someone from the news media interview me, I'd been dismayed by the watered-down, garbled version that appeared in the paper. Plus, I'd had enough notoriety to last me a lifetime. I deleted the message.

The next message was from Annie. There had been a development in the case and could I meet her later? That wasn't going to be easy. I had bumper-to-bumper patients all day, a late afternoon committee meeting, and paperwork that I'd already put off for two weeks. I called back and left a message that I'd meet her at nine for a late dinner at the Stavros Diner.

Four superstrength Advil downed with a large coffee barely made a dent in a headache that started late that afternoon, around the time the sky turned gray and the temperature dropped thirty degrees in an hour. When I finally finished up and got out to my car, the wind was tossing around tree branches, and I could hear distant thunder. By the time I got out onto the main road, it had started to rain. Hard. My old BMW's wipers were having a hard time keeping up with wind-driven sheets of rain.

What should have been a five-minute drive took thirty. At least there were parking spots on the street. I pulled into one and groped around on the floor of the backseat, hoping to come up with a forgotten umbrella. No such luck. I sat for a few minutes in the car. Maybe the rain would ease up and I could make a run for it. Instead, it started to come down harder.

A flash of lightning lit up the windshield, followed seconds later by the crash of thunder that reverberated through the steering wheel.

I was only a half block away. What the hell, I thought, as I got ready to open the door. The windshield lit up again. I waited for the thunder. I could barely hear a siren over the pelting rain. A dark sedan with a blue bubble flashing in the back window raced by, sending a wave of water over my car. The sedan double-parked in front of the Stavros, and two men jumped out.

I jerked open my car door and got out just in time to catch the wave from an SUV moving by me at top speed. I cursed and slammed the door shut, not bothering to lock it. I barely noticed the ankle-deep puddles I was galloping through.

When I got into the Stavros, Jimmy wasn't in his usual spot working the grill. No one was. I scanned the place for Annie. Though the restaurant was half full, no one was eating. They were all turned, like a pack of hunting dogs, noses pointing toward the door to the restrooms where a dozen or so patrons were bunched up.

"Police," the man in front of me bellowed as he and the other man pushed their way through the crowd and into the men's room. I rode their wake.

The voice belonged to Detective Sergeant MacRae. "Just stand up, nice and slow. Take it easy and you won't get hurt," he said, his hand poised over his gun.

"You guys sure as hell took your good sweet time getting here." It was Annie. She had her knee pinned to the back of a young man sprawled on the floor. He was wearing a yellow rain slicker, the kind of thing my mother insisted I wear to elementary school, much to my chagrin. Annie had his arm twisted behind his back. A green canvas book bag was on the floor, its contents strewn across the dirty tile.

Annie stood.

The man got to his feet, holding his hands up. "I tried to tell her. It's a job," he croaked, pushing long, stringy strands of dark hair out of his face. "My glasses," he said and got on his hands and knees and groped about for them. A pair of dark-rimmed glasses were lying behind a white metal trash bin. I handed them to him.

He put them on. He was just a kid, maybe eighteen, wearing

jeans and an MIT T-shirt under the slicker. His sneakers had once been white, but now they were ratty looking and water-logged. A sparse crop of hair was trying to grow on his face. "My Palm!" he bleated and stooped to pick up a handheld computer. He pressed a button, and after a moment, it beeped at him. "Thank God," he said dramatically.

He put the gadget reverently in his pocket and blinked at us, eyes enlarged through the thick glass. "Honest to God, I didn't do anything," he said and started to collect the papers that had spilled out of his bag. Photocopies on hot pink paper. Annie grabbed them from him and the top sheet tore. He looked at the half sheet he still had in his hand, the figure of a woman in a leather bomber's jacket and jeans. "What is with you, any-way?" Then he looked at Annie, back at the paper, back at Annie. "Damn."

Annie returned his gaze. She seemed disappointed. She'd caught him, but now she looked as if she wanted to throw him back.

MacRae took the kid by the arm. "Why don't we go have a quiet talk about this so-called job of yours," he said.

MacRae's partner took the canvas bag. Annie picked up her leather backpack, which had landed under the urinals.

"Show's over, folks," MacRae said, as he led the way back into the restaurant.

Jimmy came over to us, an apron tied around his middle. "Peter? What's going on?"

I'd been coming to the Stavros for moussaka and spinach pie ever since my days as an intern at the Pearce. I explained about the notices that were being posted in men's rooms. Outraged, he fussed over Annie, who assured him that she was fine, just fine.

MacRae started to lead the young man out. "Hang on," Annie

said. MacRae halted and gave her a questioning look. "I want to hear what he has to say."

"Take a booth," Jimmy suggested. "Coffee's on me."

The five of us traipsed over to a round table tucked into the corner of the diner. The kid stared at the table, unsure what to do. He was a concave person, his forehead protruding, knees bent, while the rest of him was scooped out, his chest caved in. My mother would have insisted on feeding him.

"Slide in," MacRae barked at the kid. "You in the middle."

"Name?" MacRae asked him, when we were all seated like it was Saturday morning family breakfast at the IHOP. Jimmy brought coffees all around.

"Aaron Spatola." He looked like he was hoping the red-plastic seat cushions would swallow him up.

"Well, Mr. Spatola," MacRae said, "you got any ID?"

The kid fished a blue canvas wallet out of his back pocket, zipped open the Velcro, and handed over a card. I could see from across the table that it said MIT across the top. A student ID. It reminded me of the time I was doing about eighty through some remote part of Louisiana. I gave the officer who stopped me my Harvard ID along with my driver's license, hoping it would make an impression. It impressed him, all right. So much so that he brought me into their local jail to show the other officers what he'd caught. Kept me overnight. MacRae didn't seem overly impressed, either.

"So, what were you doing in the men's room?" MacRae asked.

"Nothing," Aaron said. "I wasn't doing anything."

"I caught you, putting up those disgusting ads," Annie said.

"It's a job."

"What do you mean it's a job?" MacRae asked.

"You know, like I get paid?"

"Who pays you?"

"I don't know."

"You don't know?"

"I never even met the guy. Hell, I don't even know if it's a guy." He looked around at blank faces. "I get jobs off the Web. You know, the In-ter-net?" He pronounced it real slowly. "Bos-jobs dot com. They advertise odd jobs in the Boston area—like, suppose you want someone to wait on line for you for 'N Sync tickets?" He must have realized he had the wrong audience. "Or maybe a Celtics game? Anyway, this guy wants someone to put up ads for him. In men's rooms. He's got a list of places. Easy money."

"What guy?" Annie practically shouted.

"Hell, I don't know who he is. All I know is he's got an E-mail address and he pays me through the Net. I been doing this for him for weeks."

"Weeks," Annie moaned.

"What places?" I asked.

"It's in the bag," he said, nodding at MacRae's partner. The officer pushed the canvas book bag over to Aaron. He rummaged around and came up with a piece of paper.

Annie snatched it from him. "Oh, God," she said and handed it to me. It was a list of just about every nightspot and bar in Cambridge, Brighton, Somerville, and Allston.

"How'd you get the flyers?" MacRae asked.

"He E-mailed me the file. I printed it."

"Can you prove—" MacRae began.

"Sure," Aaron said, brightening. "I got all his E-mails. I got the file he sent me."

MacRae gave Annie a perplexed look. "Want us to arrest him?"

"Aw, hell," she said. "Just get the E-mail and let him go. But if I catch you—"

"Listen, lady, you don't have to worry about that," Aaron said.

"Like, I don't need money this bad, believe me."

As he was leaving, he added, "Problem is, if I don't do it, he'll just find someone else. The pay is real good."

After Aaron left with MacRae and his partner, Annie snorted. "Lady!" Then louder, "Lady?"

"You'll have to bring your Harley next time, show him the real you."

"It's easy for you to make jokes about this," she said. "He didn't call you Mister."

"Lay-dee," I whispered, taunting. "Oh, lay-dee."

Annie laughed. "Come on, this is serious. No one's ever called me that. And did you see that list he had?" She put her head down on the table and groaned. "How the hell am I going to make this stop?"

"Maybe they can track the E-mail."

"Right. And you believe in the tooth fairy too. All you need is a mail account on Hotmail or Yahoo, and no one can tell who you are."

"But he's got to do a funds transfer to pay Aaron, doesn't he?" I had no idea what I was talking about, but it sounded plausible.

Annie picked up her head. "Good thought." Then she pointed her finger at me. "You're late."

"Sorry, things ran over and it's raining." Just then, lightning lit up the windows. My wet socks were beginning to rub against my feet, and wet pants were starting to itch as they stuck to my legs. "A monsoon, actually. So what's the news you were going to tell me?"

Just then, Jimmy came over with a plate of his famous olives, a couple of beers, and a basket of warm pita. It was the best thing I'd seen all day. We ordered stuffed grape leaves and shish kebab. Then Annie pulled a folder out of her backpack.

"They've analyzed all the prints and blood at the crime scene," she said. "Blood all belongs to Lisa Babikian. Fingerprints are either hers, or Nick's, or his mother's. There's not even a lot of background noise—you know, prints belonging to friends, the cleaning lady." That didn't surprise me. Someone as distrustful as Nick wouldn't have lots of friends. He wouldn't trust a cleaning person in his house when he wasn't there.

Annie went on, "It's the bloody footprints that are interesting. We've got Nick's shoes. His mother's bedroom slippers. Lisa's bare feet. And look at this." She opened the file and showed me a Xerox copy of a photograph of a footprint. "Boley let me have this."

The wavery pattern of ripples looked familiar. "What is it?" I asked.

"Rubber soles," Annie said. "Probably duck boots."

"Duck boots?"

"Not the outdoor type, are you? You know, like from L. L. Bean. They're rubber, usually navy or green with brown leather, whitish rubber soles. High tops or low. They were originally made for hunting, slogging around in the swamp."

"Gardening?" I asked.

"As a matter of fact. And they found dirt mixed in with the blood. It's not Weston dirt."

"They can tell that?" I said.

"Apparently they can."

I stared at the footprint, at the pattern. I remembered the green rubber shoes with whitish treads standing outside Teitlebaum's office door. The recently turned soil. The bushes waiting to be planted.

Was it just a coincidence? Kwan said Teitlebaum testified in the Ely murder case in Rhode Island. There were a lot of similarities between the Ely and Babikian murders. A controlling husband, acquiescent wife. A gruesome death scene. Mutilation. The husband's odd behavior after the murder. And a psychiatrist with a connection to both cases.

"What are you thinking that you're not telling me?" Annie asked.

"Lots of people have boots like these, right?"

"That's the problem. They were practically the uniform when I was in high school. They got passed from sibling to sibling, like ice skates only unisex. Even my mom had a pair. These are big. Probably a man's."

"Nick?"

"Doesn't own a pair."

"When I went to see Dr. Teitlebaum, there was a pair of duck boots outside the door to his office. And I just found out that Teitlebaum testified at the Ely murder trial down in Rhode Island."

"Shit. Why didn't I know that?" Annie asked. "That's the kind of thing I'm supposed to know. Damn." Annie thought for a moment more. "You've got to tell the police right away. They'll send someone over there to get the shoes, see if the treads match. Test for traces of blood."

I fished Boley's business card out of my wallet. And I'd been so sure I wasn't going to trip over any evidence. I called and left a message. Boley called back a few minutes later, and I told him about the shoes. He sounded annoyed.

# 15

As I headed home, I recalled my meeting with Teitlebaum. From the beginning, I'd felt uneasy, that his relationship with Lisa Babikian had been too intense, too personal. Teitlebaum skated easily from disclosing information about the couples therapy, where he had permission, to disclosing information he'd gleaned from treating Lisa alone, where he didn't. Now, Teitlebaum had a pair of duck boots that might match bloody footprints found at the scene, and he'd played a role in a similar murder case.

I wondered if the police had already been to Teitlebaum's. Had the footprints matched? Had there been blood mixed with the not-from-Weston dirt? Would he be arrested for the murder of Lisa Babikian?

I turned onto my street feeling exhausted, looking forward to a hot shower and bed. I promised myself that the next morning, I'd walk over to the public library and look up news reports on the Ely case. Who had Teitlebaum testified for in the case?

I was jolted from my thoughts by emergency lights flashing at the end of the block, near my house. My tires peeled rubber when I downshifted and accelerated. I told myself it was probably another car accident. They happened all the time because the street was so narrow and had cars parked up and down both sides. By the time I got close enough to see that one of the cop cars was in my driveway, my heart was racing and my stomach had gone queasy with dread. Please, not a special-delivery package that I was too late to intercept.

I double-parked in the street, jumped out, and ran up the walk. My mother was out on the porch in her bathrobe, flapping her arms at a pair of uniforms. Pulsing in time to the police lights was a *whappa-whappa-whappa* sound. Took me a moment before I realized what it was—our newly installed alarm.

"There's my son," she told one of the officers. The gauzy scarf she had around her head, knotted over the forehead, was coming off. She looked completely frazzled. "He knows the whatever-it-is to make this—you should excuse the expression—goddamned thing stop!"

I gaped. I had never in my life heard my mother use that word.

The door to my house was open. I hurried in, punched in the code, and the alarm went silent.

"New alarm?" said one of the officers, a craggy-looking fellow who looked as if he had an easy smile.

"Just had it installed," I said.

"Sometimes they need to be adjusted. A blowing curtain can set it off."

"I don't have curtains."

"We can go in and check again," he said. "Went in before and didn't find anything."

"Nah," I said.

"Peter," my mother said sharply, giving me a gimlet eye.

"Sure. Please. That would be great if you'd have another look around."

A white van from the alarm company pulled up and double-parked behind me. A guy in blue jeans and a T-shirt rolled out of it and trotted up the walk. "Everything under control?"

"Probably a false alarm," I said.

"Such a noise," my mother said. "I'm inside, minding my own business, and it starts. You think I could remember that code with that noise going on? I couldn't remember my own name."

"Was my door open?" I asked.

"It was" — Mom glanced at my front door — "closed." She felt in the pocket of her robe and came out with a key ring. "I used my key."

"The door was locked and you unlocked it?" I asked gently.

She closed her eyes and thought about that. "Locked, unlocked, who knows?" she admitted. "I got distracted. While I'm trying to get it open, my phone starts ringing."

"That was probably us," the guy from the alarm company said. "Standard practice. An alarm comes in, we call the homeowner. No answer, we call the backup number you gave us, usually a neighbor. That was probably you."

The cops reappeared in the doorway. "Looks all clear," the second cop said, a freckle-faced kid who reminded me of Opie from the old TV show. When had cops gotten so young?

The guy from the alarm company asked, "You got a dog?"

"Nope," I said.

"Any pets at all?"

I shook my head.

"No rodent issues at the present?"

Delicately put. "Not at the present."

"Windows closed or open?"

"Closed?" I looked at the police officers. Officer Opie nodded.

The alarm company guy scratched his head.

"Maybe there *was* a break-in?" I suggested.

My mother's hand gripped my arm.

"If there was, he hightailed it." The cop even talked like Opie.

"Probably just the alarm system's set too sensitive," the guy from the alarm company said. "We'll adjust it."

After they'd all left, I gave my mother a hug. We went over the code again together—her code was the same as mine.

"Maybe I should have it tattooed on my wrist," she quipped. It was a grim joke. "This is the kind of thing that makes me feel old. Old and incompetent." I tried to hug her again but she pushed me away. "But not pitiful."

My mother went back to her side of the house, and I went to mine. The police had left the lights on in every room. I was relieved that they hadn't found anything, but I wanted to check for myself.

I went up to Kate's studio first. Everything seemed as I'd left it. I turned off the lights and came down to the second floor. I checked my study, the bathroom, my bedroom. I checked in the closets and even pulled the covers off the bed while trying to stay at a respectful distance. No horse heads.

Then I checked the basement. No signs of anything unusual. I brought a bottle of everyday red up to the kitchen. The adrenaline rush that had pumped me up had ebbed. I wanted to go from hyperaware to numb.

I foraged around in the drawer where I keep my corkscrew. It wasn't there. I checked the counter. Not there either. I started opening drawers. I found it where I keep my silverware.

I opened the bottle and poured myself a glass of wine. I leaned against the counter, swirling the wine in the glass. There were crumbs on the counter. I tried to remember when I'd last had crackers or cookies out on the counter, and couldn't. Maybe it had just been a while since I'd wiped it down.

I picked up the morning paper, turned to the sports section, and went into the living room. I settled into my morris chair, leaned back, and almost spilled my wine. I sat bolt upright, dropping the paper to the floor. The chair back was set reclining farther than I ever keep it.

What was it Nick had said? *Bypassing that system — piece of cake.* He was right about one thing. If I had video surveillance cameras in place, now I'd know if someone had broken in.

I opened my briefcase and found the test protocol I'd been using with Nick. There in the corner was written Argus Security and a phone number. I called and left a message asking for someone to call me first thing the next morning.

Then I went through the house again, meticulously inspecting every nook and cranny, every closet from top to bottom. I pulled the blinds in every window and turned on the outside lights. That night, I barely slept.

· · ·

The next morning, I went through the house again and opened all the blinds. I checked in on Mother. She looked as tired as I felt. "Don't forget, you can always beep me if you need me," I told her.

"Fine. More numbers," she complained.

I would have accepted her offer of French toast, but the man from the new security company had arrived.

"So, Nick Babikian recommended us," said the good-looking man with graying temples and a ramrod-straight back that screamed *retired military*. He extended a hand. "Bill McCutcheon."

Bill wore a white-knit collared shirt with lettering stitched over the chest, ARGUS SECURITY, and the image of a small peacock. Argus. It was a name I knew from when I'd been obsessed with Greek mythology in grade school. A giant with one hundred eyes, Argus had stood guard over Zeus's mistress. This irritated Zeus's wife, who killed Argus, then she took his hundred eyes and gave them to the peacock. It was the perfect logo for a security company.

"Peter Zak," I said, shaking his hand.

"Nick's one of our best customers."

"Quite a setup he's got," I said. "Did you folks do the installation for him?"

"We helped." Bill looked around, like he thought someone might have overheard. "A little. Mostly he just bought the parts from us. Did the setup himself. The guy knows what he's doing as well as any pro."

Of that I had no doubt. "I'll tell him you gave him a vote of confidence."

"Uh, thanks, but . . . do me a favor, would ya? Don't mention I said anything. Likes his privacy. And like I said, he's a good customer."

"Sure. No problem."

Bill checked out my new system and proclaimed it "adequate." Suggested a few ways to beef it up. Then he told me about the video surveillance cameras they could install to monitor the front and back of the house.

"We can hook it right into your cable system. You're watching TV, the doorbell rings, it interrupts with a picture of the person at the door. You don't even have to turn your head away from the TV." Apparently a major selling point for couch potatoes.

"Sounds wonderful, but I don't think so," I said.

"High-speed Internet? We can hook it up to your computer."

"I'd really rather not."

He looked crestfallen.

He wrote up an estimate for the surveillance cameras transmitting time-lapse images to their offices. I couldn't help gasping when I saw the price. Bill reminded me it included the cameras, the wiring, a year of service, and archiving of old data to CD. They kept it for six months.

As I wrote out a check for the deposit, I wondered why I was doing this—following the advice of a delusional paranoid. I hoped I wasn't fast becoming one myself.

No, I reassured myself. Someone who's delusional is convinced of threats that don't exist. The threats that haunted me were real. I had the broken pieces of Kate's pot to prove it. I wasn't paranoid, just cautious. I felt threatened and was protecting myself. Then it struck me. Wasn't this just the kind of rationale someone with paranoid delusions would offer up?

I'd hoped to get to the library that morning to look up Teitlebaum and the Ely case. But by the time the Argus Security van had pulled away, I had just enough time to get to the Pearce for my morning appointments.

# 16

JEFF GRATZENBERG had offered to show me the game that had made Babikian his reputation as a game designer. He had time late the next afternoon.

After work, I stopped at home first. There were no police cars out in front of my house. No alarm going *whappa-whappa*. I stood on my porch and wondered whether I'd be able to see the security cameras once they were installed. Bill from Argus had promised, "You don't know where to look, you won't know they're there."

Why hadn't it occurred to me that security surveillance was a two-way street? Sure, I could monitor visitors. But how easy would it be for someone to tune in on the stream of video images being transmitted to the folks at Argus Security? Could Ralston Bridges somehow monitor my comings and goings? Had I improved my safety, or had I handed another tool to my tormenter?

That's when I realized, if Nick was as paranoid as he seemed to be from all the evaluations I'd done, then why would he trust me? And if he didn't trust me, then why was he being so helpful about my home security system?

I tried to shake myself out of it. That was the problem with paranoia — it was like a serpent feeding on its own tail.

Gratzenberg was living with his mother on a street that dead-ended at the Mass Pike. The house was a bungalow, badly in need of some TLC. The white and turquoise paints were peeling, and one of the gutters hung loose at one end. Four-foot maple saplings grew up through the front hedge.

I rang the bell. Gratzenberg opened the door. His pale face glowed in the murky light of the hallway. He called over his shoulder. "It's for me, Ma."

A small woman in a dark house dress and carpet slippers came padding timidly from the back of the house. The sounds of a television game show were barely audible. "Jeffrey?" she said, her voice querulous. The house breathed out the smells of cooked cabbage and furniture polish.

"It's just someone for me."

She backed away.

"Come on in," Gratzenberg said.

He led me into the kitchen, through a door, and down a flight of stairs to a paneled rec room. A fluorescent ceiling fixture lit the middle of the room with its wood-trimmed, brown plaid couch resting on a field of green indoor-outdoor carpeting. A lava lamp on the floor in a corner glowed, the orange gunk undulating, rising, and going over with a *blup*. Shallow horizontal windows ran along the edge of the ceiling. The place smelled of mildew and ripe sneakers.

"Sorry about this place," he said. "It was this or the street. Get you a drink?"

He headed to a bar at the far end of the room, opened a half refrigerator, and leaned over into it. "Mountain Dew? Gatorade? Beer?" He stood. "Water?"

"Thanks. A beer would be great," I said.

The bottle gave a little sigh when I twisted the top. It had been at least a decade since I'd had a Rolling Rock. Nothing subtle about it.

Gratzenberg's long skinny arms stuck out of his tired black T-shirt. I read the words on it: SOMEONE SET UP US THE BOMB!

"It's from the intro to a cheesy old Japanese computer game," Gratzenberg said, noticing my confusion. "*ZeroWing*. A 2-D shooter?" I still wasn't getting it. "The game was an outdated hack, even when it was released. Great soundtrack, though. Too bad they can't make any money off all the T-shirts it spawned." Jeff peered down at his chest. "Weird mangled mistranslations. I've got a whole bunch of 'em."

He perched on a stool at the bar and set his beer down beside a computer flanked by huge speakers. "So you're a forensic psychologist? Do you, like, testify in court?"

I fished a business card out of my pocket and gave it to him. "When someone's accused of a serious crime, I'm often asked to come in and evaluate the person's state of mind. Does he know the difference between right and wrong. Does she understand the consequences of her actions? Is there something wrong with his brain? That kind of thing. And yes, I often testify as to my findings."

"So you evaluated the Beak?"

"Nick Babikian?"

Jeff nodded. "But don't ever call him that to his face. He'd go nuts." Jeff turned over my card. "The Pearce Psychiatric Institute. I had a friend ended up there once. Drug rehab."

"Yeah. We've got a pretty good program."

He put the card on top of the bar. "So you want to see *Run-*

*ning Scared*? You have to remember, it came out about six years ago. At the time, no one had seen anything quite like it. Now there's all kinds of clones, a multiplayer version, plus a million MODs."

I hoped it didn't matter that I hadn't a clue what he was talking about. I got on the other stool and wedged my leg up against the bar to stay facing forward. "I really appreciate you doing this," I said.

"I just hope I can help get that bastard what he so richly deserves," Jeff said. He jiggled the mouse and the screen came to life.

There was a graphic of the same face Nick had sketched for me. The Seer leered off the black screen in bold strokes of gray and white. Above the face pulsed the words RUNNING SCARED, with flames leaping from them.

Jeff turned on his speakers, and on came a deafening drum-beat and dissonant electronic music that sounded something like a metal bed scraping across a linoleum floor. The sounds reverberated through the bar counter.

Jeff had his long, thin fingers poised over the keyboard, like a pianist ready to launch into a Chopin piano concerto. He clicked the mouse, and the game fell silent as LOADING . . . appeared on the screen. Then some menus came up and he made a bunch of clicks. A knife with a curved blade appeared, spun around, and then stopped, pointed away from us. Then a hand grenade appeared.

"This is all you get to protect yourself to start," he explained.

His fingers danced spiderlike on the keys as the knife flew through the air, slicing left, right, up, and down, and then around in a circle. Then the face of the Seer reappeared. "Welcome to Earth-2," said a sonorous voice.

"Usually I skip this part," Jeff said.

The voice went on to explain that we were on a planet where

survivors of Earth's final war had taken refuge. Once again, humans were under siege, this time from a force of alien invaders.

Then the face of the Seer was replaced by the interior of a cave, walls and passageways lit by torches. Jeff did something with the mouse or the keyboard—he was moving so fast I couldn't tell which did what—and the knife reappeared. We were propelled forward, through a series of dark tunnels, up a rough-hewn staircase, onto a ledge. Then a leap, and we continued through a new tunnel, around stalagmites.

"Hear that sound?" Jeff asked.

I hadn't noticed it before but there was a steady beating, sharper than a drum sound, more like boot heels on cement. "Is that our footsteps?" I asked.

"It's the guy following us. No need to worry. Yet."

From behind a boulder, a red creature leaped out, pincers lashing. It looked like a scorpion crossed with an octopus. With a sweep of the knife, Jeff cut off an arm. Green blood spurted from the wound. Then the sound of an explosion. All that was left of a second alien was a green puddle with bits of red in it— the handiwork of the grenade, I assumed.

A human figure emerged from behind the rock, a woman in dark clothing with her hands tied. Jeff clicked on her and the bonds came free. An array of green numbers hovered briefly in a corner of the screen.

"What was that?" I asked.

"That was our score. I fragged two aliens, freed a hostage. Now I get a quantum generator."

Fragged? Quantum generator? Jeff was already moving forward again, and now he had a new weapon that looked like a machine gun with a glowing red trigger. The sound of footsteps had grown louder.

"This was one of the first games where the object wasn't to frag everything in sight," he said. "You've got to watch out for the hostages. If you frag one of them, you die . . . Shit."

An alien had dropped down from overhead. Jeff shot but missed. A smoking hole appeared in the stone wall alongside the creature. "This is a cool weapon. It opens up a vortex that sucks in anything nearby. Got to be careful, though, not to suck yourself in." Jeff shot again. This time, there was an explosion and the alien shrank to a candle flame that went out with a sizzle.

It was odd watching Jeff, who'd up to now impressed me as a passive kind of person, so completely in charge and aggressive in the context of the game.

The aliens disposed of, Jeff freed two more hostages. Then he knifed one of the hostages.

"I thought you said you died if you kill a hostage."

"This one's not a hostage. Watch."

As the dark figure lay on the ground, it morphed into another alien.

"How'd you know?"

"Experience. You play the game long enough, you figure out which things are bogus."

He clicked on a little whirlpool of mist. The cave dissolved and the sound of footsteps ceased, replaced by the sound of rushing water and echoing chimes. We had emerged into a vaulted chamber, a waterfall in the background. I knew it was my imagination, but I could feel the temperature drop.

Two small circles of yellow glowed in a corner. We approached them and the figure of the Seer emerged from the shadows. He had his arms extended. The glowing yellow orbs had been his eyes.

"He's offering us a choice," Jeff explained. "Body armor or a gas mask. And he's showing us a map of the new level." The faint outlines of a maze floated in the air.

"So which is the right choice?"

"That's the cool thing about this game. There isn't one. It's just different, depending on which you choose."

"How do you win?"

"There's two ways. Kill all the aliens. Or save all the hostages before you get killed yourself."

That was a novel twist.

"Most players don't get that far," Jeff said as he chose the gas mask. A moment later, we were hurtling forward through a new cave. The new level was darker. The footsteps following us were louder.

For the next twenty minutes, I watched mesmerized. To get out of the nearly unlit cave, Jeff had to annihilate a band of aliens who were building a fire at the cave's mouth. Without the gas mask, he explained, we'd have been asphyxiated. From there, he ran through a forest with new aliens that looked like apes in S&M leather, to a partially destroyed castle complete with ramparts and a neon pink sky. In a basement dungeon, hostages were kept behind bars. They reached their arms out, begging to be released as we sped past. Over the edge of a cliff, dead bodies floated on a river of red.

As I watched Jeff play, I could feel the claustrophobia of confined spaces, the relief of emerging into the open. I could almost smell the rooty coolness of the cave's interior. Hearing those footsteps, like relentless pistons getting louder and louder, made the tension build. With the continuous adrenaline high, I could see how players got sucked into playing for hours on end.

By now, Jeff had lost his quantum generator and gas mask and acquired a blade-shooting machine gun, more grenades, and a flashlight. He paused the game and showed me which keys on the keyboard controlled the weapons, the beam, how the mouse controlled movement through space. Then he handed me the controls and turned the game back on.

Thirty seconds later, I'd aimed the gun at an alien, fired, and the game went black for a moment.

"No big deal," Jeff reassured me. "Everyone's a newbie at first."

The game's eye retreated until it showed a body lying on the ground, bleeding. On the cave floor beside it lay a gun, a flashlight, and several unexploded grenades. "That me?" I asked.

"That's you. You killed yourself."

"Huh?"

"You fired the blade-thrower at a brick wall and it ricocheted, killing you."

The footsteps reached a crescendo, slowed, and stopped. A dark figure appeared and hovered over the body. It was the Seer. He gathered up the fallen weapons. "Sucker," a voice sneered, and hollow laughter seemed to echo off the cave walls.

• • •

That night, I lay in bed, images from the game romping through my head. I had the physical sensation of hurtling forward, lurching sideways. Cave walls and torches rushed up to meet me. I felt the stomach-dropping sensation of leaping from rocky ledges. The vertigo of looking off a cliff at dead bodies floating in red water.

I remembered Nick's mother's tale of a forced march, of corpses floating down a river of blood. Her mother—Nick's grandmother—had probably told her the same stories she'd spoon-fed to Nick. Those constant messages had formed Nick's character and convinced him: Trust no one. I wondered—having used those images in his game, did they haunt him less?

I tried to turn off the game, to think of something else. But when I closed my eyes, I kept hearing "Sucker." In my head was Nick's voice. He had to pop back in and taunt players who failed. He'd designed his game so that the only way to win was to be hypervigilant and anticipate, to assume everyone was out to get you.

As I was drifting off to sleep, I remembered Jeff Gratzenberg's comment: *You play the game long enough, you figure out which things are bogus.*

# 17

THE NEXT evening, I'd just poured myself a glass of wine and sat down to the paper when my doorbell rang, followed immediately by loud knocking. It was not my mother's shave-and-a-haircut.

I flipped on the porch light and peered out through the glass panel alongside the door. It was Richard Teitlebaum. His suit looked like he'd slept in it.

I pulled the door open. Teitlebaum was glancing back over his shoulder. There was a Statie parked across the street, its parking lights on.

He turned back to me, wild-eyed. "I get back from the APA meeting and the police have my house staked out. Search warrant."

I felt a pang of guilt. "Come in," I said, backing away. "Take it easy."

He stepped inside. I closed the door.

"You're working on this case, aren't you?" He didn't give me a break to explain that I didn't work for the police. "What are they looking for? What in the hell are they—?"

"Duck boots," I said. "There were footprints at the murder scene—"

"Everyone and his mother's got a pair of those," he exploded. Then he stopped. "Are you saying they think *I* did it? I'd kill my own patient? That's insane." There was a pause. "And how the hell do they know I've got a pair of duck boots?"

Now I was wishing I hadn't answered the door. "When I came to talk to you after the murder, there was a pair of them in the driveway outside your office door. I had to tell them what I'd seen."

"Outside my office?" Teitlebaum blinked. "*You* told them?"

"I had to, when I found out that there were prints from shoes like that at the murder scene."

He leaned heavily against the door. "He's setting me up. The bastard, that cunning son of a bitch, he's—"

"Hey, take it easy," I said, putting my hand on his arm. "You look like you could use a drink."

I led him into the kitchen. He dropped into a chair. I dug around in the cabinet and found a bottle of bourbon shoved to the back. I poured some and gave it to him. He knocked it back and set the glass down on the table. Then he closed his eyes for a moment. When he opened them again, the eyes that had been so startlingly blue seemed dead gray.

"I keep those shoes in the shed," he said, his face grim. "I always put them back after I finish working." He paused. "Christ. That's around the time my gloves went missing too. And . . ." He stopped short.

"And what?"

He swallowed. "And when I went to finish planting the bushes, my shovel wasn't on the hook where I keep it. It was lying on the floor."

"Who's setting you up?" I asked.

"Who?" Teitlebaum looked at me like I had the IQ of an amoeba. "Nick Babikian. And now I've got the cops after me."

"They're just making sure you don't leave town before they see if your shoes match the footprints."

"And you think there's a chance in hell that they won't?" he asked. "Paranoid, rabidly jealous, smart. What did I want him to do, wave a gun at me too? Why the hell didn't I tell them I was too busy? Or refer them to someone else?" His head jerked to one side. "Christ, who am I kidding? I would have taken Charles Manson if he'd asked. Since I moved up here, the world hasn't exactly been beating a path to my door."

"I'm just guessing," I said, "but I'd say it was also because you realized Lisa Babikian needed all the help she could get."

He pushed away the glass and rested his elbows on the table. "I kept telling myself, no history of physical abuse. There's always physical abuse first. Now she's dead, and the bastard's fixed it so it looks like I'm the one who did it. He's fixed me good."

I wanted to ask him, Why not tell the police? Surely he could explain. But the doorbell rang.

Teitlebaum leaped to his feet. "See." His eyes darted about the kitchen, from the doorway that led to the front of the house, to the door to the basement, to the back door. "Told you it was just a matter of time."

"Wait here," I said. "Okay?" I squeezed his shoulder.

He shook me off. "It's your fault. If you hadn't told them—"

The bell rang again.

"Wait," I said and headed for the door.

When I looked out, I couldn't see anyone. From the shadows, I knew at least one large person was standing alongside of the door. The cruiser was still across the street. Now its lights were out.

The bell rang a third time, long and insistent. "Open up. Police," said a disembodied voice.

"Show yourself," I called back.

Two police officers emerged from either side of the door. With their caps on, their faces were in shadow. One of them flashed a badge.

I opened the door. "We're looking for Dr. Richard Teitlebaum," one of them said. "He's wanted for questioning."

"He's here," I said, leading them through the front hall and into the kitchen. But when we got there, the room was empty.

One officer yanked open the basement door. The other officer was out on the back porch. "He's out here," he bellowed.

In the dark, I could see Teitlebaum trying to hoist himself over my neighbor's chain-link fence.

"Halt! Police!" the officer yelled.

He grabbed hold of Teitlebaum's ankle. Teitlebaum kicked, and the officer swore but held on. By now the other officer was outside too. He had his gun out and was pointing it at Teitlebaum.

Cornered, Teitlebaum inched his way down from the fence and landed with a thud. He turned, his face ashen.

One of the officers explained the advantages of coming along quietly. They just wanted to ask him a few questions.

Teitlebaum's eyes seemed to glaze over. "Call your attorney," I told him. "Don't say anything until your lawyer's with you."

I couldn't tell if he heard me, or could process what I was saying. "Do you have a lawyer?" I asked as the officers started to lead him away.

Still no response. The officers were walking him out to the street. "Do you want me to call one for you?" I called out.

His shoulders sagged. He looked as if he was giving up.

One officer opened the back door to the cruiser, put his hand on Teitlebaum's head, and pushed him in. The door slammed shut and the officers got in front. Teitlebaum pressed the side of his face against the glass.

"Get a lawyer," I yelled as the cruiser slid away.

I trudged back to the house. The porch lights were on and my front door was standing open. I went to my mother's door and rapped. "Mom?" I called out, so she'd know it was me.

The door opened immediately. "You had visitors?" she said. She loves to state the obvious.

"You okay?"

"Why shouldn't I be okay? A little yelling. A person is climbing over our back fence. The police. This business of yours, helping criminals?" She screwed up her face. "Why shouldn't I be okay?"

"He's not a criminal. He's a psychiatrist," I said.

My mother raised her eyebrows. Like what else would she expect? "A friend?" she asked.

It hit me. I did feel a kinship with Teitlebaum. Shrink kills patient? It was like man bites dog. It did happen—occasionally. But like Teitlebaum suggested, it was usually the other way around.

"Maybe. Kind of," I admitted.

"And you didn't go with?"

Trust my mother to be able to rearrange my priorities with a firm smack. She was right. If anyone was in need of help right now, it was Richard Teitlebaum. More than that, he needed to call himself a lawyer. But that meant he'd have to want to fight back, and it looked as if anything resembling a survival instinct had been sucked out of him. Without someone there as his advocate, the cops would steamroll him. I'd done what I had to do. But still, if he *had* been set up to look like a murderer, then I'd helped ensure that the setup worked.

"Actually, I thought I would. Go with, that is. I just wanted to be sure you're okay alone."

"I'm fine," she said. "I'm not alone."

"You aren't?"

"Why does this always surprise you?" she asked and closed her door.

I locked up the house, jumped into my car. But where to go? I hadn't a clue where they'd taken him.

Then I remembered. I still had Boley's card. I took it out. His office was at the state police homicide office on the second floor of the Middlesex County Courthouse. I hoped that was where they'd taken Teitlebaum.

• • •

I screamed up Mem Drive doing sixty, checking my rearview mirror every so often and praying that the patron saint of speeders and scofflaws was on duty. I made the trip in record time, slid into a parking spot on the street. Even at this hour there were people ahead of me, getting their credentials checked and passing through the courthouse metal detectors.

The homicide unit was on the second floor, just around the corner from the elevator. Go the other way, and there was the cafeteria, now closed but still oozing the smell of stale coffee. Up a few floors were courtrooms. The floors above that housed the jail.

There was a small reception area with an oversized metal desk. The American and state flags were the only color in an otherwise gray room. The desk sergeant, a woman, was talking on the phone. She had dark hair, medium-length, a lot of shoulders, and no ring. She gave me a quick glance and a tight nod, and continued her conversation. Then she turned to a microphone and barked some instructions, listened to some static, then barked some more.

I couldn't remember if there had been any female cops at the Babikian crime scene. Another officer came out and mumbled something to her. I didn't recognize him either, couldn't tell you if he'd been at the Babikian house two weeks earlier, or if he'd been at mine an hour ago. I'd make a lousy eyewitness.

Finally, she turned to me. "Yes, sir?" She was giving me that blank look cops give you when you roll down your window and they've got out their pencil poised to write you up.

"Dr. Richard Teitlebaum was just brought in?" I said.

"And you are?"

"His"—if I were his lawyer, I'd be able to get in; but I wasn't—"colleague. Has he called a lawyer?"

She gave me a look, like, *How the hell should I know?*

Just then Boley came striding through.

"Detective Boley!" I said.

He stopped. Recognition turned to wariness. "What are you doing here?"

"They picked up Teitlebaum."

"Yeah, thanks for the tip." He started to walk off.

"He was at my house."

He paused. "So?"

"He's distraught." I knew I sounded crazy. First I'd ratted on the guy. Now I was doing an about-face and worrying about his welfare.

Boley gazed back at me, like why was this his problem? Looked like "Easy Al," as Annie called him, was going to blithely trade Nick for Teitlebaum and nail the sucker.

"In my professional opinion, he's in shock. He's not making rational judgments." I waited for that to sink in. "If he hasn't asked for a lawyer, then he's not acting in his own best interest. Anything you get from him now will get thrown out in court."

A look of annoyance passed over Boley's face. He glanced toward the back. The room they had Teitlebaum in must have been back there somewhere. "I'm sure Dr. Teitlebaum appreciates your concern."

Just then, an officer came through carrying a box. Boley pulled him over. They talked, heads bent together.

"They found something?" I asked, when Boley turned back to me.

"Shoes," he said. His face gave me nothing. "Just like you told us."

"He should have an attorney present."

"You already said that." Boley turned and marched away.

If Teitlebaum's state of mind hadn't miraculously improved over the last thirty minutes, then he was undoubtedly satisfying his interrogators' craving for raw meat. Short of storming the examining room, there wasn't much I could do. At least I could try to get him an attorney.

I went into the hall, got out my cell phone and called Chip. Yes, he could recommend an attorney. But Teitlebaum was going to have to ask for it. No attorney was going to show up without knowing he had a client who wanted to be represented and who was good for the bill. For free, Teitlebaum would have to ask for a public defender. But he'd have to ask.

I hung up, discouraged. I stuck my head back in the homicide unit. The woman officer at the desk looked up and glared at me, her look saying, *Go home!* I went back out into the hall and sat on a bench.

Suppose Teitlebaum did have an affair with Lisa Babikian? Suppose he killed her? As a psychiatrist, he'd know just how to create a crime scene that pointed to Nick Babikian. But then, after all the careful planning and flawless execution, why wear such distinctive shoes? And then how colossally stupid of him to leave those shoes outside his office door.

I wondered what Annie would say. When she'd met Stuart Jackson, an innocent man accused of shooting his ex-wife in the head and killing her boyfriend, she'd said, "If he's a killer, then I'm the Easter Bunny."

I contemplated what seemed like zero options. At least I could hang around and give Teitlebaum a ride home if the cops grilled him and then let him go.

It was after midnight when Teitlebaum emerged. He looked as if they'd leached bodily fluids out of him.

"Can I drive you back to your car?" I asked.

"My car?"

"You left it at my house."

He gave a dull nod. Then he seemed to come to. "Why are you here?"

I started to say, *My mother shamed me into it*, but thought better of it. "Thought you could use a friend."

"Huh?" He seemed stunned. "Thanks. Thanks a lot."

We started out to my car. "You should know better than to talk to the police without your lawyer. I work with a criminal defense attorney. I called him. He said he could refer you to one of his colleagues."

He didn't respond. We got into my car.

"They found traces of blood on my shoes," he said in a monotone.

The street was quiet. I pulled out. A car pulled out behind me.

"Took my fingerprints," he said.

"They ask you a lot of questions?"

"Mostly where was I at one in the morning the night of the murder. And what was my relationship with Lisa Babikian."

"And you told them?"

"Home asleep. Therapist."

I turned on my blinker and turned onto First Street. We passed the Galleria—the mall was deserted, shuttered for the night. The car behind me followed. Once on Mem Drive, I stayed in the right lane and cruised at thirty-five. Cars whizzed past. The car behind me fell back. I didn't doubt that Boley was having us followed.

Teitlebaum rested his head back and closed his eyes. "You ever lose a patient?" he asked.

"We all have," I said. I remembered the BU undergrad, the first patient I'd "lost." The first time I saw him, the police had just fished him out of the Charles. He'd dropped some LSD, then settled back to read *Welcome to the Monkey House*. Maybe it was Vonnegut's despairing view of the future that got to him. Whatever it was, he'd taken off his clothes, walked outside to the parking lot, and tried to bury the book in the asphalt. When that didn't work, he went down to the river to throw the book in but forgot to let go.

Hard as I tried, I couldn't help him. When I told his parents that he might be schizophrenic, they bundled him home. A few months later, I heard that he'd thrown himself off a bridge.

"Some people think that just because we're paid to listen, we don't care," Teitlebaum said. "With Lisa, I thought I could make a difference, she was just like—" He broke off.

"Like what?"

He shook off the question. "I fucked that one up. I told myself I was getting a second chance. This time I could make it come out right." His voice turned angry. "Idiot! I can't believe this is happening."

Anger is a vast improvement over despair. "We all have our ghosts, the ones that got away," I said.

As we drove up Mass Ave and passed through Central Square, I realized I'd lost track of the car that had been following us.

Teitlebaum said, "It's what I tell my patients. You can't run away from your problems. They have a way of reappearing with new faces."

When I pulled into my driveway, a car trailing behind me pulled into a parking spot a half block back. "I think we've been followed," I told Teitlebaum. He twisted around in his seat. "Back about a dozen houses."

"Oh, God." He groaned and collapsed in the deep bucket seat, his chin sunk into his chest, despair once again taking control. Finally, he roused himself and opened the door.

"It feels as if you're giving up," I said.

"And I suppose you'd be doing better in my place?"

"I know one thing. I wouldn't be talking to the police without an attorney." I was beginning to sound like a broken record. "If they can't make the charges stick to Nick Babikian, they're going to be looking for someone they can make them stick to." Sometimes a little paranoia is a good defense.

That seemed to wake him up.

"At least call," I said. I slid a card out of my wallet and wrote Chip's number on the back. "Call, tell him you're the one I told him about. And don't forget, if they stick it to you and you didn't do it, then Lisa's murderer is going to get away with it."

• • •

First thing the next morning, I walked over to the main branch of the Cambridge Public Library, determined to find out about Teitlebaum's role in the Ely case.

The library was tucked into a park on this side of Harvard Square. The outside was all rich ochers and reddish-browns, brownstone walls and arches, turrets with multipaned windows. I stepped under the dark, cool archway to the entrance, eager to get some answers. The library had just opened.

I took the passageway from the nondescript, bureaucratic front desk to the back area with rows of computers. The brilliant architect who'd gutted and reworked this interior—it now resembled the inside of a cardboard box—deserved to roast in hell.

I got into the on-line newspaper archives and did a search on

"Ely" and "Teitlebaum." I got six hits. The first one told me what I wanted to know. It was from a front-page article during the trial. "The defense claim that Ely is mentally ill and therefore not criminally responsible for his wife's death picked up momentum yesterday with testimony from psychiatrist Richard Teitlebaum . . ." I scanned the paragraphs. Then reread them to be sure I hadn't misunderstood.

Teitlebaum hadn't been a forensic witness for either the defense or the prosecution. He'd been Angela Ely's therapist.

No wonder Teitlebaum was so upset over Lisa Babikian's death. For a second time, it looked as if his patient had died at the hands of a delusional husband whose grip on reality had slipped.

Teitlebaum had testified that Henry Ely telephoned him after the murder. Ely had sounded confused and disoriented, claimed his wife was an alien, intent on murdering him. Ely believed aliens, like vampires, drank blood. He told Teitlebaum that he'd cut his wife open and driven a stake into her heart to prevent her from chasing him.

In his opinion, Teitlebaum said, "Ely was in the throes of a psychotic episode. His progressive preoccupation with his own health and the loosening links between his thoughts and reality foreshadowed his breakdown."

*Loosening links between his thoughts and reality*—the words Teitlebaum had used about Nick Babikian.

The trial had ended six weeks later. Ely was found guilty and went to jail for life. A year after that, Teitlebaum moved to Newton. Six months later, the Babikians showed up.

As I walked home, I wondered once again: What were the odds of a therapist having two patients in two years killed and mutilated by their husbands? Like Uncle Sigmund, I wasn't a fan of coincidence.

IT WAS nice to have an uneventful week. The new home security system minded its own business. And Annie reported that
her late-night phone calls had stopped.

Patients came and went on the unit. I was covering for Kwan
while he was in Geneva lecturing on psychopharmacology and
aging. Mrs. Smetz was becoming a whole lot more rational, but
she still had her moments of Mother Mary–ness. It would be at
least another week before she was completely grounded in reality.

The papers were running stories every other day about the
Babikian case. A feature article focused on the "leads" that were
being developed. According to "unnamed sources," a "promi-
nent Newton psychiatrist" was under investigation.

Then Friday, I got beeped in the middle of the afternoon. It
was a number I didn't recognize. I called back.

"Hello?" It was a man's voice.

"This is Dr. Peter Zak, returning—"

"They're digging," he said. It was Richard Teitlebaum.

"Who? Where?"

"The police. They're back. Now they're digging up my yard." Then, in a whisper, "I'm afraid of what they're going to find. Jesus, I'm afraid."

His voice had a kind of ragged quality, a sound that sets off alarm bells when you hear it in the voice of a profoundly depressed patient.

"Are you there by yourself?" I asked.

"You think I have any patients still willing to see me?" Teitlebaum gave a hollow laugh. "They read the paper. Not too hard to figure out. They've all canceled."

"Any friends you can call? You shouldn't be alone."

"Don't you think I know that?"

"Have you contacted a lawyer?"

No answer.

I was already looking at my schedule. I had a patient who'd be arriving any minute. Then a meeting I could probably skip. And I'd hoped finally to finish editing a research article that I'd promised to deliver to *The Journal of Neuropsychology* more than a week ago. That could wait.

"Oh, God," he said. His voice sounded far from the phone.

"What? What is it?"

"I think they found something."

There was a knock at my door. "Hang on." I stuck my head out and told Matt Ciampi, a patient I'd been working with for several months, that I'd be a minute more.

I checked my watch. "I can be there by four, but I've got to see a patient first."

I heard him breathing.

"Richard," I said sharply.

"Uh-huh."

"Did you call Chip Ferguson? Have you talked to a lawyer?"

"Jesus Christ, they're bringing something up. I can't see . . ."

Matt was waiting for me. With any other patient, I'd have canceled the appointment. But Matt's world was fractured and fragmented, his weeks disorganized and chaotic. If I canceled our weekly appointment, it could topple what little fragile order he'd managed to erect, removing one of the steady things he could count on as he began to recover from depression.

"Richard, will you be okay until I get there? I should be there by four."

"Four?"

"Earlier, if I can."

He hung up.

Quickly I called Annie and left her a message, asking if she could, to get over to Teitlebaum's before me. Then I sat and tried to stem the flow of adrenaline that had me snapping static.

When I was feeling grounded, I opened the door. "How you doing?" I said amiably and ushered Matt in.

"Fine, I just . . ." he started to answer and froze. "You all right?"

People say a horse can sense a rider's anxiety. Some patients are the same way. I reassured Matt and we sat down to our hour.

As soon as he left, I called Teitlebaum. The phone rang once and I got his voice mail. I left a message that I was on my way. Then I hurriedly locked my office and went down the hall. I punched the elevator button. It responded with a faraway groan. I took the stairs instead, flying down as fast as I could. I knew Teitlebaum shouldn't be alone.

Even though I hit the road just after three-thirty, rush hour was in full swing. My cell phone went off while I was in bumper-to-bumper traffic, everyone crawling, halting, and creeping homeward. I fished it out. It was Annie.

"Sorry, I just picked up your message," she told me. "I'm up in Manchester, heading out now." It would take her at least an hour to get back. I told her I was going over to Teitlebaum's and I'd call her later.

If anxiety could levitate a car, I'd have leapfrogged my way into West Newton. Finally, I found myself in the maze of streets near Teitlebaum's. The yellow clapboard house looked pristine and tidy.

Today the garage was closed, and the silver Volvo had been backed into the driveway and parked parallel to the house. I parked on the street and hurried to the office door. The whole area along the side of the house was a mess, the ground dug up. Someone had knocked over the PARKING sign. Three of the recently planted bushes, the ones nearest to the office entrance, had been uprooted. Pieces of yellow crime-scene tape had been trampled into the earth.

I knocked. "Richard!" I yelled.

I waited, then knocked again.

Clumps of pink and white petunias were wilting in the pile of dirt that was crisscrossed with footprints. I banged on the door. "Richard! It's me, Peter. Let me in."

Still nothing.

I peered in through the window. I could see Teitlebaum's office. The phone on the desk was off the hook. I banged my knuckles on the window and shouted some more.

I glanced across the street. Next door. The corner of a curtain in the window of the neighboring house dropped into place.

"Hey!" I called out. I hurried across the two driveways and knocked at the side door. A pale, dark-eyed woman opened the door. She held one hand out flat in front of her, fingers splayed, and blew on the nails. There was tinny, raucous laughter in the kitchen — sounded like the portable TV on the kitchen counter behind her was tuned to an afternoon talk show.

"I'm looking for Dr. Teitlebaum," I said, jerking my thumb back toward Teitlebaum's house.

"I already told the police," she said. "I don't know anything." She blew on the nails of the other hand. "But he never was very friendly. Kind of a loner. Very peculiar." She must have thought I was a reporter. I've always been amazed by the awful things people are willing to say about their neighbors the moment there's a whiff of scandal.

I cut her off. "Did you see him go with the police?"

She peered out into the driveway, back at me. "Who are you, anyway?"

"I'm a friend of his."

"Oh. A friend," she said, pursing her lips in distaste.

Police had badges to give themselves legitimacy. I gave her my business card. It was what I had. "I'm a psychologist. Do you know where he is?"

"I . . . I'm not sure. I've been really busy. I didn't notice." She waggled her fingers.

"How long ago did the police leave?"

She waved one of her hands, vaguely. "An hour ago, maybe more. Oprah wasn't on yet." She squinted across the driveways. "Who's going to clean up that mess?"

I returned to Teitlebaum's house and attacked the front door. It was locked. Then I circled around to the back. The back door was standing open.

I put my head in and called out. I entered the kitchen. There was dirt tracked all over the white ceramic tile floor. Three coffee cups sat on the table. I touched one of them. Cold. The light on the coffeemaker was on, warming the inch and a half remaining in the pot.

"Richard," I bellowed. He'd been distraught, despairing, unable even to summon a lawyer to defend himself. If he'd been my patient, I'd have made him sign a contract, agreeing not to harm himself.

I quickly checked the first floor. Where the hell was he? I

took the stairs two at a time up to the second floor. I checked the bedrooms, the closets, the bathroom. The rest of the house was *Better Homes and Gardens* spotless, and no one was anywhere.

I returned to the kitchen. I looked out the window. White paint was peeling off the clapboards of the garage, and the structure listed slightly to one side. Apparently Teitlebaum hadn't gotten around to renovating it.

I raced out the back door and tried to pull open the garage door. It was either locked or stuck. A window in the side was already broken. I got a stick and broke away the remaining bits of glass and climbed through.

Inside was gloomy, and it smelled of dry leaves and loam. I waited as my eyes adjusted. Despite its falling-down exterior, the interior of the garage was as orderly as the interior of the house. I could make out a twin mattress leaning up against the wall, an old hot water heater shoved into a corner. I walked across the concrete floor. Bags and boxes of gardening supplies were neatly stacked in shelves alongside a lawn mower and wheelbarrow. Other tools hung from hooks on the wall.

I continued around. In the back was an old closet with a number painted on it, 31. It was taller than me. I unlatched it and pulled the door open. Empty.

I crawled back out the window, trying not to snag my clothes on the sill. I walked slowly back, trying to figure out what to do next. I leaned up against the Volvo. That's when I realized it was running. I tried the door. It was locked. I peered inside. Empty.

Odd, how close to the house it was parked. I went around to the other side. "Shit," I said, as dread gathered in my chest. There was a hose, one end stuck to the tailpipe, the rest of it snaking its way through a basement window.

I yanked the hose off the tailpipe and raced back into the

kitchen. There I found the door to the basement. I pulled it open, groped for a light switch, and flipped it on. Dirt had been tracked on the off-white carpeted steps. I hurried down.

I found myself in an exercise room, the floor covered in padded black rubber, free weights against the wall, a bench and a treadmill. Now I could smell it, the faint odor of automobile exhaust. The wall on the side bordering the driveway was paneled in cedar stripping. It had a door with a window in it. Looked like a sauna.

I peered in. I could just make out Teitlebaum collapsed on the lower bench, pressed against the wall. I had to get him out of there, and right away.

I took a huge gulp of air, pulled the door open, and propped it with a chair. Then I dragged Teitlebaum down off the bench. I grabbed him under the arms and had him all the way to the basement stairs before I inhaled again. I yanked and pulled him, trying not to think about the damage I might be doing to his head and back as I bumped him on the steps. His face was bluish-gray, not the cherry-red that I remembered reading was a sign of carbon monoxide poisoning. We both needed to get out of the basement. In a closed space, carbon monoxide could quickly reach toxic levels. Within minutes after that, it starts killing brain cells.

I pulled Teitlebaum into the kitchen, slammed the basement door shut, and opened the outside door. I leaned on the counter, trying to catch my breath. Then I picked up the phone. No dial tone. Chills went down my back—had someone cut the phone lines? Then I remembered. When I'd peered into his office, the phone had been off the hook.

I didn't want to leave him alone, so I got out my cell phone and called 911 and told them to send an ambulance right away. The dispatcher asked if he had a pulse. I pressed my fingers to his neck. There might have been a faint one. Did I know CPR? She said she'd wait on the line while I started.

I'd learned CPR years ago but never actually had to use it. I laid him out on his back. Today his sweater was yellow, and the shirt under it pale blue and still crisp from the laundry. I knelt over him, placed the heel of one hand in the center of his chest and the other hand on top of that one. I pressed down, then released. Press. Release. Press.

I put my fingers in his mouth to be sure the airway was clear. I pinched his nose, opened his mouth, and started mouth-to-mouth. I exhaled, watching his chest rise, then fall. I did it again, and again. "Breathe, goddamnit," I whispered.

I didn't hear the ambulance until the siren's wail was dying and someone was banging at the front door. I jumped to my feet and let them in. I waited as the team of paramedics worked over Teitlebaum. I asked one of them about his coloring. Why wasn't he red? That was a myth, the paramedic explained. Only a small percentage of carbon monoxide poisoning victims turned cherry-red. Most were cyanotic, like Teitlebaum.

While I was giving him what information I knew about Teitlebaum, the other one said, "He's breathing."

Teitlebaum was still unconscious when they lifted him onto a gurney, an oxygen mask strapped over his face. I hoped I'd gotten to him soon enough. Carbon monoxide poisoning had a particularly devastating effect on the frontal lobes and limbic system. A psychiatrist who couldn't control his emotions, who swung back and forth from euphoria to apathy, would be as hard up for clients as one accused of murder.

I watched the ambulance pull away and heard the siren start up again. The woman next door was standing halfway out of her back door, transfixed by the drama.

I went back inside. The dispatcher was still on the phone. I thanked her and hung up.

The quiet house was still full of Richard Teitlebaum's presence. There were large photographs of sailing yachts on the walls, bookcases filled with modern fiction and nonfiction. The smell of coffee wafted in from the kitchen.

I walked into the kitchen and turned off the coffee. I was wiped, like I'd just run a mile in knee-deep mud. I poured what was left in the pot into a cup.

I leaned against the refrigerator and took a sip. How long had he been down there? Would it have made a difference if I'd gone to the basement first instead of farting around, upstairs and down, chatting up the neighbor, climbing in and out of the garage?

I wandered into his office and sank down in a chair. I'd sat there when I first met him. I could picture him pitched forward, kneading his hands together. He'd been upset. Stunned, grieving as if he'd lost a friend. *You don't have to be a psychiatrist to know that husbands kill wives.* Had it all been an act?

I thought about Teitlebaum. A Newton Hill yuppie with callused hands. A calm professional who crackled with anxiety. I tried to envision Teitlebaum creeping into the Babikian home in the dead of night when he knew Nick would be working in the basement, knowing that the only witness to worry about wouldn't be able to tell anyone what she saw. He finds Lisa . . .

That's where I hit a wall. Teitlebaum may have crossed a few boundaries in his relationship with his patient. But in my heart of hearts, I couldn't picture him as a murderer. And though he knew that it would incriminate Nick to have Lisa found with a mask on, I couldn't imagine him inflicting that final, dehumanizing indignity on a young woman he'd treated and for whom he seemed to care deeply.

Teitlebaum's desk was bare. No neatly folded suicide note providing the explanation we all crave when someone takes his own life. Only two mugs—one full of pens, the other full of pencils all sharpened and pointing up—lined up alongside the receiverless phone.

I picked up the handset from the floor, put it back in place. Who would grieve for Richard Teitlebaum? Did he have relatives in Rhode Island? On the shelf behind the desk were some framed photographs—looked like a family reunion, maybe Teitlebaum with parents, brothers and sisters, nieces and nephews. At least I could call and let someone know.

I scanned the room for an address book. I tried the top center desk drawer. It had a neat stack of stationery, envelopes, extra pens and pencils, and in the corner a small container of stamps. I tried the top side drawer. I remembered Teitlebaum opening this drawer when we'd talked here. Sitting on top of a checkbook and a calculator was a small brown leather notebook. I lifted it out and shoved the drawer closed with my knee. The book had a calendar in the front, addresses and phone numbers in the back.

I went to the *T*'s and found several Teitlebaums listed. I called the first one. Michael Teitlebaum turned out to be his brother. Michael's wife Karen was home. I told her what I could, as gently as I could. She seemed stunned, barely able to talk. Finally, she thanked me and said she'd let the rest of the family know. I gave her my phone number.

Then I called Chip to let him and Annie know what was going on. Annie got on the phone and launched into a barrage of questions. She made me take her through my every movement. Finally, she asked how I was feeling.

I gave a tired laugh. "Feeling?" As usual, I'd been trying not to feel anything. "Just beating myself up for not getting here earlier."

"He may make it," Annie said.

"And he may be sorry that he did," I said. "Carbon monoxide can cause permanent brain damage."

"Maybe you should go over to the hospital. After he regains consciousness. You might get some closure." She was beginning to talk like me. "Let me know if you want company."

I hung up and opened the drawer again to put the datebook back where I'd found it. I remembered Lisa Babikian's calendar, her biweekly appointments. If she'd been alive, she'd have had an appointment with Richard Teitlebaum today, Friday, at four o'clock, right around the time Teitlebaum had been sitting in the sauna losing consciousness.

I opened the datebook to today's page. Lisa Babikian's name had been crossed out. All of the other appointments today were scratched out too. Being suspected of murder hadn't just damaged Teitlebaum's practice. It had destroyed it.

# 19

THE HEADLINES Saturday morning: "Suspect in Brutal Killing Clings to Life." There was a picture of a professorial-looking Richard Teitlebaum. I scanned the article. When the paper had gone to press, Teitlebaum had been alive and in intensive care. There were no details about what the police had dug up from Teitlebaum's garden, just that they'd brought back several boxes of evidence.

There was an interview with his next-door neighbor, Barbara Small. She described him as "weird" and "spooky." "You'd say hello, and he'd just have this distant look on his face. And he had all these strange people going in and out of his house at all hours." With neighbors like her, who needed enemies?

She also claimed that a large, paunchy person had been skulking around the car, kicking at the dirt in the driveway. She said it might have been before Teitlebaum got taken off, might have been after. Paunchy? I looked down at my stomach. I most certainly was not paunchy, though I wasn't being as religious about rowing every morning as I'd once been.

I made up my mind to visit Teitlebaum at the hospital. I called Annie to take her up on her offer to go with me. We agreed to meet in the hospital lobby later that morning. I was hoping the visit would reassure me that I hadn't been too late.

It was just after eight o'clock and the day was already heating up. It promised to be a scorcher—almost ninety in May. It sometimes happened in New England, and when it did, it was not a pretty sight. Unseasonable heat cooked magnolia blossoms right off the trees.

I threw on shorts and sneakers, grabbed my water bottle and Walkman, put in a Jess Klein CD, and went out for a run on the river. I did a circuit, up and over the Longfellow Bridge, then down along the Boston side and back over the Mass Ave Bridge. Then home. As out of shape as I was, I still resisted the temptation to rest along the way. Running gives the mind a break while the body takes over.

I got back dripping with sweat, as if I'd taken a dive into the river. I smelled almost as sweet.

When I got out of the shower, the phone was ringing. It was Detective Boley. "Just a formality at this point," he said, but could I go over to the police station and give a statement about finding Teitlebaum?

I told him I'd be over around noon. "What did you find at Teitlebaum's?" I asked.

There was a pause. "I'll be holding a press conference in a half hour. Tune in and find out," he said and hung up. The arrogant bastard. He'd be enjoying center stage.

I drove to the hospital with the heater on high so my engine wouldn't overheat, the windows down, and news radio blaring. At least the roads were empty. I was rolling into the hospital parking lot when the breaking news bulletin came on. The police had found bloody gardening gloves and human tissue buried in Dr. Richard Teitlebaum's garden. Maybe Lisa Babikian's unborn baby.

I bashed the radio into silence and peeled myself off the seat. Annie was waiting for me under a potted palm in the blessedly cool lobby. She had on jeans and a black scoop-neck T-shirt under an unbuttoned white cotton shirt. "Did you hear the news?" she asked.

I nodded. Annie had her hair up, and tendrils curled down the back of her neck. That's where I kissed her. Her skin felt cool and damp.

"Chip's preparing a motion to get Nick released," she said.

If this were any other case, I'd have been pleased. Getting our defendant off without a trial was a win-win all around. Good for the defendant, good for the state, and Chip got paid. But I'd have felt a whole lot better if I thought Teitlebaum was going to get a fair shake from the criminal justice system. For once, I appreciated the way Chip usually shielded me from information I didn't need to know. Now I craved the tunnel vision I didn't have.

We took the stairs to the second floor. Then down a long corridor, following the signs to the ICU.

"I just heard what else they found when they searched Teitlebaum's house," Annie said. "A miniature surveillance camera."

"Yeah, I saw it there," I said. "It was in Richard's desk. He said Nick planted it in his office so he could spy on his wife's sessions."

Annie started to say something else but stopped. We'd reached the closed double doors to the ICU. A uniformed police officer was seated just outside. He harrumphed to his feet and asked who we were there to see.

"Richard Teitlebaum," I said. "We're friends. Dr. Peter Zak. Annie Squires."

"Hey, Annie," the officer said, turning a warm smile on Annie. "How you been keeping yourself?" Half the police officers in the Western world seemed to know Annie.

"Hey yourself, Eddie. I'm good. Peter's the one who found Dr. Teitlebaum and called the ambulance. Okay if we go in?"

"They only let one person in at a time."

"That's cool. You go ahead," she told me.

The officer glanced through the window in the door. "He's unconscious."

I pushed the intercom next to the door. The nurse, a middle-aged woman with graying hair who looked like she'd seen it all, came over. She asked who I was there to see and buzzed me in.

The beds in the ICU radiated out from a central nurses' station in separate, glass-walled cubicles. The nurse indicated Teitlebaum. She gave her head an infinitesimal shake. "A shame," she said, "young man like that."

Teitlebaum lay inert in a hospital bed, a tube up his nose and an IV in his arm. Wires snaked from under the covers, others were attached to his head. They connected to the monitors that surrounded him, each one making its own sinusoidal graph.

"Has he regained consciousness?" I asked.

She took the chart off the end of the bed. She shook her head.

I went over to his bed, pulled up a chair, and sat. I was breathing shallowly, through my mouth, trying not to swallow the smell of the place—denatured alcohol and gardenias.

"Richard?" I said. A monitor alongside the bed was beeping. A machine, breathing for one of the other patients, hissed and clanked. "Richard," I said a bit louder, putting my hand on his arm. The nurse's shoes made a squishing sound as she moved from one side of the room to the other. But Teitlebaum didn't stir.

I felt a new surge of anger. Why the hell couldn't he have waited for me to get there? Suicide was the ultimate stupidity. It left so many unanswered questions, so many people blaming themselves and each other. The police would assume they had their killer, and that he'd taken his own life. Case closed. Everyone goes home happy.

But I knew in my gut that this case wasn't closed. Sure it was hard to swallow, Teitlebaum treating two patients who were both brutally murdered. But maybe for once, that's all it was. A coincidence. Nothing in Teitlebaum's demeanor, in his reaction to Lisa Babikian's death, suggested that he killed her.

I thought about the occasional psychopaths I'd met over the years, killers who managed to mask their malevolence. Wasn't it a shame about that woman he was accused of killing, Ralston Bridges had asked when I evaluated him. Did I know that she had a five-year-old daughter, now left without a mother? It made him so sad to think about it. He had a little girl himself. He'd been there when she was born. It was the most incredible experience of his life. As he said this, as if on command, a single tear appeared at the corner of a dead, emotionless eye. I'd met only two other real psychopaths, and they had the same dead eyes.

When Teitlebaum's eyes went dead, it was from despair, not emotional impotence. I was convinced that he genuinely cared about Lisa Babikian.

I asked the nurse if I could borrow a piece of paper. Then I scribbled a note. In case he came to, I wanted Teitlebaum to know I'd been there and wished him well. I left it folded on the nightstand.

I left the ICU and Annie and I started down the hall. A

dapper-looking man, skin the color of light coffee, moved toward us with the fluid grace of a dancer. It was Naresh Sharma, another public defender with whom I'd worked over the years.

"My good friend Peter!" he said. His voice was flat Midwest. Careful word choice—he picked his words as one would pick up shells on a beach—was all that remained of what must have once been an Indian accent. "And is that Annie Squires?"

He and Annie embraced. Then she stood away from him. "You're looking swell," she said.

As always, the tall, somber-looking fellow was dressed, if anything, more elegantly than my good friend Kwan, in polished wing tips and a dark suit that fit as if it had been made for him.

Naresh and I shook hands. "How are you? How's Lakshmi?" I asked. I'd never forget the extraordinary shrimp curry and homemade chutney his wife, also a lawyer, had cooked to celebrate the end of a trial.

"She's fine. I'll tell her you asked after her," Naresh said. He glanced toward the ICU, then back at me with concern. "Your mother? She's well?"

"She's fine," I reassured him. "Alive and kicking. I was here to visit Richard Teitlebaum."

"You're acquainted with Dr. Teitlebaum? He's my client."

"He hired you?"

"A few days ago. You know I'm in private practice now too."

The three of us moved to the end of the hall. I lowered my voice. "I didn't realize he'd hired an attorney. That's great. I'm the one who found him and called the police. I've been working with Annie and Chip, defending Nick Babikian, the man who . . ." Naresh put up a hand to let me know he didn't need it explained.

"I know it sounds bad," I said. "And after they dug up his garden and found what they did. But there's something about this that doesn't feel right."

"You don't think this was suicide?" Naresh asked sharply.

"Actually, the attempted suicide is the only part that feels right about it. What I can't figure out is why."

"He was pretty distraught," Annie said.

"Not why the suicide. That makes sense. But why would Richard Teitlebaum kill Lisa Babikian, then slice her open and bury her unborn child in his own garden?"

There was a pause. "Well," Annie suggested, "suppose it was his child."

"Okay," I agreed. "Say he and Lisa are having an affair. She gets pregnant. Hysterical. Wants to leave her husband and go off with the man who truly understands her. Teitlebaum freaks out, kills her, then destroys the evidence that would show their relationship was more than doctor-patient. Buries it in his own garden because he is, after all, the baby's father. He can't just throw it away."

"That's certainly what the DA would have us believe," Naresh said.

"That baby is not Teitlebaum's," I said, surprised at the conviction in my own voice. "I'll bet you anything that a DNA test—"

"I don't bet when it comes to my clients," Naresh interrupted.

"If he dies," I said, "he'll be condemned in the court of public opinion, based on circumstantial evidence confirmed by his own final act. But he's not dead now. A DNA test would at least show he didn't abuse his position as her therapist."

Naresh didn't look convinced. "I don't know, Peter. I always say, never open a door unless you're one hundred percent sure what you're going to find on the other side."

"They've already taken fingerprints, interviewed him," I said. "I tried to get him to call a lawyer when they questioned him. But he ignored me. I warned the detective in charge of the investigation, told him Teitlebaum wasn't acting in his own best interest."

"You told him that?"

"I went to the police station where they were holding him. I told Boley that anything they got from him would get thrown out of court. We argued about it—lots of people overheard."

"Very interesting," Naresh said. I could see the wheels turning as Naresh strategized about how to prevent the police from using the evidence Teitlebaum had given freely while overwhelmed by despair.

• • •

We left my car at the hospital and Annie drove, her Jeep's A/C on full blast. "You have to admit, the evidence is stacking up," Annie said, as she barreled along winding back roads to get to the Middlesex County Courthouse and Boley's office.

She was right. Bloody shoes. What looked like Lisa Babikian's unborn child and bloody gloves buried in his garden. And a suicide attempt that made him look guilty. "On the other hand," I said, "no witnesses. Unless you count Mrs. Babikian. Too bad that surveillance data is missing."

"That's what I forgot to tell you," Annie said, swerving around a dead raccoon. "They also found the hard drive that was missing from Babikian's computer."

"Where?"

"In Teitlebaum's desk."

"Shit." I felt as if the ground had been yanked out from under me. Here was yet another piece of evidence implicating Teitlebaum in Lisa Babikian's murder.

Wait a minute. I'd been in Teitlebaum's office. Watched him go through that desk. Gone through it myself. Could I have seen the hard drive there and not realized? "What's a hard drive look like?"

"About so big." Annie made a frame with her thumb and index finger. "Flattish. Looks like computer hardware. It's got an actual disk on it, like a little record. It had been smashed, maybe with a hammer. They're trying to recover the data."

Annie circled the courthouse four times before she finally gave up and went into a parking garage. She slid into a spot on the fifth floor, pulled the parking brake, but didn't get out of the car.

"Peter," she said, giving me a long look. "You ever worry that after doing this work for so long, you'll wake up one morning with your feelings for other people paralyzed?"

"You worried that's what's happening to you?"

Annie shrugged. "Maybe. A little. I mean here I am, talking about a buried fetus like it's nothing."

"I guess the work you do, investigating crimes, isn't so different from the work I do, poking around in people's heads. If you let yourself feel too much, you'd never be able to do your job. You've got to keep your distance." I put my hand over hers. "It's healthy. More than that, it's essential. But it doesn't make you insensitive. I know that for a fact."

Annie slid me a smile. She opened the car door. Warm air rushed in, like tepid swamp water.

Inside the courthouse, it was only marginally cooler. The desk sergeant—the same woman who'd been presiding last time I was there—had a fan set up on her desk blowing air right in her face. She had her shirt button undone, showing some compressed cleavage. This morning, she was writing on a clipboard.

"Peter!" It was Boley. He'd emerged from the inner area. Today he had the chummies. "Annie!"

"Hey, Al," Annie said. "Seems like they're keeping you pretty busy."

He gave Annie a lazy smile. He looked refreshed, the tension from around his eyes gone. "Thanks for coming in," he told me.

"Like I said, just a formality. I need a statement about how you found Teitlebaum. Should pretty much tie things up."

"Tie up what, exactly?" I asked.

"Looks like we've got our killer, and he might even save the taxpayers the cost of a jury trial."

Boley seemed so smug, so sure of himself. Were they even considering the possibility that Teitlebaum had been set up? "He's not dead yet, Detective Boley," I said, trying to put a little distance between us. "And have you considered the possibility that he's innocent?"

Boley did a slow blink. "How the hell do *you* think Lisa Babikian's blood got on his shoes? You think someone else buried those remains and the gloves in his garden?" He stood there, trying to stare me down.

"Brilliant strategy for getting rid of evidence — bury it in your own garden. And leave the shoes lying around. The guy must have at least a high school diploma."

Boley narrowed his eyes at me. "You can't believe he did it because he's a shrink. You people." His complexion was going from red to purple. "Stick together, don't you?"

Did he get extra brownie points if he could blame it on someone with a fancy degree? Still, I wondered if there wasn't some truth to what he said. Was I so sure Teitlebaum couldn't have done it because of my own biases about the basic goodness of the mental health professions? I pushed away the thought. "Anyone can come and dig in a garden," I said. "You still haven't got a witness."

Annie broke in. "Maybe this isn't something you two need to discuss right now?"

Boley ran his index finger around the inside of his collar. I could feel his anger tick down a notch. Nick Babikian's words came back to me: *Find the father.* Teitlebaum insisted he wasn't having an affair with Lisa, and I believed him.

"You *are* going to push for a DNA test, aren't you?" I asked.

Red seeped back up from Boley's neck and into his face. "What?" he exploded. "You must be out in La La Land. Why the hell would we be doing a DNA test? He tries to kill himself. We find the missing hard drive right in his goddamn desk drawer. Who do *you* think is guilty?" It was full-fledged fight-or-flight—gaze intensified and pupils constricting, capillaries dilating, sweating. "What the hell difference would a DNA test make?"

I ignored Annie's look telling me to back off and took a step toward Boley. We were inches apart. "If it didn't matter, then why would he take the fetus? And whoever the father is, I'm sure you'd want to talk to him. Wouldn't you?" Boley blinked in spite of himself. "If it's not Teitlebaum, and it's not Babikian, then it's someone else. I'm just saying it's important to find out who that someone is."

Boley took a step back and looked away. He rubbed his hand back and forth over his mouth. Seemed as if he was trying to regroup. "We don't do frivolous DNA testing. It's expensive. Especially when there's no direct connection to the murder. Ties up resources that could be used on real cases."

"This *is* a real case," I found myself shouting. "You don't know there's no connection. And Richard Teitlebaum could be innocent. It's just easier, isn't it, to let him take the blame? Gets one off the books for you."

"Gets one off the—?" Boley glared at me. "How dare you suggest . . ." He swallowed. "People who are innocent don't try to kill themselves. It's not natural."

"How the hell do you know that?"

"I know," he said, hooking his thumbs in his belt loops. "I'm a homicide detective. It's my job to know." Boley pulled himself up and accordion-pleated his chin until it disappeared into his neck. "This is none of your goddamn business anyway."

He wiped the sweat from his forehead with the back of his hand. "I asked you to come down and give a statement about finding Dr. Richard Teitlebaum. You're just a witness. That's all."

"Al," Annie said, "maybe one of these gentlemen wouldn't mind taking Dr. Zak's statement?"

Boley looked around, noticing that we had acquired an audience. About a half dozen people, officers in uniform and staff, were hovering. Boley jerked his chin at one of them who came over and took me back to his cube.

I gave my statement.

On the way home, I barely heard Annie say, "It's like I told you before. Easy Al. Once he's got what he considers enough evidence, he wants to ram it home. Doesn't want to be distracted by anything else. If Teitlebaum dies, easier still. Boley doesn't even have to testify."

"There's something else that's bothering me," I told Annie. "That hard drive that investigators found in Teitlebaum's desk drawer. Teitlebaum went through those desk drawers when I talked to him right after the murder. I went through them again after they took him to the hospital."

"Maybe you missed it. It's not that big," she said.

"I never saw any smashed computer innard," I insisted.

Annie thought about that. "Are you saying someone planted it for the police to find *after* Teitlebaum tried to kill himself?"

That would have been one way to explain it.

# 20

MONDAY THE heat broke with spectacular thunderstorms. The temperature dropped twenty degrees and it turned clear and crisp. I was on the unit most of the day. When I got to my office I checked my messages. Naresh Sharma had called. "I wonder if I might impose on you," he said. "Dr. Teitlebaum has regained consciousness." He left his cell phone number.

I felt a surge of relief. If Teitlebaum was conscious, that was a positive sign. I called Naresh.

"Hello, Peter. After our talk at the hospital, I thought you wouldn't mind if I ask your advice."

"Of course. You said Dr. Teitlebaum is conscious?"

"He's awake."

"Communicating?"

"Yes. I had to tell him about the suicide attempt. He didn't remember."

That wasn't unusual. With head injuries and coma, there was always some retrograde amnesia, forgetting what happened around the time of the injury. How much of it returned depended on how much his brain had been poisoned by carbon monoxide and the length of the coma. Four days wasn't all that long.

"Can I see him?" I asked.

"I was hoping you'd suggest that."

"Have they done any brain imaging?"

"I have no idea."

"Well, it would be good if you could find out. If they haven't, see if you can get them to do a CAT scan or, better yet, an MRI. And if they have, I'd like to see the pictures."

• • •

I met Naresh later that afternoon in the hospital lobby. Teitlebaum was out of the ICU and in a private room. When we got there he was dozing, his eyes open a slit and his head dropping off to one side, then righting itself. I pulled a chair over to sit, my face level with his. "Richard?"

His eyes opened. He saw Naresh hovering behind me. He blinked at me. "Peter?" Recognition. That was a good sign.

"Hey. Glad you're awake."

"Yeah, though this feels like a bad dream." He licked his lips. "Heard you saved my life." His voice was thick.

That was good too. He was taking in new information and remembering it. "Know where you are?" I asked.

He gave a wry smile. "This a test?"

I nodded.

He pushed against the mattress to raise himself and groaned. "God, am I sore. My head. My back. Feels like someone hit me on the head and pushed me down a flight of stairs."

"Up."

"Huh?"

"Up a flight of stairs. I had to get you out of the basement."

"Thanks." Groggy, he touched the back of his head. He glanced about the room. "Actually, I don't know where I am. But Mr. Sharma tells me I'm in Newton-Wellesley Hospital."

This simple statement was actually quite telling. It showed he was self-reflective — he didn't know where he was, but he recalled he'd been told. He knew his lawyer's name. That suggested that his critical faculties might not be in too bad shape.

"Do you remember Lisa Babikian?"

He turned still. "She was my patient."

"How long had you been treating her?"

"I already told you this," he said.

"So tell me again."

He took a deep inhale and winced. "Since October with her husband. And alone for the last four months," he added.

Longer-term memory seemed to be intact. "What's the last thing you remember before you woke up here?"

He closed his eyes, opened them. "Last thing I remember . . . talking to you on the phone."

"Do you remember the police coming to your house?"

"I didn't at first. But it's coming back to me. They were digging."

That was good too. Memories were already starting to return.

"Do you know what the police found?"

"I do now," he said. I thought I saw a flicker of anger in his eyes.

"Any idea how it got there?"

"Not the slightest."

"Were you having an affair with Lisa Babikian?"

He sat forward. "For God's sake, no!" The look of outrage quickly turned to pain. "Ow, shit." He eyed me. "That, I would remember."

"Someone was. I think you know who."

Teitlebaum's eyes widened, his pupils dilating. "You sound

like them. That's what that detective . . . Boley . . . kept asking me."

"What did you tell him?"

"That I didn't know. Which is true. Between you and me, if she'd told me who she thought she was in love with, I'm not sure I would have told Boley."

"*Thought* she was in love with?"

"Lisa Babikian was vulnerable. Easily taken in by a little kindness. Easily taken advantage of, I'm afraid. And she was quite unhappy."

Just then, Naresh tapped me on the shoulder. He was holding a folder. Teitlebaum's CT scan. "We need to leave anyway," Naresh said. "There's someone here to take a DNA sample. I'm having it analyzed first by a private lab." That was smart. If the results came out the way we thought they would, Teitlebaum could agree to give the state a swab and make it official.

"They took some CT scans," I told Teitlebaum. "Mind if I have a look?"

"Help yourself."

I left and Naresh ushered in the fellow from the lab. I went to the end of the hall, pulled out the film, and held it up to the light.

The oval-shaped, thickish layer of white was Teitlebaum's skull. In it, the textured gray was brain. There were light gray areas at the inside edge of the skull. These indicated contusions, bruises where there was bleeding and swelling inside of the brain where the head had been struck.

Naresh joined me and perched on the windowsill. "He's suffered some brain damage," I told him, pointing out the darker gray spots on the image. "We call them lacunae, a fancy word meaning holes. Carbon monoxide poisoning acts like a moth, eating away at the limbic structure of the brain—subcortical areas that mediate emotion and memory. But I've seen much worse, and in a patient who eventually recovered most of her memories."

I wondered how long it would be before Teitlebaum remembered forming the plan in his mind to kill himself. How long before he remembered attaching the garden hose, starting the car, and closing himself in the sauna? Would he remember sitting on the bench, leaning against the wall, and waiting for the end?

．　．　．

The next day, I was back at the Pearce early for rounds. There was a package addressed to me in my morning mail. It looked innocuous enough — about the size of a shirt box, brown paper, tape. It was heavy for its size and seemed to be padded around the outside.

I dropped it onto the table and stared at it. The label to me was typed, and the return-address label was typed too: S. ZAK in Pittsburgh. My brother. I'd talked to him on the phone a few weeks earlier and he hadn't mentioned sending me anything.

I remembered what the police had said to do if I got another unexpected package. *Don't open it. Call us immediately.*

While I was hovering between ignoring the warning and opening the package, or paying attention and calling the police, Kwan arrived. "I didn't know it was your birthday again. Though you do seem to be getting older more quickly than I am."

"Yes," I said. It took an effort to keep my tone light and come back at him. "Just a few more birthdays, and we'll be the same age."

He looked at the package with interest, obviously sensing nothing sinister about it. "Hey, aren't you going to open it?"

Gloria arrived, her crisp white shirt tucked into khaki pants.

"He got a present, and he won't open it," Kwan complained.

"It's just something from my brother . . ."

"Aw, come on Peter," Kwan said. "Be a sport."

"Kwan, you're just bored," Gloria said. It was true. Now that Mrs. Smetz was on the mend, our remaining patients were a fairly tame bunch. "Let's see what you got."

For a moment I was paralyzed. Common sense told me I was being ridiculous. It was just a package from my brother. More common sense told me it was foolhardy to open a package I wasn't expecting. Especially not when I could be endangering others.

"You don't look so good," Gloria said.

"Actually, I just realized I left something out in my car," I said. If I was going to be foolish, at least I could do it where it couldn't hurt anyone but me.

Before either of them could reply, I picked up the package and hurried off. I let myself out the back door of the unit, crossed the parking lot, walked into the woods behind the building. I set the parcel down on a rock.

It looked innocuous enough. No rattle. Didn't bomb squads put suspicious objects under water? Maybe it was worth the precaution.

I sprinted back to the unit and ran up the stairs. In my office, I tucked a pair of scissors into my back pocket. Then I emptied the trash from my wastebasket and carried it into the bathroom. It was too big to fit under the tap, so I had to go down the hall to the custodian's closet. There was a deep sink. I filled the wastebasket a third of the way with water and started back down the stairs, water sloshing up the side of the wastebasket with each step. I was grateful I didn't run into anyone. I wouldn't have wanted to have to come up with an explanation.

Once I was outside I could move more quickly. When I got back to the rock, I set the wastebasket down. I lowered the package into it. Little bubbles rose as the water penetrated.

I got out the scissors and snipped the string. Then I pulled open the paper. The thing inside was wrapped in bubble wrap. I pulled it away.

Inside was a book. I pulled it gingerly out of the water. It was old, bound in green cloth. On the cover, in spidery black Victorian lettering, it said *Heads and Faces*. Beneath that were the words *How to Study Them*. I flipped through. It was a wonderful old book from the nineteenth century on phrenology, the pseudoscience of how to infer character traits from the shape and features of someone's skull and face. Before I'd dunked it, it had been in pristine condition. Now the edges of the pages were rimmed with wet.

On the title page, there was a yellow Post-it. "Hey, Peter — Thought you'd get a kick out of this. A new specialty for you? Got it in a box-lot. Steve"

I felt sheepish. Of course. Steve was an inveterate yard-saler who also went to the occasional auction. Damn.

I dumped the water out of the trash can and walked back to the unit. I went inside, avoiding Kwan and Gloria. In my office, I put some newspaper on the floor and lay the book there to dry.

I went back downstairs for rounds. After that, I had a meeting. Then I did my good deed for the month and took a group of visiting doctors on a tour of the hospital.

I was back in my office, eating a Greek salad and reading the latest issue of *JAMA*, when Kelly from the *Globe* called again. I hedged when she asked if I'd gotten her message about the article she was putting together about obsessions and compulsive behavior. She went through her pitch again. She sounded sweet, earnest, and very young. "We're writing about the line between healthy coping strategies and compulsive behaviors. I'm sure your expertise can help others."

I told her no, sorry, I didn't have the time. At her insistence,

I took her name and phone number. Just in case I changed my mind.

I'd barely hung up when the phone rang again. It was Naresh. "You were right," he said. I doodled NARESH on my yellow pad. "The DNA test results are back." I wrote DNA. "Richard Teitlebaum is not the father." I circled the DNA and drew a line diagonally through it, then two exclamation marks alongside. I wasn't surprised, but it was nice to be vindicated.

I knew Nick had staunchly refused to offer up his DNA for comparison. He knew he wasn't the father, and once the government had your DNA, he said, there was no telling how they might use it. Trace your movements. Experimental cloning. I thought he'd been watching too many X-*Files*.

I went down the hall to the bathroom to wash the smell of olives off my hands before settling down to work. I needed to stop thinking about the Babikian case and start working on that journal article I'd promised to edit.

When I returned, I was startled to find Nick Babikian waiting for me. He reminded me more than ever of his game character as he sat hunched over in the chair, staring out at me from under the brim of his baseball cap.

I hadn't been thrilled when Chip told me he wanted me to finish testing Nick. "Even though he's been released from jail," Chip had said, "he's still a suspect. If he's arrested again, I want to be prepared."

I'd been putting off calling to schedule a time to finish my evaluation. Seeing him appear unexpectedly in my office, I was quickly reminded of how uneasy he made me feel.

"Did we have an appointment?" I asked, trying to keep my voice neutral.

"What did you do to her?" he asked.

"Her?"

"My mother. I went to Happy Acres to take her home."

"Westbrook Farms."

"Whatever." The words were flip, but his body language conveyed hurt.

"What makes you think I did anything to her?"

"She wouldn't come with me."

Why was this my problem? "I assure you, I didn't do a thing to her. Maybe she likes it there. Transitions are very difficult for people like your mother.' "

" 'People like my mother'? What's that supposed to mean?"

"For older people with Alzheimer's disease, change is frightening."

"But being in *there* is change. Going home isn't."

"She doesn't know that. She lives in 'now.' Change is anything that's different from now. She's become comfortable with the staff, with the routine."

"How do you know that?" His eyes sharpened. Did he think I was spying on his mother?

"Well, I'm just assuming she would be. You know I work with a lot of Alzheimer's patients." His hypersensitivity was getting on my nerves. "If she resists leaving, then . . ."

"She belongs at home! Now that I'm back, I can take care of her there. I've always taken care of her." He was building up a steaming head of self-righteousness. "You got her in there. Now you gotta help me get her out."

"I did not *get* her in there. You got her in there yourself. Actually, you're the one who left her on the steps of a place that was in no way equipped to take care of her." Immediately I regretted rising to the bait. This was only escalating the confrontation. And at some level, I admired Nick's devotion to his mother. Not many sons would do as much in the same situation.

"What are you saying?" Nick growled.

"I'm just suggesting that you think about what's best for your mother, not what's best for you."

"I know what's the best thing for my mother," he said, his voice rumbling. "I'd expect you, of all people, to understand that."

"I barely know you," I said, getting exasperated and wanting him out of my office and out of my face.

"You live with your mother too."

I started to say, "She doesn't live with me. She lives next . . ." I couldn't believe I'd been suckered into explaining my life to this man. And how the hell did he know who I lived with, anyway? I took a breath and tried to calm down. "Your best resource is the staff at Westbrook Farms. I'm sure they'll be more than happy to help you move your mother home."

"The nurse over there suggested that I ask your advice," he said. He stared into his lap. Asking for help stuck in his craw.

"You might have said that to begin with."

"Once she's home, she'll be fine. I've already got someone to come in and help out." He looked up at me. "You probably don't like me very much. People don't."

Nick had just pushed the guilt button. It was working. "It's not my job to like or dislike you."

"It won't take long. Just meet me over there. Help me out on this."

Reluctantly, I agreed. "Oh, one other thing," I said. "We didn't complete the test battery, and Chip feels we should finish up, even though you've been released."

"I don't know why he thinks . . ." Nick said, grumbling. "Waste of time, if you ask me. Can't it wait until I've got Mother home and settled in? I feel like I can't really concentrate on much until that's taken care of."

Not a problem, I told him.

He stood and slowly scanned my office, tracing the line of the dormer, across the bookcases, my Wines of Provence poster, the table with its stack of journals and assortment of knickknacks given to me by patients. Now there was a wet circle in the gray industrial carpet around my trash can where I'd stuffed the wet brown paper and bubble wrap.

He eyed the book my brother sent me, still on newspaper on the floor. It had started drying out. Too bad. It had been in beautiful condition. The book, with its watermarked pages, promised to be a potent reminder of what happened when I let paranoia get the better of me.

Then Nick's eye snagged on the yellow pad on my desk where I'd been doodling. Even across the desk and upside down, he'd be able to read what I'd written. "DNA results?" he asked, putting it together.

"You didn't know?"

"No, I didn't. They got him, didn't they?"

"Him who?

"Teitlebaum."

While I was saying, "Dr. Teitlebaum's not the father," Nick was saying, "That's just what I . . ."

Then he seemed to process my words. "No," he said, and sat down so fast he almost missed the chair. It was as if someone had chopped his knees from behind. Then he narrowed his eyes. "Who did the test, anyway? Someone Teitlebaum hired?"

I opened my mouth and closed it. There wasn't anything I could say that would convince Nick that the test by a private lab was trustworthy.

"And one day, I'm sure the police will explain the miracle of the hard drive," Nick went on, "how mine ended up in Dr. Teitlebaum's desk."

That was the thing about Nick. He'd be off on some rant, completely paranoid about bogus DNA tests or me poisoning his mother's mind, and then he'd throw out something I'd been wondering about myself. The disk drive. At least the DNA test was something I was sure about. "Why would they fake the results?" I asked, though I knew rationality couldn't make a dent in Nick's suspicions.

"He's a doctor. He knows people."

"When a doctor's accused of murder, he's just like anyone else in the system."

"Then who the hell . . ." Nick's eyes darted about. I imagined him cataloging suspects.

I stood. "So when do you want to get your mother?" I said.

"I'll call you after I talk to them." Nick got to his feet. "Maybe tomorrow?"

"After five."

Nick nailed me with a dark look. "Doctor, it's not paranoia if they really *are* out to get you."

He left without good-bye or thanks. I watched him scuttle down the hall, head down as if he were having an intense argument with himself. He turned the corner. Usually I can hear footsteps. But I couldn't hear Nick Babikian's. Just the ding as the elevator door opened, the ding again when it closed.

I shut my door. I didn't want colleagues or a patient to catch me as I did a careful search of my office shelves. I even poked up a few ceiling tiles to be sure he hadn't secreted any surveillance cameras up there.

I sat back in my desk chair, feeling uneasy. For every therapist, there's at least one kind of patient he or she shouldn't be treating. For me, that kind was Nick Babikian. Maybe I might have been less sensitive if it hadn't been for the special-delivery packages, or if Annie hadn't been getting lewd phone calls, or if no one had broken into my house. But there was a reality factor that made Nick's paranoia contagious. I could have called it by its technical term — projective identification — but that didn't make it feel any less virulent.

• • •

Later that day, Nick left me a message. Something had come up. He'd be busy tomorrow and the next day. Could we meet Saturday instead? One o'clock. Westbrook Farms. I called back and told him fine.

The next day, I called Dottie Grebow at Westbrook Farms to get her perspective. "It was unfortunate," she said. "He obviously cares a great deal about his mother, but he frightened her. Maybe it's that hat he wears. Or his perennial scowl. All I know is he filled out the paperwork for us to discharge her, went down to get her, next thing I know she's screaming. He's angry with us. Like it's something we did to her to make her the way she is. I tried to explain, it's not unusual for our residents to react like that. He just needed to be patient."

"You suggested that he consult me?"

"Not me. Maybe Carole did. We could have helped his mother if he'd let us. A little advance warning wouldn't have hurt."

I remembered Nick's mother with her salt-and-pepper frizz. How she'd howled when she first saw me, and then how she'd been waiting for her Nicky to come home so she could feed him milk and cookies. With patients who've lost their mental moorings, an old habit is a good starting point. "We'll be there Saturday one-ish. Would you mind having some milk and cookies on hand?" I asked Dottie.

"We always have milk and cookies."

# 21

"THERE'S ANOTHER package from your brother," Gloria told me when I arrived at work two days later.

Maybe he'd mailed them both at the same time and this one took longer. This time it was a box about a foot square and six inches deep. It was neatly wrapped, just like the last one, with typed mailing and return-address labels. This one felt too light to be books.

I was about to carry it up to my office when Kwan appeared. "Another present? Since when are you so popular?" He eyed the return label. "Something new from your brother? Let's have a look."

This time I figured, hell, why not. I set down my other mail and started to work on the package. I ripped off the brown paper. Underneath was a brown cardboard box. It was taped shut. Gloria handed me a pair of scissors. I slit the tape.

I opened the box flaps, peeled back some tissue paper. A doll's leg and arm were on top. That was odd. I poked them aside.

Underneath was a half a doll body, cut up the middle. Inside the hollow of its chest was the doll's head, the eyes popped out.

I pushed the box away and gagged on the smell of vinyl and vanilla.

"Your brother's got a strange sense of humor," Gloria said.

I spread out the paper wrapping. It looked just like the package I'd gotten earlier. But the postmark wasn't Pittsburgh, it was Cambridge. And the date was October. When I looked more carefully, the postage meter strip on the package looked as if it had been glued on.

"I doubt this is from him," I said.

Gloria pulled out the doll's head. It looked sinister with its empty eyeholes. "This was a nice doll, once upon a time. I had one just like it when I was a kid."

I felt like the floor fell out from under me. I remembered Annie's baby doll sitting in the chair in her kitchen.

"You okay?" Gloria asked, as she tucked the doll's head back in the box. "Want me to throw this out?"

I didn't reassure her that I was okay because I wasn't. I went up to my office and called Annie. I told her what had happened. She confirmed what I was hoping she wouldn't—that her doll was missing. She wanted to come right over.

When she got to my office, I made her sit. Then I handed her the box. She took one look, swallowed. Tears started down her cheeks. "Bastard. Lousy son of a bitch bastard," she said, her voice barely a whisper.

I drew her up into my arms and held her tight. We rocked slowly, back and forth. She took a tissue and blew her nose. "My dad gave me that doll," she said, "for my fifth birthday. I named her Jenny." Annie gave a weak laugh. "Very original. Grandma made clothes for it—a pink polished cotton dress with a lace collar she crocheted herself. Jenny used to sit in a rocking chair in my room. I was sure that whenever I left, she'd climb down off the chair and watch me from the windowsill." Annie blew her nose again. "Sappy, I know. And I don't even like dolls!"

"When do you figure —"

"I don't have to figure. I know. It was two days ago. I got home and my front door was closed but not double-locked. I'd left in a hurry that morning, so I thought maybe I'd forgotten. Nothing else was missing or looked like it had been touched even. You know how when there's something regularly there, you don't even see it? Wasn't until this morning when you called that I realized Jenny was missing."

"I think it's that damned Ralston Bridges," I said, "taunting us from jail. It wouldn't surprise me if the flyers in the bars were his handiwork too."

"He's got to be getting help. Someone on the outside. Someone he knows." She said this the same way a rock climber on a stony cliff face searches for a toehold. "A professional."

"You should get an alarm system," I said.

"I'll do no such thing. I hate having to live that way, like I'm in some kind of war zone." Now she was sounding like Kate. "It's infuriating." Anger was better than terror. Empowering rather than disabling. "Whoever's doing this," Annie said, "we're going to get him. *I'm* going to get him. I've just got to figure out how."

I called the police and dropped the package off at police headquarters later that night. It was dark when I pulled my car into the driveway. As I got out and started up the walk, I felt as if I were passing through a flashing strobe. Click, as the little video camera saw me come out of the shadows. Click, as I stepped up on the porch. Click, as I put my key in the door. For all the money it had cost, for all the work it had taken to install, it only made me feel more vulnerable.

• • •

Saturday I met Nick in the lobby of Westbrook Farms. The greeting committee of elderly ladies, mostly in lilac and pale blue pantsuits, gabbled at us from the sofa and chairs at one end of the lobby.

"Ooh, visitors!" one of them said.

"My Louie was tall like that," said another.

"Young people today," a third one said, sniffing. "Don't they know it's not polite to wear a hat indoors?"

"Maybe he's orthodox?" another suggested with a hopeful, upward inflection at the end.

Nick swiped the baseball cap off his head and stuffed it into a back pocket.

We went up to the second floor. Nick started down the hall to his mother's room. "Hold your horses," I told him. "You asked me to help. Now let me help."

He looked as if he were about to argue.

"Let me explain what I'm going to do," I said. "Last time I was here, your mother thought you were still a little boy, and she was waiting for you to come home."

"She does that all the time," Nick said.

"That's typical of people with Alzheimer's. Often, they don't have access to recent memories, although their past remains readily accessible. As a result, they're overly responsive to the environmental cues in the present that trigger those past memories.

"I know that for your mother, milk and cookies bring back the anxiety of waiting for you to come home, but also the pleasure of having you return safely. I can use milk and cookies as a cue, use the promise of seeing Nicky home safe from school to put your mother in a receptive state of mind for going with you. In a sense, I'll be lying to her. But we do it so often working with Alzheimer's patients, there's even a word for it. A therapeutic fiblet. A little lie that's harmless and helpful at the same time. You need to become little Nicky and follow my cues. Okay?"

"Okay," he agreed, though he didn't seem convinced.

I found Dottie. She poured a cup of milk and gave it to me along with the plate of cookies on a little bed of napkins that she had ready. I asked her to keep anyone in a uniform out of the halls for the next half hour. She escorted Nick to the lounge to wait for me.

Just like last time, I loosened my shirt collar and rolled up my sleeves so I'd look as unofficial as possible. Armed with the milk and cookies, I headed to Mrs. Babikian's room.

She was standing at the window. She wore a loose house dress, her pocketbook clutched to her chest. As I drew near, I could hear, "My mother was a little girl when the Turks came to her house. The soldiers' eyes were empty."

It was the story she'd recited last time I was here, told in practically the same words. This was another piece of the past that Mrs. Babikian had stuck in her present along with the milk and cookies.

I cleared my throat so I wouldn't startle her. Her voice died and she looked at me. Her eyes widened in terror, and I could hear the beginning of a howl working its way out of her belly. I held out the milk and plate of cookies. "Where's Nicky?" I asked.

Fear vanished from her face. "Nicky?" She looked at me, her eyes bright. "I'm waiting for him to come home." Her face broke into a broad smile. "Milk and cookies! Nicky loves his milk and cookies."

"Is he coming?"

"I don't know. He should be." She turned back to the window.

I joined her. "Is that him?" I asked.

A couple was walking from the parking lot into the building.

"Oh, look," I said. "There he is. He just came into the building."

"Nicky. Nicky," Mrs. Babikian keened, straining to see what wasn't there.

"He should be up here any minute," I said. "Shall we bring him his milk and cookies?"

I handed Mrs. Babikian the plate of cookies. Then I took her other arm. "He's waiting for us," I said, coaxing her out in the hall.

Once I had her started, it was easy to guide her to the lounge, the promise of Nicky propelling her forward. Nick was sitting in a corner beside an artificial ficus plant. He stood. "Mom!" he said.

"Nicky! You're home!" She brought the cookies over and stood beside him, beaming. "How was school?"

He smiled and shook his head. "Fine, Mom. It's always fine."

"Those boys? They give you trouble again?"

"No trouble."

She pushed the plate of cookies at him. "Eat! You're always so hungry when you get home." Nick took a cookie and munched on it.

I went back to Mrs. Babikian's room and got the black, soft-sided suitcase that the staff had packed in preparation for our visit. When I got back to the lounge, it was Mrs. Babikian who was drinking the milk. She put down the cup. Nick took the napkin and gently dabbed at some that had dribbled down her chin. "Let's go home, Mom."

Mrs. Babikian went happily along, out to the parking lot. She got into Nick's car without a murmur.

"You okay now?" I asked Nick.

"Thanks," he said. Gratitude. That was a first.

• • •

When I got home, there was a note stuck to my door. It was my mother's handwriting: "You have company. She's with me."

Maybe Annie had discovered something else gone missing and didn't want to be alone. Or maybe something more had happened. I knocked on my mother's door. When she answered I pushed past her and into the living room. No one was there. I whipped around. "Where's Annie?"

"Annie?" she said. "What happened to Annie? Is she sick? Did she have an accident? Is she all right?" My mother peppered the questions at me, her eyes sharp with anxiety.

I realized my mistake and tried to downplay it. "She's fine. Healthy and all in one piece. Nothing's the matter. I just thought she's who was here."

"Nice try," my mother said. "We'll talk more about this later. Right now, Mrs. Gratzenberg is in the kitchen."

"Mrs. Gratzenberg? Why on earth?" It was the last thing I'd expected.

"She tried calling you at work, but she doesn't like leaving messages. I agree. Terrible inventions, answering machines. And she didn't understand how to beep you. Electronics, feh."

Figured, a computer geek's mother would be a technophobe. But I wondered how she'd found her way here. Again, my mother anticipated. "She found my number in the phone book. I *answer* my phone." My mother said this as if it were an accusation.

We'd had this problem before, someone looking for me and finding my mother. I'd tried then to get my mother to unlist her phone, but she didn't want to be out of reach of long-lost relatives, or friends who'd misplaced their address books or their glasses.

"You know I don't list my phone number because I don't want my work coming home," I said.

"This," she said, "I know. What else I know is how beside myself I'd be if you disappeared."

"If I disappeared?" Then it dawned on me. "Jeff Gratzenberg is missing?"

My mother put her finger on her nose. I followed her into the kitchen.

Mrs. Gratzenberg was perched on a chair. A cup of tea was on the table in front of her. She stood. I remembered her as the shadowy figure who had emerged from the back of her house when I'd gone to see her son. She was about my mother's height but seemed much smaller. She held out a card, her hand trembling. I took it from her. It was my business card.

"You know my Jeffrey?" she asked.

"Yes. Remember, I met you at your house? I came and Jeff showed me some software."

"Ah, yes. I remember now. I saw you, but for just a moment. Jeffrey hasn't come home." She held her palms up in despair.

"Maybe he's staying with friends?"

Mrs. Gratzenberg set her mouth in a determined line. "No. He tells me if he's going to stay out."

"When's the last time you saw him."

"Day before yesterday. In the afternoon." She peered up at me. "You had work for him?"

"I wouldn't have had any work for him. Why do you ask?"

"He was excited. He'd found work. He left. Said he was going to meet the people. I made him dinner but he didn't come home. Not that night. Not the next day. He always calls."

Now I understood. After her son didn't come home, Mrs. Gratzenberg looked around in Jeff's basement room, hoping to discover where he might have gone to. She'd found my business card and tracked me down, thinking I was his new employer.

"Did you call the police?"

"I tried. Yesterday. Again today. They say he's not gone long enough. He's young. It's probably nothing. But I know, it's not nothing."

"Can't you help?" my mother said. "You work with the police. Can't you make them do something?"

I picked up the phone and called the Cambridge PD and asked for Detective Sergeant Joseph MacRae. The angels must have been with us, because he was there. I told him the story and asked if he could lean on whoever needed to be leaned on to take Mrs. Gratzenberg's story seriously.

MacRae pointed out the obvious: A twenty-five-year-old who's been missing for a day and a half is an unlikely missing person. I told him I knew that, and would he do it anyway. He said he'd try. Ten minutes later he called back. An officer from missing persons would be on his way over to Mrs. Gratzenberg's house shortly.

I thanked him. I hated thanking MacRae. "It's nothing, Peter. Don't sweat it," he said. I hated that even more.

"You'll drive Dobra home?" my mother asked, tilting her head my way after I told her a police officer was on the way. "And help her with the police?"

These only sounded like questions. They were actually commands.

• • •

A police cruiser was waiting for us. Mrs. Gratzenberg glanced at the neighboring houses, then across the street. I could read her face. What would they think? That her Jeffrey had another run-in with the law?

The officers introduced themselves and Mrs. Gratzenberg hurried them inside. She darted about in the living room smoothing cushions and straightening bits of lace that rested on the backs and armrests of her sofa and one stuffed chair.

The officers sat. One flipped open his pad. Sitting in the soft, deep upholstered chair with his knees up around his shoulders, he made the furnishings seem doll-sized. Neither one of them was a day older than Jeff Gratzenberg.

"You say your son is missing?" the one with the pad said.

Mrs. Gratzenberg slowly explained how two days ago, he said he'd gotten a call about a job. He'd gone off and hadn't come back. She described what he'd been wearing—jeans and a black T-shirt with white letters, some kind of slogan on it.

"That's what he wore to a job interview?" one of the officers asked.

Mrs. Gratzenberg shrugged.

"He's a computer programmer," I explained. "That's what they'd expect him to wear. If he showed up in a suit, he'd lose his credibility."

They asked about her son's friends. Girlfriends. Mrs. Gratzenberg knew next to nothing.

"You should tell them about the incident a few months ago," I told her. "When Jeff was arrested."

"You know about that?" she asked me.

I nodded. I wished it didn't matter, but I knew it might.

Mrs. Gratzenberg looked tired, her eyes sad. "You tell them. Please."

Mrs. Gratzenberg leaned back and shut her eyes, her mouth trembling, as I told the police that a few months ago Jeff Gratzenberg had been arrested for breaking into his employer's company and making a bomb threat. I told them that his employer was the man who'd been under suspicion in his wife's murder. That got their attention.

The officers asked to see her son's room. Mrs. Gratzenberg opened the door to the basement. The smell of mildew wafted up. She turned on the light. The police officers followed her down.

The lava lamp glowed orange in a corner and the refrigerator hummed. Mrs. Gratzenberg pulled a string and the fluorescent ceiling fixture flickered to life.

One of the officers started to work his way around the paneled rec room, just as the investigators had done at the Babikian house after the murder, spiraling in from the outside.

Gratzenberg's computer sat on the bar in the middle of the room. The screen was black with a glowing red, blue, and black drawing at the center. Tiny blue stars pulsed away from images that changed every few seconds. The images—the inside of a spaceship, an explosion in space, and so on—were comic book-ish and flat.

I jiggled the mouse. There was an E-mail on the screen. "Hey, look at this," I called to the officers. They came over. The E-mail contained a job description. It was from FRODO177@HOTMAIL.COM.

While the officers checked out Gratzenberg's computer, I wandered around the room. On a small plasterboard bookcase was an array of sci-fi cyberpunk novels, from William Gibson's *Burning Chrome* to Neil Stevenson's *Snow Crash*. He also had what looked like the complete works of C. J. Cherryh. His taste in literature wasn't half bad.

I went over to a shadowy corner of the room where a twin mattress sat on a box spring. A T-shirt, jeans, and jockey shorts lay in a crumpled heap on the bed. On the bedside table was a clock and a comb. At one end of the bed, stuck to the cement wall, were some strips of cork. Pinned to them were ticket stubs, a couple of postcards, some photographs. I turned on the gooseneck lamp so I could see better.

In the middle of the hodgepodge was a photograph cut from the newspaper. It was Lisa Babikian. And above it, stuck under the pushpin, was a dried clover flower. Was this a little memorial to an acquaintance? A friend? Or something more?

# 22

THAT NIGHT, Annie and I went to the movies. I was quickly
reminded why I avoided Saturday night movies—long lines and
kids running around inside, throwing popcorn at each other.
Annie had wanted to see a new Chinese martial arts flick. By
the time we got to the front of the line, it was sold out. We
decided to go down the street for sushi instead.

Over a bowl of steamed edamame, I told her about Gratzenberg. Annie put one of the soybean pods in her mouth and
pulled it out between her teeth. She chewed. "You think Jeff
Gratzenberg was Lisa's lover?"

"I don't really know what I think. He liked her. It made Nick
jealous the way he chatted her up. More than that? Maybe."

"If Gratzenberg did it." Annie said, tossing the empty pod
into the bowl, "don't you think he'd have buried the fetus in
Nick's backyard? To incriminate him, not Teitlebaum."

It was a good point. He'd want to get back at Nick for setting him up for burglary. "But it leaves us with the question: Where's Gratzenberg," I said.

"Probably with a girl. Or he had a car accident. Or maybe he's been working seventy-two hours straight. I've heard those guys can work through day after day and subsist on pizza and Mountain Dew."

I hoped it was one of the above. I'd barely met him, but I liked Jeff Gratzenberg. He deserved a break. I wished him better luck choosing his new employer.

I reached for Annie's hand. I tasted one of her fingers. It was salty and moist. Annie smiled and offered me a pod of edamame. I took it in my mouth and bit down as she slowly pulled the pod out through my teeth, releasing the nutty-tasting beans.

That's when I realized Annie looked tired. There were dark smudges under her eyes. "You having trouble sleeping?" I asked.

"I got new locks, but it isn't making me feel any safer. You've got to feel safe to sleep well."

"You should have called me. I'd have come over and . . ."

"Peter, I've been living alone ever since I got out of school. I'm a big girl. I don't want to feel like I need someone to take care of me. I want to fix the problem, make whoever is doing this stop. Not change my lifestyle."

"It's got to be Bridges," I said. "He bragged to Nick that he knew about the 'special-delivery packages,'" I said, drawing quote marks in the air. "But he's in jail."

"He couldn't be orchestrating this unless he's using a phone to contact an accomplice. Or maybe he's sending E-mail from the prison library computer. If we can get his phone and computer privileges suspended, that might shut him down."

"I like it. But other than what he told Nick, we haven't got any proof that it's him."

"I think he could get a stranger to post notices in bars. But to break in, steal, mail those packages—I say it's someone he knows. An accomplice." Annie took an edamame pod and gestured with it. "If we could lure him out." She split the pod open with her fingers. A soybean dropped onto the table. "Catch him." Annie pressed her thumb down on it. "Then squeeze until he admits that Bridges is behind all this." There was a little popping sound as the skin burst and the bean flattened.

I winced. "How?"

"You're the psychologist," she said. "What would he find irresistible?"

Past behavior was a potent predictor. He put up degrading posters. He'd defaced my father's grave marker. Destroyed Kate's pot. Dismembered Annie's doll. And rubbed our noses in the damage he'd wrought. "He's targeting the people I care about. Finding their vulnerable spot, and . . ." Nick's comment about Ralston Bridges came back to me. *Bastard like that. Knows just where to stick it, and how to twist it.* "So we need to offer up a spot so soft and vulnerable that he can't resist. Something he knows I care about, have labored over. And then wave it in his face."

We said it in unison. My car.

"I don't know," I said, immediately having second thoughts. "All that work    " I'd spent hundreds of hours working on the 1967 BMW, painstakingly restoring it until it was like new, inside and out.

"Come on, Peter," Annie said. "It's perfect. You know it's perfect. It's in your garage, not in the house. We can get the place wired so even a pro can't detect it. The only question is, once we lay the trap, how to get him to take the bait?"

I'd worked on the car to keep myself from thrashing around half the night, unable to sleep because the bed was too big and too empty without Kate. To keep myself from obsessing about what I should have sensed, how I should have acted. A benign variant of classic obsessive-compulsive behavior, working on the car served me as a distraction.

That was it. The answer to how to get Bridges's attention. I told Annie about the call I'd gotten from a journalist asking if she could interview me about obsessions and the compulsive behaviors people use to deal with them. I could do the interview and talk about the less debilitating obsessions that help turn an ordinary person into a performing artist, a collector, or as in my own case, a car restorer. The article might draw Bridges's attention.

"Maybe they'll even run a picture of you with your car," Annie said.

I groaned. I hated it. But it could work. It had to work. And it felt a whole lot better than cringing behind a barricade.

• • •

Monday morning I scanned the paper for news about Gratzenberg's disappearance. There was nothing. After rounds, I went up to my office and found the scrap where I'd scribbled Kelly from the *Globe*'s phone number. I called and told her I'd changed my mind.

She said the article was already written, ready to go in the Science section this week.

I knew I sounded certifiable as I explained to her that I could talk about obsessions and compulsive behaviors as a therapist, and also as someone who'd seen the positive aspects of it. I told her about my car. "It's extremely rare. A 2000 TC. There were only about nine hundred made, and mine is one of about two hundred imported into the country. Maybe the only one in New England," I added, laying it on thick. "A pile of scrap metal when I first got it. You could even run a picture of me and my car," I said, putting the cherry on top.

"Oh, God, that would have been so great," she said. "If only you'd changed your mind a few days ago."

"It's really too late?" I asked.

"Maybe not," she said. "Hang on." There was a moment of dead air before a Muzak version of "New York, New York" came on.

She came back on the line, breathless. "They'll hold it until tomorrow. Can I interview you this afternoon?"

"This afternoon?" I said, swallowing any second thoughts. "No problem." We agreed to meet after I'd finished work.

Now all I needed to do was get the garage wired to trap an intruder. I remembered Nick's advice: Install infrared cameras that could see in the dark; hook up the alarm to my beeper. I called Argus Security. I told Bill approximately what I wanted, and he said he could have it installed in a couple of days, easy.

That left me only one detail to take care of. I called my mother and asked if she had any lunch plans. There was silence on her end of the phone. Then, "Lunch?"

"Why? You've eaten already?"

"It's ten-thirty in the morning. I'm still digesting my oatmeal."

"So you'll be hungry by twelve or one?"

"And why exactly is it that you want to take me to lunch?" my mother asked. "It's not my birthday. It's not your birthday."

"We can go to Carberry's." No response. "Or the S&S?" I could just barely hear her breathing. "Why can't I just take you to lunch? Does there have to be a reason?"

My mother sighed. "Just come here, why don't you? I'll make you a nice lunch, and you tell me whatever it is that you don't think you can tell me on the phone."

Later, I sat in my mother's kitchen and drank coffee while she cooked cheese blintzes. Alongside the stove, she had a plate of a half dozen yellowish pancakes. Her metal bowl held a mixture that looked like creamy cottage cheese and smelled like vanilla. She sliced a hefty chunk off the end of a stick of butter. It sizzled when it hit the pan.

One by one, she lay each pancake in the skillet and warmed it on both sides, ladled on the cheese filling, folded it, and set it on a plate warming in the oven. There are no cheese blintzes between here and Brooklyn that can hold a candle to my mother's.

When she'd finished cooking, we sat together at the table. She put three blintzes, now browned at the edges, on my plate. Then another. I started to protest but didn't, promising myself instead that I'd row an extra Head piece, from the boathouse past the Cambridge Boat Club, to pay for this lunch.

I spooned a few dollops of sour cream over the blintzes and dug in. I closed my eyes and savored the thin, resilient pancakes tasting of egg yolk, the sweet filling, and the tang of sour cream. My father would have had them with a glass of hot tea with a teaspoonful of marmalade stirred in.

"So," my mother said when I pushed back from the table feeling uncomfortably full. "You wanted to tell me?"

I plunged in. "You know the break-in I had? The packages we've gotten?"

"So?"

"Well"—I hadn't quite figured out how I was going to say this so it wouldn't sound as if I'd be setting out the welcome mat for a career criminal—"I'm having them wire the garage too. In case someone breaks in there."

"And why on earth would anyone want a car that's thirty years old and falling apart?"

I laughed. "It's not falling apart! It's probably working better now than when it was brand-new. And it's worth twenty times what it cost brand-new."

Her look, the way she had her lips pursed together and raised her eyebrows, said I'd be trying to sell her a bridge next.

I went on, "And also because there's going to be an article in the paper about how I've been working on it."

My mother's look turned incredulous. "My son, the mechanic?" Minnie Sadowsky would not have been impressed.

"Actually, it's an article about obsessions, and the compulsive behaviors people use to deal with them. The car's just a sidelight."

"But why in the paper?"

"They asked me to do it."

She didn't say it, but I could hear her thinking: *And if they asked you to jump out a window?*

"Anyway. I wanted to warn you. About the article. About the garage. Just in case you decided to go looking for those boxes in the back . . ."

"The ones with Uncle Louie's postcards from Florida? And your father's harmonica collection?"

"Because if you go in there, an alarm will go off. You won't hear anything, but the police will be coming . . ."

"Before I could play 'Pop Goes the Weasel' on the harmonica."

"I didn't know you could play the harmonica."

"I can't."

She tilted her head and gazed at me. It was like watching a Pachinko game, when all the silvery balls rain down and find their way into the slots. "You *want* him to break in," she said.

"No. I don't. I just don't want you to set off the alarm. Or get frightened. Or be upset when you see the article."

She folded her arms over her chest. "This is an excellent plan. I approve. Then maybe when we're rid of him, we can get rid of these foolish alarms and cameras and keypads. And I can stop worrying about forgetting where I put the little piece of paper I keep in case I can't remember the pass code."

As I was leaving, she handed me a videotape. "Mr. Kuppel

recommends," she said. It was *The Conversation*, a Gene Hackman movie I'd seen when I was in high school. I vaguely remembered the dark story of a guy who's hired to tape a conversation between a young couple in a park.

"I already saw it," I told her and began to hand it back. Then I remembered more. Like the Gene Hackman character in the movie, Nick Babikian was an expert on surveillance. And like Nick, the character had become paranoid about his own life. "On second thought," I said, "I wouldn't mind seeing it again."

• • •

Kelly Quinlan turned out to be a tiny brunette who weighed about as much as a large housecat. She had glasses that slid down her nose when she got excited. She got excited when I showed her the car. She ran her hand over the fender. When I opened the door and she sat in it, she sighed and sank back into the leather seat and closed her eyes. Then the photographer who'd come with her took a picture of me with a chamois cloth in my hand, polishing the chrome.

We went in the house. She sat at my kitchen table, switched on a tape recorder and set it on the table between us. We talked for a while about the differences between healthy and unhealthy habits, when normal behavior shades over into obsessive behavior, and how to tell when habits become compulsions. I talked about my car and how working on it was a habit that helped me when I needed to be distracted.

"How long ago was it that your wife was murdered?" she asked.

I felt as if I'd been sucker-punched. The answer was three years, two months, and a couple of weeks. I gritted my teeth and reminded myself: I'd asked for this. There was a greater good. "Three years. I'd rather not talk about my personal life," I said.

She looked genuinely pained. She turned off the tape recorder. "I'm sorry. I just thought your working on the car might have been a way of working through your grief."

"It was very painful," I said, not wanting to get into it more deeply than that. "I don't think there are words that can do it justice."

"I know," Kelly said. "My fiancé was killed in an airplane crash. Do you ever get over it?"

She closed her notebook and looked at me. Had the sadness been there in her eyes all along and I just hadn't noticed? I smiled at her. So many of us wounded souls were walking around looking whole.

"Not really," I told her. "When you lose someone you love, it creates a hole. Grief shrinks the size of the hole. The loss never stops being there. But after a while, you can keep yourself from falling into it. Eventually, you get to where you can get on with your life without thinking about it every godamned minute"—I heard my voice rising but I couldn't help it—"of every stinking day."

The interview only took forty minutes, but it felt like two hours. Kelly gave me a hug when she left.

Bill from Argus Security arrived as Kelly was leaving. He took his measurements and gave me an estimate.

After he left, I closed the garage and stood inside in the dark. It was just a car, I told myself. If there was one thing I knew, it was that cars could be fixed.

• • •

The article ran on the front page of the Health and Science section of the paper. I couldn't read it. I barely glanced at the picture of me polishing my car and looking like I'd rather be giving blood.

Annie called me that morning. She'd told me it was fine. It could do the trick.

The phone started ringing before I'd left for work. I let the answering machine accumulate the messages from well-meaning friends who'd seen the piece.

I drove to work in a rented Toyota, hoping the BMW left in the garage all day would make an irresistible target. Even though I didn't think he'd take the bait right away, whenever my beeper went off it was an electric shock that didn't subside until I checked the readout to see that it wasn't the security company. Gloria noticed. She suggested a couple of Valium.

As the end of the week neared and work at the Pearce wound down, no alarms had been tripped.

# 23

NICK WAS supposed to come to my office to finish up the tests. At the last minute he called to say his mother's caretaker had called in sick and asked if I could come over to his house instead. I wasn't happy about doing it there. Though there was no time pressure from Chip, the last thing I wanted was for the testing to be seriously interrupted, giving Nick the opportunity to fortify his psychological defenses. In my office, I could control interruptions.

The security gates were closed when I pulled into Nick's driveway. I opened the car window and pressed the button on the intercom mounted on a post. I waited. His neighbor's yard was abloom with newly planted pansies, and the air was fragrant with lilacs that reached out into the driveway on either side. It was the last place you'd have expected to find a gruesome murder.

The gate clicked and swung open, and I drove through. In the daylight, the low-slung house with its harsh angles seemed like a scar on the landscape. The bushes that flanked the door had been pruned as they were into cubes and spheres.

As I pulled up, the garage door swung up to reveal Nick, standing in the shadowy interior. I got out and walked up to meet him. It was one of those garages that look as if no one had ever parked a car in them for fear of soiling the concrete floor.

He led me in through a laundry room. It smelled of detergent, the way it had the night of the murder. The dryer hummed, and there was a stack of clean laundry on the top. In the kitchen, the counters were clean and bare.

"Coffee?" he asked, opening the refrigerator door and pulling out a carton of whole milk. In his pressed pants and white oxford shirt with a button-down collar, Nick reminded me more of an accountant than a computer geek.

The photographs of babies were gone from the refrigerator. The calendar had been turned to June, and the photo was of a fluffy white kitten peering out from a basket of pink and turquoise yarn balls. Each day's space had chores carefully written in, like I'd seen on May's page. Lisa Babikian hadn't expected May to be her last month.

"How's your mother doing?" I asked, pouring a cup.

"She's fine. We got back and it was as if she'd never left."

I took my coffee and followed Nick through the living room and into the family room. The wood floor gleamed, but I remembered where the blood had been smeared. When I looked up, Nick was staring at the same spot. He looked at me and immediately away.

Nick sat at the edge of the leather couch. I took a chair and put my briefcase on the glass coffee table. All the masks in here were lacquered, some white-faced, others gilded. They were arranged on the wall in clusters. Did a camera lens peer from any of the eyeholes, beaming my image into Nick's basement work-room? "I've got them turned off," Nick said, reading my thoughts.

"Really?"

"You don't believe me?"

I shrugged and sipped the coffee. What did it matter if he was recording the session, anyway? I took out the inkblot cards and a blank test protocol. I clicked my pen open.

Nick looked at the cards with distaste. "Let's get this over with," he said.

"You've got the phone turned off?" I asked. "I'd like to get through this without interruption."

"No one calls me except telemarketers. If it rings, the answering machine will pick up."

The Rorschach is a sensitive test. It has no right or wrong answers. It taps into the basic personality structure of the unconscious. As the test goes on, card after card, the subject's defenses tend to become more permeable, and the person's underlying character and issues surface. With someone who's more fragile, I might administer cognitive tests as bookends around the Rorschach, starting and ending with their more structured, less emotionally charged content. I didn't do that with Nick. His defenses didn't need shoring up. If anything, a bulldozer might have helped get past them.

I started the test the way I always do. "When I was a kid, I used to lie on the beach and look at clouds. Their shapes reminded me of other things. You ever do that?"

"You want me to look at inkblots and tell you what I see."

"Right. Have you ever taken this test before?"

"No. But everyone knows how it works."

"Good, then," I said, handing him the first card.

Nick examined it. He turned it over and back. "Looks like a horseshoe crab. There's bumps on the back. And maybe gills on the sides. Or maybe a vampire mask." He pointed to two white spots. "Eyes." Then to jagged outcroppings on the bottom edge. "Teeth."

Vampires. Hermit crabs. These were pretty standard—what many people see, in fact. Although Nick had given it a twist, calling it a mask.

I showed him the second card. His eyes flicked over it. "Two men in red masks, dancing," he said. The "red masks" part was a bit more unusual. Still, this was close to another popular response. He'd integrated a card with lots of different parts into a single idea—something you see in high achievers.

Several cards later, Nick was staring at a vividly colored ink-blot. "This is fire," he said, pointing to an orange and green shape at the bottom, "and smoke." He indicated a gray area above the green. He stopped abruptly when the phone rang. The second ring was broken off by a click.

"And here," he pointed to one of the red shapes on either side, "are the bloody bodies of two lions that . . ."

There was another click from the kitchen. Then the distant sound of a man's voice. "Nick, Chip Ferguson calling. We got back the results . . ."

Nick leaped to his feet and raced into the kitchen. He grabbed the phone. "I'm here," he said, then lowered his voice so I couldn't hear what he said next.

This was what I'd been afraid would happen. Now Nick was pacing the kitchen. For a moment his voice got louder, angry. "That can't be!" Then quickly he quieted again.

A minute later, he returned and sat. His face was blank.

I showed him the card we'd been doing. "Anything you want to add?" I asked. He seemed to be looking at it but didn't say anything. "You need more time?"

He peered into my face. "You knew, didn't you?"

"Knew what?"

"That Chip was going to call with the DNA results. That's why you wanted to see me today."

"What the hell are you talking about? You're the one who made *me* come *here*."

Logic didn't ruffle him. "We could easily have finished the testing last week. Just like you had to come to the jail to see my reaction to the autopsy. You think I don't get it?"

"I don't know what you're talking about." Then I stopped myself. Belatedly I processed what he'd said. "*You* got a DNA test?"

"Don't pull that crap on me. You knew all about it."

I wondered why he'd agreed to one, after all his suspicions about the testing labs. Clearly, the results had surprised him. "Is it your child?" I asked.

"Of course not!" Nick exploded. He started to say something, then stopped. He looked confused. Then a wave of anger crossed his face. He leaned back and collected himself. "Maybe . . ." He gave his head a shake, dismissing whatever it was. "If it's not Teitlebaum's," he said slowly, "and it's not mine, then who the hell . . ."

"You want me to finish the tests another time?" I asked, though I didn't especially want to have to come back to this house, the atmosphere thick with Nick's barely controlled paranoia and echoes of Lisa Babikian's violent death.

"Just give me a couple of minutes." He put his head in his hands. "I'll be okay."

"Take your time," I told him, though I knew it was wasted effort to stay. Even if we finished, the results would be pretty empty with the flow interrupted and Nick as distracted as he was. Coming back wasn't a great option, either—he'd already seen most of the inkblots.

Nick sat there motionless, his fingers making tracks through his hair as he pressed his forehead deeper into his hands.

"I'll go outside," I told him. Maybe a walk would freshen my mood. I was surprised when he didn't object. Then I reminded myself: He probably had cameras out there watching me.

I went through the atrium doors to the back. In a little building to one side of the pool, a compressor pulsed and hummed. I crouched at the water's edge, near the spot where Lisa Babikian's body had floated, bumping up against the edge of the pool. I wondered if the pool had been drained and scrubbed down since then.

The garden around the pool was landscaped with little pathways through the bushes. Mrs. Babikian emerged from one of the paths. She was holding a spray of lilacs in one hand, the blossoms already drooping off the woody stems. She came toward me, holding out the flowers.

"Lilac," I said. "So fragrant."

She handed me the flowers. I took them, feeling her cool, hard fingers.

She put her hand heavily on my shoulder and lowered herself. She let her knees collapse until she was kneeling alongside the pool. I put my arm around her, afraid she might tip over into the water. But she seemed quite stable as she reached out, dipped her hands in the water, and drank from cupped hands.

When she looked back at me, her face was wet with tears. "She had to drink. What else could she do?" she said.

I remembered the heartbreaking story Mrs. Babikian had recited, of her mother's forced march with the Turkish army, and how, parched with thirst, they'd drunk from the river that ran red with the blood of relatives and neighbors. Now Mrs. Babikian drank from the pool that had gone red with her daughter-in-law's blood.

"Of course," I said. "What else could she do?"

Mrs. Babikian's eyes were focused on the air, somewhere above the water. "My mother hardly remembered her uncle, except for the way the Turks killed him. They burned his home, and he and his neighbors fled to the caves." The story was told in a singsong. "The Turks followed. Stacked wood in the mouth of the cave. Lit a fire. And waited. When someone came out of the cave, they shot him. Inside, my great-uncle and his wife, their five-year-old son and a baby, were asphyxiated. They were never buried."

Nick's grandmother had immersed both Nick and Nick's mother in her horrifying memories. In Nick, they'd found new life in his computer games. It was a way to make himself feel as if he had some control over the violence that had been visited upon his family. Now the images came back to Mrs. Babikian as forcefully as her own memories of waiting for Nicky to come home from school.

"They had to hide. They thought it was the only way to survive," Mrs. Babikian whispered. "My mother saw a place. This was a place where many skulls were piled very high. Not bodies. Just skulls."

Mrs. Babikian pushed herself up, leaving wet handprints on the concrete apron at the pool's edge. She drifted off through the garden. I followed, not knowing if it was safe to leave her alone. The everyday world was a dangerous place for an Alzheimer's sufferer. I'd seen patients eat flowers brought to them by caring family members, and a garden was full of poisonous plants. Even in a confined space, it was easy to become confused and lost.

She walked around to the back of the house, humming to herself. Here, the ground sloped away, and there was a door standing open to the basement. I followed her inside.

First we passed through a corridor. Midway along it, a door was ajar. Through the opening I could see what looked like an office—file cabinets, bookcases.

We emerged through a door at the end of the corridor into

a large space. The room had black and white checkerboard tile flooring, white walls, dropped ceiling with recessed fluorescent lighting. It had no basement smell of damp or mildew. I realized why, at first, the police hadn't found Babikian's workroom. Closed, I'd have assumed that the door we'd just passed through led to the outside, not to a corridor and an office.

I followed Mrs. Babikian up the stairs. "Nicky?" she called when she emerged into the kitchen.

"Can I get you a drink?" I asked her.

She jumped at the sound of my voice.

"Juice?" I asked.

She nodded. I found a cup, opened the refrigerator. There was a bottle of apple juice. I opened it and poured. I followed Mrs. Babikian to the back of the house. Her room was large and sunny, and it overlooked the pool and garden. She sank into a wing chair opposite the TV and I handed her the cup. She drank, set the cup down on the table, turned on the TV, and began to watch a rerun of I Love Lucy, her eyes blinking and then glazing over.

I returned to the family room, hoping Nick had collected himself and was ready to finish up. He wasn't there.

"Nick!" I called out.

I waited. There was no answer. It was annoying that he'd just vanish like that, leaving me to cool my heels.

I went into the living room. The masks on the walls stared impassively back at me. There seemed to be an empty spot between one mask that laughed and another that howled with rage. I wondered if the one Lisa Babikian had been wearing when they'd pulled her from the pool had hung there. And which ones were hiding miniature cameras? I approached the leering, red devil mask. Had Nick really turned the cameras off, or was he in his basement workroom now, keeping tabs on me, taking his good sweet time to reappear?

I headed back down to the basement. I passed through the door and into the short corridor. I knocked on the door. No response. I pushed it open. Nick was sitting at his desk, staring intently at a row of computer monitors on a shelf above eye level. Sure enough, one of them showed his living room, empty now. Another watched over the front of Nick's house. Every five seconds or so, the images updated. A third monitor was blank. On a fourth was the back of the house, the pool and garden. He'd probably been watching me outside with his mother.

But he wasn't watching that monitor now. He was watching the last one, another mask's-eye view of his living room. These images must have been captured earlier, because he was running them fast-forward, figures streaking past, the living room going from light, to dark, to light again. It reminded me of the time-lapse photography you see in nature programs where a seed sprouts, flowers, and dies in a matter of seconds. Only in Nick's living room, though day and night passed, people moved through, sat, and vacuumed, nothing changed.

Nick paused and watched Lisa sitting on the living room couch. She was reading a magazine. Her paleness was lost in a baggy gray sweatshirt and sweatpants. Her long blond hair was pulled back at the nape of her neck.

Jerkily, the image advanced as the time-lapse camera took a picture, then another. If the images were snapped every five seconds or so, she must have sat there reading her book for thirty minutes. Then she vanished.

Nick pushed the video into fast-forward, then slowed it again. Now, two figures were standing in the living room. Jeff Gratzenberg was talking to Lisa. He had a white sweater over his arm, in the next flash she had it. The image was too fuzzy to make out facial expressions. There was a quick embrace. A few more frames of conversation. Then the room was empty. Nick replayed it.

"Nick," I said.

He whipped around. "What the hell are you doing down here?"

"Looking for you," I said. "Remember, we were going to finish the test?"

Already his eyes were drifting back to the TV monitor, as if drawn by a magnetic pull. "Just give me a couple of minutes, would ya?" He shifted the video into fast-forward. "Hang on."

Nick fast-forwarded through more days, pausing here and there, then pushing on. Only Lisa, Mrs. Babikian, and Nick made appearances.

Finally, he pushed a button and the computer's CD drive slid open. He lifted the CD from the drive, slipped it into a plastic case. Then he rolled over to a wide metal cabinet that had a stereo system and speakers on top of it. He pulled open one of three narrow drawers. It held six rows of CDs, lined up front to back.

I wondered if the police had checked the surveillance data on the CDs in this cabinet. Or had they overlooked it, thinking all the CDs were music?

He found a spot in the drawer and slipped the CD in. Then he lifted out the one behind it. He hesitated, staring at it. Instead of opening the case, he set it on top of the storage cabinet. Then, with a few clicks, Nick shut down the program.

How many places in the house could Nick watch from this hideaway? Could he flip the channels and see his bedroom, then check out the goings-on in the kitchen? Could he spy on his employees from here?

"Impressive setup," I said.

"Pretty simple. Cameras collect the images, transmit them here."

"And you back it up on CD?"

I didn't hear Nick's answer because just then, my beeper went off. I unhooked it from my belt. I stared at the readout. At first I didn't recognize the number. Then I remembered—the security company. Saturday, middle of the day. A time I'd least expected a break-in.

Nick pushed a phone over to me. I set down the beeper and dialed. A woman from Argus Security picked up right away. She told me an alarm had gone off at home. They'd already called the police.

I hung up. I wanted to call my mother to be sure she was okay, but I didn't want to waste any time getting home. At least there wouldn't be much traffic. I could call her from the car once I got on the highway.

"You going to finish the test?" Nick asked.

"I've got to go. Someone's breaking into my garage."

Nick smiled. I didn't have time to think what the hell that was about. I raced up the stairs, detoured to the family room and threw the remaining test materials and pencils into my briefcase, and hurried out. I ran out to the rental car, got in, and started it. There was a beeping. Instinctively, I reached for my beeper. It wasn't hanging on my belt. I stared at the dash. A red icon was blinking at me—the beep was reminding me to fasten my seat belt.

Shit. For about two seconds, I considered taking off without my beeper. But I couldn't leave the staff on the unit and my patients without emergency support. Cursing, I got out of the car and ran back to the house.

The front door was locked. I rang the bell and banged on the door. I waited. Rang and banged some more. Where the hell was he? And why the hell couldn't he see me on one of his computer monitors? The garage was still open. I went inside. The door to the house was unlocked.

I hurried in and down to the basement. The door to Nick's office was open. He was still at his desk, staring up at one of the computer monitors. At first, all I could see was a dark blur, a figure moving in a closed space that was nearly filled with a large object. A car. Then I realized what it was—the interior of my garage.

"What the hell are you doing?" I said, exploding.

Nick whipped around. He glanced up at the computer monitor. Then back at me. "Hey, take it easy. It's not what it looks like."

"I don't have time for this shit," I said. I reached for the cables that were snaking off the shelf and yanked, intending to pull the plugs. The monitors rocked forward.

"Stop!" Nick bellowed. He leaped up on the desk and held them in place. "You asshole! I haven't been watching you."

"Like hell you haven't."

"Well, just now, yeah. You said Argus got the alarm. I wanted to see . . ."

Could he have tuned in to any of the images beamed from any of the cameras that Argus monitored? The ones at my house? The ones at my mother's? In trying to secure my boundaries, I'd made them more permeable. The thought left me feeling cold and exposed.

"It's like cell phones," he went on, climbing down from the desk. "Or shortwave. Or radio, even."

I checked the monitor again. The guy in my garage was moving around. He raised something like a large mallet and brought it down. I cringed. There went my windshield. As he brought the weapon up again, a rectangle of gray light appeared behind him—it must have been someone opening the back door to the garage. Was it the police already? Didn't look like a cop. The shadow in the opening was a small figure.

"Oh, shit," I said under my breath. It looked like my mother. And she had what looked like a baseball bat over her shoulder.

I grabbed my beeper from Nick's desk. I had to get out of

there. I wheeled around and charged into the hall. Nick followed me up the basement stairs, protesting. "You just have to know how to pick up the signal." Now I was in the kitchen, Nick still on my heels. "Why would I be spying on you? You have to believe me."

I didn't respond. We were in the laundry room when he grabbed my shoulder. I stopped, looked down. "Take your fucking hand off me. I don't *have* to do a goddamned thing." I flung his hand away, knocking over some laundry that had been stacked on the dryer. Nick lunged for the pile of dark pants, socks, and T-shirts, and I almost fell over him trying to get past.

"Would you just get the hell out of my way!" I pushed him aside and left.

Driving out of Weston, I ignored the stop and yield signs. Drivers on all sides honked at me as I zigzagged around them, crossing over the double yellow line to pass. I was being the quintessential Boston driver, driving with my middle finger instead of my brain. I kept seeing my mother's silhouette, the baseball bat wavering. My own voice screamed in my head. Go faster! Get home *now!*

When I got on the highway, I called Annie. I told her what had happened and that I was on my way home.

"Meet you there," she said. "I'll use my scanner to tune in to the police dispatcher."

The hair on the back of my neck stood up. Was everybody in the world eavesdropping on everybody else? Maybe paranoia wasn't a disorder — maybe it was a sensible adaptation to the realities of life.

I stayed in the far right lane on 128, pushing ninety — I hate people who do that. When one of the quarters I tossed missed the collection basket at the tolls for the Pike, I cursed and blew on through, ignoring the blaring buzzer. Fortunately, there wasn't a cop lurking to pick off toll evaders.

It wasn't until I was back in Cambridge that I'd calmed down enough to think about how odd Nick's behavior had been. How he'd chased me up the stairs. Scrambled to collect the pile of laundry, like he was hiding something. Conjurers do that. They create a flurry of activity to divert your attention from the thing that's right in front of your face. Nick was trying to keep me from noticing something. But what?

Just then, I reached my street. Annie was a few cars in front of me. I followed her. There were two cop cars, nose to nose in front of my house, and an ambulance was pulled into the driveway. A precaution, or was my mother hurt? I double-parked, leaped out of my car, and raced up the walk.

The garage doors were open. Broken glass littered the ground. A pair of paramedics were huddled around someone lying on the cement floor alongside the car. Annie was pushing her way inside.

"Stand back," a man's voice boomed.

Then I heard, "No, you can't have it." It was my mother.

The relief I felt was nearly a physical blow, throwing me momentarily off balance. Mom was in the front yard, engaged in a tug-of-war with a large policeman. "It's a family heirloom," she said, tugging at my old baseball bat. Her voice rang with the same authority it had had when she ordered my brother and me to stop using the living room couch as a backstop. "You most certainly *cannot* have it!"

"It's evidence, Mrs. Zak," he said, pulling the bat his way. "I promise, you'll get it back."

"You'll forgive me if I tell you that I don't believe you," she informed him, holding on tight. I watched with my mouth open. "And who says I used it to knock anyone out?"

"Well, the guy in there has a helluva bump on the head. And you're carrying around a baseball bat."

"And he's carrying a sledgehammer. Maybe he hit himself in the head."

"Mrs. Zak," the officer pleaded. Gently, he peeled her fingers from around the bat. "I promise, you'll get it back."

My mother saw me. She relinquished the bat. "I should live so long."

"What happened?" I asked.

My mother started to answer and stopped. She jerked her chin at the police officer. He took the hint and disappeared into the garage.

"I heard a commotion. I went to see what was what."

"You heard an intruder and went to confront him? With a baseball bat?"

She looked as if this was news to her. "I didn't think. I just did." She narrowed her eyes at me. "I guess I'm where you inherited it from."

The paramedics were taking a large man, dressed in jeans and a black parka, out of the garage on a stretcher. He had on reddish-brown construction worker's boots. They lifted him into the ambulance.

"I must have been nuts," my mother admitted.

"I'm just glad you're all right."

"Fine, actually." She seemed quite pleased with herself.

Annie was standing by the open ambulance doors. I went over to her. She glanced back toward the garage. "I guess someone took the bait. He's unconscious," Annie told me. "Blow to the head. They say he's going to be okay."

"Mom whacked him in the head with a baseball bat."

Annie's eyebrows raised. She didn't even blink.

I wasn't ready to look at my car yet. "Who is he?"

"No ID."

"You sure he's going to be okay?" I asked. I wanted the guy to recover so I'd know, definitively, that Ralston Bridges was responsible for the break-ins, for the special-delivery packages. "They'll be able to question him?"

"These guys think so," she said, indicating the pair of paramedics. "And they've had a lot of experience with people getting bashed in the head."

"And if the police can get him to admit that Ralston Bridges is responsible?"

"Then party time's over. We'll petition to get his telephone and computer privileges taken away for a good long time."

That sounded fine to me.

•  •  •

A few hours later, after the police had left, Annie and Mom and I stood in the garage. I surveyed the damage in harsh incandescent light. The roof had a couple of dents in it, and one of the front fenders had been dealt a few blows. The windshield and side window had been smashed. Ditto the head- and taillights. Stuffing and springs showed through slits in the leather. I gagged. It smelled as if cat urine had been sprinkled liberally about.

"Could have been worse," I said.

"You're taking this very calmly," Annie said.

"I knew what could happen. The point is, it worked. We caught the guy. The glass, the roof, the seats—it can all be fixed." Insurance would cover some of it. I'd have to pay for the leather upholstery. I was a lot less sure about the smell. I hoped he hadn't poured whatever stank into the radiator.

My mother looked up into a corner of the garage. I followed her gaze. "Can we get rid of those awful surveillance cameras now?" she asked. "They're making me paranoid."

"First thing Monday, I'll call and get them to come and rip them out," I told her. I blinked up at the camera. I hoped no one was staring back at me.

# 24

ANNIE SPENT the night. We made love, leisurely and without looking over my shoulder. Knowing Bridges was on the way to being neutralized, it felt as if a two-ton elephant had lifted off me.

I fell into a sound sleep but found myself wide awake at four in the morning. In my dream, I'd been the camera's eye in one of the masks hanging on the Babikians' living room wall. From there I watched Gratzenberg and Lisa talking. Just as in the video footage I'd watched over Nick's shoulder, Gratzenberg handed Lisa a black sweater. Then they hugged.

Seemed likely that the sweater was the "something" that Jeff told me he'd brought Lisa at her home. Right before he said the shit hit the fan and Nick started disparaging his work. Not long before he was arrested. I sat up and hung my feet off the bed. There was something about the dream, something I couldn't put my finger on, that was different from the actual video.

"You awake?" Annie asked, her voice soft with sleep.

"Just thinking," I said.

" 'Bout what?" Annie reached out and stroked my bare back.

I closed my eyes and savored her touch before answering. "Actually I was thinking about Jeff Gratzenberg." I told her about the dream, about the surveillance data Nick had been scanning. About Nick's odd behavior—how he'd chased me up the stairs, knocked over the pile of laundry.

"This seems like stuff the police should know," Annie pointed out. "About the CDs. Nick obsessing about Gratzenberg, who's coincidentally disappeared."

"I keep thinking I should be putting something together that I'm not."

"You think Gratzenberg was seeing Lisa Babikian?" Annie asked.

"When? Nick never let her out of his sight except when she went to see Dr. Teitlebaum." I remembered the photograph of Lisa in Gratzenberg's bedroom. "Though I have no doubt that Jeff was infatuated with her. I'm sure Nick thought it was more than that. He would."

I knew my mother was calling Mrs. Gratzenberg every few days and getting an update, urging her not to lose hope. Still, as each day passed, it was looking less and less likely that her son was off somewhere, immersed in a new job. Disappearing was like being in a coma—the longer it lasted, the less likely it was that the outcome would be a good one.

• • •

First thing next morning I called Detective Boley. "I thought you folks might have overlooked the CD-ROMs Nick's got in a storage cabinet in his home office. I'd have assumed they were music CDs if I hadn't seen him load one into his PC."

There was silence on the line. Then Boley cleared his throat. "CDs," he said.

"There's at least a hundred of them. He's probably got data from every camera in the house. Who knows how far back it goes. I only saw a few minutes of one of them."

I could hear him breathing. I imagined him calculating the hours it would to take just to figure out which CDs were relevant. And none of it was likely to help him convict Teitlebaum.

"I saw him running one that showed Jeff Gratzenberg returning a sweater to Lisa Babikian."

"Gratzenberg. That's the kid I arrested who was up for breaking and entering."

"The one who's been missing now for about a week," I said.

"You like to stir the pot, don't you?" he said. "Well, for your information, we didn't overlook them."

"You didn't?"

"No. We checked them out. There's nothing on them that's relevant to the murder case."

"Oh," I said, feeling deflated.

"But thanks for letting us know."

After he hung up, I stood there staring at the phone. I didn't believe him. He wasn't any more interested in examining the surveillance footage than he had been in DNA testing. But he'd happily gone after the duck boots, dug up Teitlebaum's backyard. Selective laziness? Or something else?

• • •

The next week got off to a busy start. We had a half dozen new patients on the unit—usually we get only two or three coming and going at a time. Gloria had jury duty, putting an extra strain on us all.

The car was back in my garage, but I hadn't had a chance to go in and inventory body damage, never mind start hammering out the dents. I'd had the car towed so the glass people could replace the car windows. Trolling the Web, I'd lucked out and found replacement headlight covers and taillights. And I'd found a place that removed the seats, promising to reupholster and reinstall them good as new. The thought of a new car with its readily replaceable parts was growing more appealing by the minute.

Friday evening, Annie came over. She'd called earlier to say that she had news. Good news. When I opened the door she was holding a bottle of champagne.

I kissed her and held her for a moment, burying my head in her neck. I loved the way Annie smelled.

"What are we celebrating?" I asked.

She gave me a mysterious smile and handed me the bottle. "Pour, then I'll tell you."

We walked back to the kitchen. I undid the wire harness. It was a bottle of Piper Heidsieck. "Must be something worthy of a celebration," I said as I eased the cork out of the bottle. At first it resisted, then began to slip. Finally, with a satisfying *thock*, it came free.

I took two champagne flutes from the top shelf of the china cabinet, rinsed and dried them. Then I poured. Annie picked up her glass and sniffed at the bubbles. She raised her glass. "To court orders!" she said, waiting for me to raise mine.

I stopped with my arm halfway up. "Bridges?"

"Yup."

"Did the guy in my garage confess who put him up to it?"

"No. He's refusing to name anyone. But remember our friend Mr. Spatola? They were able to trace who hired him. You said it yourself. Follow the money."

It wasn't quite the home run I'd been hoping for. I clinked my glass against Annie's and drank.

Annie went on. "Looks like Bridges was using the computer

in the prison library to create the flyers, using the Internet to hire someone to post them. Then he used an electronic payment service to pay him. He won't be able to do that anymore."

"Let's hope," I said. "I mean I'm relieved that he's out of commission. But I'd be happier if I knew for sure he was the one who was responsible for defacing my dad's grave. For breaking in. For my car . . ."

"Speaking of which, how *is* the car?"

"I got the glass replaced. And I'm getting new seats. I haven't started hammering out the dings."

"Dings?"

"Makes me feel better to call them that. Wanta see?"

Annie stroked my jaw. "You bet."

She followed me outside. The streetlights had come on, though dusk hadn't yet settled into night. On the porch, Annie scanned the shadowy overhang above the front door. "I had them remove the cameras," I told her.

"Glad to hear it," she said. "Those things give me the willies."

"You and my mother."

We walked across the lawn to the garage. The hinges creaked as I pulled opened the heavy wooden doors. I turned on the light. The space smelled of car wax, cement dust, and gasoline, under a thin veneer of cat urine. The car looked worse than I remembered it. Now there were holes where the headlights and taillights had been. Annie ran her hand gently across the dented roof where it looked as if he'd brought the sledgehammer down more than once.

"I'll have to take out the head liner so I can work on the roof," I told her, trying to sound like this wasn't such a big deal.

"Most of the stink seems to have departed with the seats," she said, peering inside.

"Yeah. But not all. I stripped out the carpet and I'm getting that replaced. Maybe over time . . ."

"Looks like your nights will be occupied for a while," Annie said.

"I wouldn't count on it," I said, coming up behind her and putting my arms around her waist. "You could help me. Isn't car repair something you've always wanted to learn?"

"Not," Annie said. "I like car repair almost as much as I like rowing."

"I thought you liked rowing."

"Not." Annie squinted up at the ceiling. "I thought you said you had the video cameras removed."

I followed her gaze. I shaded my eyes from the overhead light, trying to see into the gloom overhead. I thought I saw two tiny spots of yellow light, like the Seer's eyes glowing from the shadows in *Running Scared*. In spite of myself I listened, half expecting to hear distant boot heels. Get a grip, I told myself.

Sure enough, when I stepped closer the lights were gone. I could just make out a small black object mounted against the dark boards of the roof.

"Argus came back two days ago to remove their video camera," I said. "It was over there." I pointed to the opposite end of the ceiling, alongside a bare lightbulb.

"Could there have been two cameras in here, and they took only one out?"

"I . . ." It had been daytime. I'd watched them do it. Could they have missed a second camera?

"I don't like it, Peter," Annie said, grabbing my arm. "Let's get the hell out of here."

There was urgency in her voice. I welcomed it.

As we rushed out into the night air, veering away from the open doors, I thought I heard a click. Then there was a flash. It wasn't until I was on the ground with Annie under me that I registered the other sound. An ear-splitting explosion. I put my arms over my head to protect myself from the debris that rained down. I groaned as something sharp hit my back. Pieces of wood and roof shingles fell around us.

It was odd lying there. Like watching a silent movie. Through air thick with smoke, I could see cars rolling by slowly, silently. A man on a bike pulled up and stopped. He took out his cell phone. I hoped he was calling 911. I strained to look around. It looked as if the garage roof had been lifted off and squashed back down. One of the doors hung on a single hinge, and smoke billowed out.

Annie had wiggled out from under me. She was sitting up. Her mouth was moving, but I couldn't hear anything. I opened my mouth wide, put my fingers by my ears. "Hello hello hello," I said. It sounded like I was calling to myself from across a wide canyon. "You okay?" I asked Annie, mouthing the words. She gave me a thumbs-up.

As I raised up on my knees, I felt a sharp pain in my lower back. I could barely hear myself say, "Shit. What the hell . . ." I held my hand to the spot. It came away bloody.

Annie crawled over to me. She pulled my shirt away and probed gently. "Looks like you got hit by some glass," she said, her mouth close to my ear. "Hang on."

Suddenly there was an even sharper pain. Then Annie was holding out an inches-long shard of glass, looking at it as if it were some fascinating laboratory specimen, and mouthing some words that because of the explosion and the pain I couldn't make out.

She bunched up the end of my shirt and pressed it against the wound. She held my hand in her other hand. I closed my eyes.

When I opened them again, the hand in mine had turned old, the skin thin and spotted with age. I jerked my head around. My mother was alongside me. She was holding my shirt against my back, just as Annie had been doing. I wondered how long she'd been there. Her other hand pincered me in place as I strained to see where Annie had gone. Suddenly, I was cold. I could feel a glaze of sweat on my face.

A crowd had formed on the sidewalk. There were lights flashing, and people backed away and watched a hook-and-ladder truck pull up, followed by police cars and an ambulance.

A police officer was crouched beside me now. He was asking questions I couldn't hear. Now my mother was talking to him.

I wondered about my car but didn't have the stomach to look at the garage again. Two paramedics loomed over me. In short order, one of them examined my wound, rolled me onto my side, took my blood pressure. The other one talked to my mother and took notes on a clipboard. I tried to protest. I didn't want to go to the hospital. I'd be fine, I wanted to reassure them. But I found I couldn't summon the words, or move my mouth to talk. I tried to raise up on my elbows, but my muscles wouldn't work.

One of the paramedics ripped away my shirt and began to dress the wound. I bit my lip and counted backward from a hundred. It wasn't until I got to forty-three that he stopped probing and began taping.

Soaked with sweat and shivering with cold by the time he was done, I watched the crowd watching the firemen scurry about. There was the guy who ran the convenience store at the corner. My next-door neighbor and his wife. Lots of strangers. And behind one of them, a shorter man with blond hair that flopped over his face. I felt a surge of electricity through my chest. Was it Ralston Bridges?

As a police car pulled up, momentarily blocking my view, it felt as if the muffled whine of its siren was actually coming from deep inside my head. I tried to sit up, but my muscles still wouldn't respond. When the cruiser passed, the blond guy was still there. Now I could see he had a bike and was wearing a backpack. He was just a twenty-something who happened to be shortish and blond. A stranger.

SOMEONE SET UP US THE BOMB, the slogan floated back to me. Those had been the words on the T-shirt Jeff Gratzenberg had been wearing when I met him at his home. He said he had a collection of them. Where had I seen a black T-shirt with a similarly odd slogan?

Then I remembered the laundry that had gotten knocked off the dryer in Nick Babikian's kitchen, the pile he'd scrambled in front of me to grab. The garment on top had been a black T-shirt. It occurred to me that I'd never seen Nick Babikian wearing a T-shirt. He'd always dressed more accountant than nerd. Shirts with collars. On the other hand, T-shirts were Gratzenberg's everyday uniform.

There had been white lettering on the shirt. I'd seen only part of it. ARE BELONG TO US. Gratzenberg had said he had a whole collection of T-shirts with mangled translations from some old computer game. *"ZeroWing,"* I whispered, the name coming from nowhere.

I closed my eyes. I saw Jeffrey Gratzenberg handing Lisa a white sweater. Or was it a black one? No, the black one had been in my dream. That's what had been nagging at me, the detail that wasn't right.

I wondered, was that the T-shirt Gratzenberg wore to apply for his "new job"? Did he find his old enemy, Nick, waiting for him instead of a prospective employer? Why take the shirt? A trophy? And then, why launder it? Maybe to keep the police from identifying the body if it was found.

If Nick had just left the laundry there in a mound on the floor, I never would have noticed. It was picking it up that drew my attention. Typical paranoid—ends up fulfilling his own worst fear.

A firefighter was using a huge wrench to open a fire hydrant, one I'd cursed for years because it grew out of the sidewalk in front of the house exactly where I wanted to park. He hooked up the hose. In the shadows behind him was a dark figure with a cap pulled over his eyes. The loose-limbed stance reminded me of Nick Babikian.

It had to have been Nick who'd "set up us" this bomb. Who'd known all about video surveillance cameras. Who'd planted a bomb along with a camera after Argus removed theirs, then watched, waited until I was in the garage to detonate it. The fact that he didn't hesitate to push the button with Annie and me in the garage was an indication of how desperate he'd gotten. If it had worked and I'd been killed, the attack might have looked to the world like a last gasp from Ralston Bridges.

But it hadn't worked. And Nick Babikian, never one to trust anything to chance, had stopped by to see for himself. For the capped figure was still there, and I knew it was him. Still watching. I wanted to sit, to push back the fog. I struggled to sit up but strong hands pushed me down.

Now the paramedics were rolling me over on my back and hoisting me up onto a gurney. My mother was a few feet away, her eyes tense with concern. The gurney swung around and headed for one of the ambulances. I was starting to hear voices more clearly. "We're on our way," said the paramedic hovering over me. "Possible internal bleeding. Shock, puncture wound."

Nick wouldn't stop now. I had to get him. The open doors of the ambulance loomed. Shut inside there was the last place I wanted to be. I tried to tense my leg muscles, flex my knees. The paramedic who'd been holding me down yelled something to his partner and reached inside the ambulance.

There was a crash as the roof of the garage fell in. I could picture my car, transformed now into a blackened, smoking husk. It meant nothing to me. It was just a possession. In the scheme of things, it mattered not at all.

I looked back to where Nick had been standing. There was no sign of him. I searched the crowd, looking for that baseball cap and the hooded eyes, until the closing doors of the ambulance cut off my view.

# 25

TWENTY-ONE STITCHES. Stitch in the side. Stitch in time. To be in stitches. My mind meandered with the Demerol as the emergency room doc tied off the last one. I barely heard the snip as he clipped the thread. But at least I heard something. And I was starting to hear the sounds of the emergency room. My side was numb from the novocaine they'd pumped in.

Annie was there.

"I think I saw Nick in the crowd after the explosion," I told her.

I explained to her about the black T-shirt with the white lettering I'd seen in the laundry room. ARE BELONG TO US was all I'd seen. And that I thought it was Gratzenberg's.

She got it right away. "It's a slogan from an old computer game. 'All your base are belong to us.' You think he's the one who disappeared Gratzenberg?"

"Yeah. He'd know just what kind of help-wanted ad would entice him. Then when Gratzenberg shows up . . ." I stared out the window at the thicket of radio towers on the hill.

"What?"

"I don't know. Nothing good."

"Nick killed Lisa?"

"Yes."

"And tried to do in Teitlebaum?"

"That one I'm not so sure about," I admitted. At least that was one death that I'd been able to prevent.

"You're not paunchy," Annie said.

It only sounded like a non sequitur. I'd been bothered too by the neighbor's statement to the *Globe* reporter that someone "paunchy" had been hanging around Teitlebaum's house after the police left and before I discovered him nearly asphyxiated.

If she wasn't talking about me, then who? "Nick's not paunchy either," I pointed out.

Annie slid me a sideways glance. "Not to mention he was in jail while Teitlebaum was trying to kill himself."

I shrugged. "Maybe there was no paunchy person. Or maybe she just thought the person was paunchy. Eyewitness testimony is notoriously fallible. Still —"

"Still," Annie agreed.

"Up to now it's been the oldest motive in the world: jealousy and revenge. A paranoid guy finds out that his wife is pregnant. He knows it's not his child. He kills her and plants evidence to incriminate his rival. Teitlebaum. Realizes he's got the wrong guy. So he goes after the next most likely candidate. Gratzenberg. Nick thinks they were all after his wife."

"And were they?"

"Someone was. Lisa was pregnant."

"Maybe the baby's Gratzenberg's."

I didn't buy it. "Nick thought so."

Annie nodded. "So he killed Gratzenberg. And tried to kill us."

"That's what it looks like."

Annie disappeared briefly down the hall. She'd promised to call my mother with an update. She came back looking worried. She bent down to me. "No answer," she said. "Maybe she's still out talking with the cops." The clock on the wall said it was after midnight.

A half hour later, my mother still wasn't answering her phone. I'd signed off on the last of the insurance paperwork, and Annie and I were getting ready to go over to the Middlesex County Courthouse where Boley was waiting for us. I gathered up my things. As a reflex, I checked my beeper in my pants pocket. It was flashing. I didn't recognize the number.

I called while Annie drove. The phone rang once. Twice. Then a click as someone picked up. A pause. "Peter?"

My hearing wasn't back a hundred percent, but I'd know that voice anywhere. It was my mother. "Mom? Where are you—" I started.

"Shut up and listen." Now it was a man's voice. The lower register was harder for me to hear, especially with the competing car noises. I gestured to Annie to pull over.

I held the phone so we could both hear. "This is Nick. I have your mother. We need to talk."

"What the hell—"

"I said shut up and listen," he shouted. Then he lowered his voice. "No cops. I promise, you come here alone, the odds are excellent that you and the people you care about will survive. The odds drop to zero if you tip anyone off. I'm sure I don't have to draw you a map."

"Where are you?"

"My house," he said. "And don't get cute. Bring Miss Squires with you."

"Let me talk to my mother." I said. But he'd hung up.

The cell phone flew out of my hand as Annie pulled out and

made a U-turn, tires squealing. She gunned it across to Mem Drive. We made it over the Western Avenue bridge and to a red light. Annie paused just long enough to make sure there was no one coming, and tore through it.

I flashed back to my first contact with Nick Babikian. Another beep. Again an unfamiliar number on the readout. *I'm worried about this guy*, Chip had said. An understatement.

Finally we were on the Pike. I leaned forward in my seat and tried to swallow the dread rising in my throat. My mind flooded with questions. Had he really taken my mother to his home? Why? Did I trust that Nick wouldn't hurt her? What did he need to talk about that he had to abduct my mother? Should I have called the police and had them meet us there? Was his house booby-trapped? What if this were some kind of a trick?

I tried to shut down my fantasy factory. He had to be there, I told myself. And my mother had to be there too, unhurt—if frightened to death counted as unhurt. With all my goddamned degrees, so-called expert in criminal behavior bullshit, why hadn't I seen this coming?

"Shit," Annie said. Traffic clotted and we had to slow down to pass a work crew in the right lane. Huge racks of white lights blazed, steam rising, and a backhoe delivered its load into a dump truck. "You'd think with all the equipment they've got over there at the Big Dig there wouldn't be any left over to torment us here."

"Big Dig Schmig Dig." That's what my mother muttered every time we tried to make our way through downtown, on foot or in the car. I wondered what she was muttering now. Something to give her courage, I hoped.

"Your mother's incredibly smart," Annie said, reading my thoughts. "She's got great instincts for handling people."

It was after one. Why was there a line at the toll booth? Annie swerved and sped through the EZ Pass lane. The Jeep shimmied as it rounded the on ramp to 128. At least traffic was light and moving.

The air in the car seemed to thicken as we neared Weston. I rolled down the window. Annie downshifted for the off ramp, then sped up again.

She gave a tired laugh. "The guy's completely paranoid. Then, turns out he's right. Someone *is* banging his wife. If he hadn't been paranoid, trying to control his wife's every move, maybe she wouldn't have needed to break free, to sneak around."

That was the insidious thing about paranoia—its power to shape reality to match delusions. "If you think you're surrounded by assassins, eventually you will be," I said.

"Now what's he going to do?"

I thought about Nick, his eyes constantly shifting beneath the brim of his cap. Like the Seer in *Running Scared*, his mind was constantly anticipating, strategizing, defending. He'd surprised me once. It wasn't going to happen again. "He's gone to a new level. Now it's about surviving. He only seems out of control. Random. There's got to be a plan."

By now we were zipping along the winding road that led into Weston. Finally, Annie turned and headed up the hill. The street was dark, silent. Annie stopped at the end of the driveway.

"Why don't we get out here," she suggested. "Give us a chance to see what's what."

She parked the car and doused the lights. Nick's house was through the trees. We walked up the driveway, keeping to the edges where there was grass to muffle our footsteps. The security gates were open. A breeze riffled through the leaves. We emerged from the thicket.

The house looked very much as it had the first night we'd been here. Innocuous on the outside. Spotlights at the upper corners of the flat roof lit up the front lawn and brick path to the house. Lights inside were visible through the narrow ribbon windows just below the roofline.

We stood, frozen at the edge of the shadows. The front door of the house was standing open. I stared at the open door, light spilling out from the entry hall. I tried to spot the video cameras, but they were too well camouflaged. Nick was expecting us. Was he watching from his basement workroom? Would entering trip another explosion? I pushed away the thought. He had my mother, and the invitation to enter wasn't optional.

"You sure you don't want me to hang back?" Annie asked. "You can say I wasn't with you."

"I—" I couldn't stand to lose Annie if it all turned to shit. But I knew it was dangerous to underestimate Nick. He knew Annie and I would be together. I could lose before I got started if I tried to tell him otherwise. "No. We go in together."

I took a deep breath, filling my lungs with the cool night air. My back throbbed as my chest expanded. I reminded myself— only dead people feel no pain.

We stepped out of the shadows and into the spotlights' glare. If Nick were watching, I wanted to seem calm. I let my arms swing, willing the tension from my neck and shoulders. Closer now, I could see the surveillance camera mounted behind the front light.

We reached the open front door. "Nick?" I called out. I had no intention of surprising him. "Mom? You in there?"

I stepped into the house, my heart pounding. There was no explosion. Annie followed. All I could hear was the sound of a television set going somewhere deep in the house. Probably it was Mrs. Babikian's.

"Hello!" I called again, as I started through the entry hall and emerged into the living room.

Nick was sitting on the couch. Hair was matted to his head, and his eyes were manically bright. My mother was next to him.

She was sitting ramrod straight, her legs crossed at the ankles, her hands demurely folded in her lap. She looked at me, then deliberately her gaze trailed down to one of Nick's hands. He was holding something about the size of a small apple. He had his index finger threaded through a metal ring. My stomach lurched. Though I'd never actually seen one in the flesh, it looked to me like a hand grenade. I glanced at Annie. She had her eyes locked on the device as well.

"I have no intention of using it," Nick said. The masks leered down at me from the wall behind him. I could almost hear the red devil taunting me behind the mask's sneer, and the lacquered Mardi Gras faces snickering. The faint smell of decay seemed to ooze from the bird-feather masks.

Nick opened his palm. "It's just insurance."

"Mom, you okay?" I asked.

"I'm all right, Petey," my mother said. Her voice was surprisingly strong. For once, I didn't mind her calling me that. She gazed up at the gallery of masks. She looked at Nick with distaste. "I could be worse."

"You didn't call the police, did you?" Nick asked. "I don't want any fucking police showing up here. Not until I've got what I want."

"Which is?" I asked.

Nick ignored the question. "Sit," he said. Annie backed up into a chair. I went to the other chair to sit. "No, lower the lights first."

I found the dimmer switch on the wall. I pulled until the room was in half-light, then sat.

Nick slumped against the sofa cushions, but I knew he wasn't relaxed. His index finger twitched inside the metal ring. It made me queasy.

"I know it's over," Nick said, his voice a rasp in the quiet. "I thought I had it figured out. But it's no use. I'd rather give myself up than have them surround me like a pack of dogs." He seemed to gather strength as he talked. "And I will. Give myself up." He sat forward. "But I can't do that until I know that my mother is taken care of."

My mother stared at him. This was something she hadn't expected.

"There's plenty of money," he went on. "And of course," he clenched and unclenched his jaw, "no heirs." He looked at me. "I want you to promise me that you'll do everything in your power to see that Mother is well cared for."

"For God's sake, why me?"

"I—" Nick started.

"What about Jeffrey Gratzenberg's mother?" my mother asked. Nick looked at her as if she were one of his masks who'd suddenly started to speak. "Dobra is up all night, every night, sure that the police will come knock on her door and tell her they've found her son. Alive? Dead? She needs to know."

Nick swallowed. "Not alive."

My mother seemed to sag as she absorbed this news. "It wasn't enough you took away his livelihood? Destroyed his reputation?" she asked, her voice rising.

Nick blinked at her. "I thought he was the father of Lisa's baby. He denied it. I had to know for sure."

It hit me. Why Nick had done the sudden about-face on DNA testing. It wasn't *his* DNA that was tested in the lab. It was Gratzenberg's. That's why Nick had been so upset when the results came back negative.

That's why he'd had to delay picking up his mother. He'd been busy dealing with Gratzenberg. He'd lured him somewhere with the promise of a job. Killed him. Hidden the body. Had he taken the DNA swab first, then killed him? It hardly mattered.

"So you killed him, and he wasn't the one," I said. "Like Teitlebaum hadn't been the one, either."

"I didn't do Teitlebaum," Nick said. "He did that to himself."

"And you don't think burying evidence, my God, burying your wife's own flesh and blood in his backyard—you don't think that played a role in his despair?"

"He was in love with her," Nick said coldly. "You never saw them together. I did."

"Just like you saw Gratzenberg."

"You saw that for yourself. He came here. He touched her."

"That was hardly making love. He's just a kid. He liked her, that's all."

There wasn't a flicker of emotion in Nick's face. "She wasn't his to like."

"Nicky? Nicky?" It was Mrs. Babikian's wavery voice. She appeared in the opening to the upstairs hallway. She peered into the darkened living room. "Nicky?" Holding her handbag, she looked as if she were ready to go shopping in her gray pleated skirt and a pink shirt with ruffles down the front. Except her feet were bare.

"I'm here, Mom," Nick said.

Mrs. Babikian came down the stairs. She stared at Nick. At my mother sitting beside him. "Rose?" she said to her.

"Rose has been dead for eight years," Nick said.

"Nicky's right here," my mother said. She touched the back of Nick's hand that had the grenade barely hidden from Mrs. Babikian. She jerked her head at him. He slid the grenade under the sofa cushion and withdrew an empty hand.

Mrs. Babikian peered at him. "You're not my little Nicky."

"Ma . . ." The word exploded with exasperation. One of the sad aspects of Alzheimer's is that victims often remember their loved ones as they looked long ago but not as they look today. "I'm not little anymore. I'm grown up."

"Nicky?" She crept close to him, reached out and touched his face. The collar of his shirt.

"Really, it's me. Did we wake you?"

She looked confused. "I want to go out." She said this to one of the masks, a laughing white face with features outlined in black, red plumes on top.

"What's your mother's name?" my mother asked Nick.

"Nairi," Nick told her.

My mother stood and went over to Mrs. Babikian, who was still talking to the mask, the sentences now fragments, some words unrecognizable. My mother took her arm. "Nairi?" she said. Then she repeated it louder. The stream of words stopped and Mrs. Babikian looked at my mother. "Did you know Rose?" my mother asked.

A smile took over Mrs. Babikian's face. She glanced back at the mask on the wall. Then at my mother. Then down at the pocketbook she had clutched to her chest. "Go out?" she said.

"Good idea. Shall we go for a little walk?" my mother suggested.

Nick started to rise as my mother led Mrs. Babikian toward the door to the yard. He looked as if he were going to say something, to try to stop them. But instead, he just hung there. My mother unlocked the door, and she and Nick's mother slipped outside.

Nick sank back onto the sofa. He put his head in his hands. "You see why I can't just end this? I have to know that she's being watched over, taken care of."

Nick took a large envelope off the coffee table. He took out some documents and spread them out. "There's two things. A limited power of attorney —"

"Power of attorney for what?" I asked.

"I've set up a fund to take care of my mother and this gives you access to it."

"Me? Why not someone who—" I started. But I knew the answer. It was the paranoia again. He couldn't trust anyone long enough to make a friendship. His so-called friendship with Chip had survived only because they'd never truly had a relationship with one another.

"They told me at the nursing home about you. All the work you've done with patients with Alzheimer's. You know what my mother needs, and you know where she can get it."

"So now I'm the one? You try blowing me up in my garage, fail, and now I'm the one to guard your mother?"

He gave a wry smile. "Plan for all eventualities."

This was the endgame. None of the other players had survived to this level. When all the options have run out, when your weapons have run out, the only way to win was to save the hostages.

"And what else is in the envelope?"

"A confession. One document for me to sign. One for you to sign." Nick took a pen out of his pocket and offered it to me.

I looked at the papers on the table. "And if this doesn't work?"

"There is another ending." He reached under the sofa cushion. "But no one likes to play a zero-sum game," he said, his expression changing from calm to perplexed. Then angry. "Shit," he said, flinging the cushion to the floor. In a moment more, he had all the sofa cushions off. "Where in the hell—"

We all looked outside. My mother was walking Mrs. Babikian around the pool, arm in arm, their heads bowed as if they were deep in conversation.

Nick rushed for the door. Annie and I followed. Nick flipped on the outside lights. Spotlights at the corner of the house lit up my mother and Mrs. Babikian, casting their shadows deep into the woods. The pool glowed aquamarine. There, in the deep end, near the drain, was a small dark object. The grenade.

It was Mrs. Babikian's voice that broke the silence. "My parents lived in Erzurum," she said.

"Mom, no," Nick said, moaning.

Mrs. Babikian stared off into space, unhearing. "The Turks came to their house." Her voice was a singsong. "The soldiers' eyes were empty, faces like masks."

"Oh, God," Nick said, staggering back and leaning against the side of the house, "please, not again."

"They took my mother and made her follow them. Tied them together with ropes. It was snowing. My grandmother . . ." Her voice wavered and seemed to float above the pool.

"No!" Nick screamed.

"My grandmother . . ." his mother whispered.

Nick shook his head back and forth.

"My grandmother . . ." Mrs. Babikian said, this time louder.

He looked up at her. She opened her palms to him, as if begging him for change. He walked over to her, took her hand.

"My grandmother," he said, taking over, his voice now low and lilting, "they dragged her into the courtyard. They dragged her and threw her onto the dirt."

Mrs. Babikian listened. She was humming under her breath.

"She was pregnant," Nick went on. "The gendarmes looked at each other. 'Boy or girl?' one of them said, like it was a guessing game."

"Brrgrr, brrgrr," Mrs. Babikian intoned. It was the same sound I'd heard her make before. *Boy or girl? Boy or girl?*

"Then, one of them sliced her open," Nick continued, his voice gliding over the word *sliced* as if it held no horror. "He reached in and took the baby from her belly. He threw it against the church wall and screamed, 'Boy!' "

The final word was shouted. Mrs. Babikian looked up, as if she were watching the word as it spiraled up into the night sky.

"Boy . . ." Nick whispered, a tear making its way down the side of his face. "It was a boy."

Mrs. Babikian only nodded to herself.

NICK AND I sat on the front steps of his house, waiting for the police to arrive. I'd agreed to ensure that his mother was taken care of, and he'd signed his confession.

"Lisa said she was going to leave me," Nick told me. "Didn't love me anymore." He gazed out at the trees surrounding his property, his voice low. "She said there was no point in arguing about it. She was going to have a baby. Another man's child. If I loved her, I'd let her go." He shook his head. "I couldn't do that."

I sat, looking down into my lap, not saying anything. I wondered why he was telling me this. It was just a rehash, almost verbatim, of his written confession.

"We argued. I was desperate. I picked up the fireplace poker. I wouldn't have hit her, but she didn't know that. She screamed and tried to get the poker from me. That's when my mother came in. She saw us struggling, shouting at one another."

Nick kneaded his hands over and over. "When the poker fell

to the ground and Lisa grabbed it, my mother must have thought Lisa was going to hurt me. She attacked Lisa. In the confusion, Lisa fell backward onto the coffee table, hitting her head on the corner."

"Why didn't you call an ambulance?" I asked. "You could have explained. It was an accident."

Nick started to say something. He faltered.

"She might not have even been dead," I said.

"I thought she was. I . . . I don't know."

"So you just left her there?"

"I made breakfast for Mother," Nick said, his face grim. "Then I went back to Lisa. I picked up the poker . . ." He closed his eyes.

"And you struck her."

"Once. Twice." He shuddered. "I kept hearing this voice in my head. *Boy or girl? Boy or girl?* I carried her out to the pool. That's where I cut her. The baby was so tiny." Nick cupped the palm of his hand, as if the unborn baby could fit into it.

Nick glanced at me. I wondered if he was gauging my reaction.

"Then I took a shower, changed clothes. I drove my mother to a nursing home, one I'd passed every day on my way to work. After that, I went to Teitlebaum's and buried their baby. He'd taken her from me. I had to make it look like he killed her."

"Then you returned home and called Chip?"

He nodded.

"What about the shoes?" I asked.

"The shoes?" At first he looked confused. Then his eyes shifted back and forth. "Teitlebaum's shoes. I—" He cleared his throat. "When I buried the baby, I saw the shoes. That's when I got the idea. It was one more piece of evidence for the police to find. I brought the shoes home, tracked them around, then brought them back."

I didn't say anything. Two trips back and forth to Newton? It would be up to the forensics experts to determine whether there had been time. I looked at the steam rising off the pool and wondered. It cost a small fortune to keep a pool heated in May when almost no one in New England swims. Had the pool been heated deliberately to blur the time of death?

"And why the mask?" I asked.

A shadow of satisfaction crossed Nick's face. This was a question he was ready for. "I couldn't cut her. I couldn't. But I had to do it. So I covered her face."

It would fit with Teitlebaum's account that Nick couldn't make love to his wife unless she was wearing a mask. It was part of his pathology, that he couldn't be physically intimate with her without covering her face. I'd never considered butchering a form of physical intimacy, but I supposed it was.

Then I asked the question that had been bothering me. "Why did you pick Teitlebaum?"

"Pick?" Nick seemed genuinely surprised. "Lisa picked him."

"She did, did she?"

He looked at me evenly. "C'mon? You think it was my idea to see a shrink? She's the one."

I had no doubt that Lisa was the one who'd initiated therapy. But would she have picked a therapist whose most famous former patient had been murdered by her husband? Or did she pick Teitlebaum not realizing his past? It was too big a coincidence for me to swallow.

"But—" I stopped short. Was this what Nick was up to? Rehearsing his story with me, working out the kinks before running it up the pole with his real interrogators?

It seemed a whole lot more likely to me that when Lisa announced she wanted to seek counseling, Nick knew the marriage was unraveling. He started to plan her murder. He put the pieces in place, just as carefully as he designed one of his games.

He picked Teitlebaum precisely *because of* his connection to the Ely case. And I was pretty sure there had been time for only one trip to Newton — to return the shoes. If Nick took Teitlebaum's shoes before the murder, that suggested planning, not an accident followed by a break from reality.

Nick had researched Teitlebaum. Found a shrink with just the weak spot he could exploit. It was probably a strategy Nick had used before. Find a weakness. Then I remembered what Nick had said when I met him at Bridgewater. *I've been reading up on you. You're the shrink whose wife was killed, aren't you?* Was that how Nick had found my weakness? Found out about my wife's murder on the Internet, then exploited my vulnerability? I wondered how much of what I'd been blaming on Ralston Bridges was really Nick Babikian's work.

Now Nick wanted me to believe that Lisa's death started out as an accident. But I knew in my bones that none of it had been accidental. Every action had been planned. Just as I had no doubt that him sitting here with me, waiting for the police to arrest him, had been planned too.

He'd accused me of arranging it so I'd be at his home when the call with the DNA results came in. But he was the one who'd set it up. He wanted me to be there when my garage got broken into, when my beeper went off. It seemed too convenient, unless it was by design. And if it was by design, that meant Nick, not Bridges, was responsible for destroying my car. If he was responsible for destroying my car, then what about the special-delivery packages? He'd been in my office the day the old book on phrenology came from my brother. He'd seen it drying on the floor. I could imagine him coming into my office, finding it empty. He'd have checked things out, the way he checked everything out. And yes, he'd even have looked in the trash can, the way he went through his employees' trash each night. He'd have found the wrapping paper, the address labels.

It would have been easy to make another package that looked like it was from my brother, containing Annie's doll.

There was the sound of gravel crunching and two police cruisers emerged from the shadows.

"And all those packages? That was all your doing?"

"Not all," he said, staring into the headlights. "I had to keep you off balance. Otherwise you'd figure it out before I made him pay."

"Him?"

Now Nick looked genuinely anguished. Here was the rub. For all his careful planning, attention to detail, watchfulness, he still didn't know who "him" was.

• • •

After the police left, I walked back into the kitchen. This was the one place in the house where I could feel Lisa Babikian. The gingham curtains. The canisters with their mushrooms and elves. The room echoed with the ticking of the cat clock, its tail twitching back and forth. I wondered what Nick had done with the pictures of the infants that had decked the refrigerator.

Did Nick still see a way out? Even if he got off with manslaughter for his wife's death, Gratzenberg's murder would be harder to wriggle out of. The police could compare the DNA evidence that Nick supplied to DNA Gratzenberg's mother could provide, perhaps a strand of his hair, and show that they were the same. Between that, the T-shirt, and the confession, surely there'd be enough to make a case. And for Mrs. Gratzenberg's sake, I hoped that the police would find her son's body.

One question remained: Who was Lisa's lover? I went over to the door to the laundry room and stood, staring at the wall calendar that still hung there. There were June's kittens, and Lisa's handwritten chores and appointments. Monday, laundry. Tuesday, grocery shopping.

When? I wondered, as I ran my finger along the calendar boxes with their neatly printed chores. When could Lisa have sneaked away to meet with her friend?

Her two appointments with DR. T. seemed to be the only times each week when Lisa wasn't under surveillance or with her husband. No wonder Nick had suspected Teitlebaum.

I wanted to kick myself. I'd been in Teitlebaum's house, had his datebook right in front of me. But I hadn't known what to look for. I glanced at the phone. Would Teitlebaum be released yet? Probably not.

I traced down the column of Tuesdays, then the column of Fridays. If I was right, then Lisa only had one appointment each week with Teitlebaum. The other one was a shill, giving her the cover she needed to meet with someone she cared for.

Which was it? I stared at the calendar, willing it to render up its secrets. I paged back a month. Then another. I found the week in mid-January when Lisa had her first solo appointment with Dr. Teitlebaum. That must have been right after the break-in. After Jeffrey Gratzenberg was arrested for breaking and entering. Right after Lisa realized she was being spied on.

The first appointment was on a Friday. There was no Tuesday appointment that week. Or the week after. It wasn't until the last week of February that Tuesday appointments got added. Tuesdays. Since February.

The doorbell rang. I went out to the front hall. My mother had answered it. It was the van sent over by Westbrook Farms to fetch Mrs. Babikian. My mother had packed her a suitcase. After reassuring me that she was unharmed, she'd insisted on riding over with Nick's mother. "Transitions," my mother had said. "They're the hardest part of getting old." Once again, I realized how much of psychology she gets intuitively.

After they left, I showed Annie the kitchen calendar and explained what I'd discovered.

"Tuesday nights," she said. The look she gave me said she'd realized something that I didn't.

"What?" I asked.

Annie pressed her lips together.

"You're not going to tell me?"

"I need to be sure. You said there's surveillance data downstairs? Let's have a look."

We went down to Nick's basement office. His computer was on. I opened the top drawer of the CD storage cabinet. "What do you think these mean?" I asked Annie, indicating the tabs separating blocks of CDs: FD, BY, LR, 01, 02.

"Maybe which camera?" she suggested. "Front door. Backyard."

I fingered the third tab. "Living room." I flipped through the CDs. They were labeled by date. Which was the one I'd watched Nick going through? It had shown Gratzenberg returning Lisa's sweater. Had to be before the break-in, before he was arrested. I pulled out the one labeled "1/1–1/16."

I took the CD out of its case, inserted it into the drive, and brought up the list of files. They were numbered sequentially. I clicked on the first one. A video window with a control panel appeared, similar to the setup of buttons on my VCR at home. I clicked and the video started.

It was the Babikians' living room. There was a date stamp at the bottom. January 1. The room was dark. I remembered how Nick had used the control bar to move the video fast-forward. I tried it. The room grew light. I watched as Nick, Lisa, and Nick's mother moved quickly through. There were long periods of no one there at all. Then dark. Then light again. Then people flashing through, in and out of the room. Then Lisa sitting with someone who turned out to be Nick.

When one file ended, I opened the next. More days passed. Then Jeff Gratzenberg was there.

I slowed the images. The date stamp was January 12. It was the scene I'd watched over Nick's shoulder: Jeff Gratzenberg talking to Lisa, giving her back her sweater. The quick embrace. Then the empty room.

Like Nick, I scanned quickly through the rest of the images. Then I put away the CD and got out the next one. It was labeled "1/16–2/3."

I started slowly, then pushed on quickly through the images. People entered and left the living room, day turned to night and back again. Nick. Lisa in her bathrobe. Lisa in a pale blue sweat suit, carrying a basket of laundry. Mrs. Babikian and Lisa. Lisa on the couch. Then I caught something I needed to go back to. A shadow in the foreground. I backed up.

Lisa was seated on the couch. A figure stood, back to the camera, just visible at the edge of the frame. Lisa talked, listened. She smiled. It was the first time I'd seen her smile. She talked some more. Then the room was empty.

The next day, the figure was there again, this time farther from the camera, closer to Lisa. It looked like a man in a suit. Most of his broad, dark back was in the frame. For a few camera clicks, Lisa did a jerky 360, staring at the walls of the room, one after the other. Suddenly, the image went dark for a few beats, then cleared to show Lisa's face hovering directly in front of the camera's eye. She backed away, her hand over her mouth. A click later and the room was empty.

I reran the sequence. The date was January 21.

"Shit," Annie said. "Boley *had* to know about the surveillance cameras."

He'd never actually looked into the camera. He'd known better. "So Boley was the one who tipped Lisa off about the surveillance cameras," I said. "I wonder how long after that before she confronted Nick with her discovery?"

"Or did she?" Annie said.

That stopped me. I'd just assumed that Nick knew. But now that I thought about it, I had no reason to assume so. Teitlebaum knew she knew. But maybe Nick didn't.

I put away the CD and pulled out a later one. I brought up February 28. That had been the first Tuesday evening appointment written in Lisa's calendar. On this day, Lisa didn't linger in the living room long enough for the camera to catch more than a flash of her passing through. There wasn't much to see, other than at sometime around six in the evening, she changed into a dress and let her hair down. "The first Tuesday night," I said.

"Poker night," said a voice from the doorway. Annie and I looked up. Detective Boley was framed in the opening. I remembered how his pals at Johnny D's had thumped him on the back, acted as if he were a long-lost friend. That had been the first Tuesday night after Lisa Babikian's murder.

"Hey, Al," Annie said.

"Hey, Annie."

"You knew we'd figure it out," Annie said.

He looked tired, whey-faced. Like if you poked him, the flesh wouldn't spring back. He smelled as if he'd been drinking.

"You were Lisa Babikian's lover," I said, putting the last piece in place.

Boley didn't bother to deny it. Now his odd behavior made sense. Why he'd been so upset at the murder scene. Why he'd gone white when he first found out what had happened. It explained why he'd want to obstruct any DNA testing. The fetus's DNA wouldn't match that of any of the suspects because it matched his. He hadn't immediately found the surveillance setup because he needed time to destroy the surveillance video, in case there was evidence linking him to Lisa. He probably figured he'd gotten it all when he smashed the hard drive. Then, when I told him about the CDs, he'd acted as if they'd already examined it.

"Been a hard couple of weeks?" I asked.

"I've had worse," he said, his voice slurred. Boley gazed at the computer screen. There was Lisa Babikian, frozen as she'd been before her first Tuesday night with Boley. "He treated her like a child. Took away her will to be anything. To want anything. She couldn't even think for herself."

"Tampering with evidence," I said.

"Yeah, well . . ." He shrugged.

"Comes with the territory?" Annie asked.

Boley flinched.

"You took the hard drive because you were afraid it might show that you and Lisa had a thing going," I said. "You even planted the hard drive in Teitlebaum's desk. Didn't it bother you, what you were doing?"

"I thought he was the one," Boley said.

"What now?" Annie asked.

Boley looked at her. "Case closed."

"And you get the credit for putting away another killer?" Annie said.

"It's my job," Boley said, managing a weak smile.

"Yeah, that's your job, all right," Annie retorted. "Find the shortest distance between two points, never mind who gets run over. And the world is full of Lisa Babikians, isn't it? Young, unhappy women just begging for what you have to offer."

"Give it a rest," Boley said.

"Sooner or later, you're going to make a mistake," I said.

"Take your sanctimonious—" Boley started.

"You almost did this time," I said, cutting him off.

"Better be more careful who you hit on. Everyone knows," Annie said. Boley looked back and forth from Annie to me. "They do. Your buddies are covering for you. Sooner or later, you're going to do something even they can't look past. And I can't wait."

Boley dismissed Annie with a shrug. "You got nothing on me."

He turned and trudged up the stairs. Annie and I followed. We watched as he wandered through the kitchen. He stopped in front of the refrigerator. He stared at the photograph of Nick and Lisa, all dressed up, her looking at him, him looking away. It was the way they'd approached life.

Boley went over to the window. He picked up a little ceramic angel from the ledge. It looked so incongruous in his beefy hand. He slipped it into his pocket.

After Boley left, Annie rested her hand on my shoulder. "See? You're definitely not paunchy."

"Guess the neighbor was describing Boley," I said. "But you already knew that, didn't you?"

# 27

A WEEK later, Mrs. Babikian had settled in again at Westbrook Farms. I'd hired a geriatric care manager to keep tabs on her. The police had found Jeff Gratzenberg's body, stuffed into a plastic barrel in a storage room behind Cyclops Productions. The autopsy results weren't back, but speculation was that death was due to strangulation. Richard Teitlebaum was at home recuperating. And there was a profile of homicide detective Al Boley in the morning paper—he'd set some kind of record in murder cases solved.

It was noon and I'd sneaked away from work. Annie had agreed to go rowing with me, and I didn't want to give her time to change her mind. She was helping me lower a double scull from an overhead rack at the BU Boathouse.

"I want to see Nick Babikian locked up until he's an old, old man," she said. "I hope to hell his attorneys don't think they're going to have a chance with NGI or dim cap."

We set the boat on our shoulders and headed out through the double doors onto the deck.

"Delusional disorder," I said. "Believing you're Mary, mother of God, is one flavor. Another is believing that the world is out to get you. I don't think there's any question that Nick suffers from paranoid delusions. Will the jury swallow that he had no control over his actions? That the paranoia compelled him to kill? That seems like a long shot to me. Especially in Massachusetts." We carried the shell upside down on our shoulders. "I'm just glad it won't be up to me to convince them." After he was arrested, Nick had been furious when Chip told him he was resigning as his attorney.

"You got pretty paranoid yourself there. For a while, anyway."

Annie was right. I'd watched *The Conversation* a few nights earlier, the movie recommended by Mr. Kuppel. What had surprised me was how I found myself identifying with the paranoid surveillance expert, Harry Caul. Like him, I never knew if I was working for the good guys who were trying to defend themselves against evil forces, or whether I'd been hired by the bad guys who were using my skills to entrap and endanger innocent people. Good and evil were more or less indistinguishable, had the same rights and privileges in the criminal justice system. And like Harry Caul, I'd come to know the insidious pull of paranoia. By fomenting my own anxiety and paranoia, Nick weakened me as a potential adversary, one less person who might see through his carefully constructed defense. I could easily relate to the uncertainty that drove Harry to tear apart his home to the floorboards, looking for planted surveillance devices.

When I'd brought the tape back to Mom, she had a package for me. I must have blanched when I saw the brown paper wrapping. "Don't worry. It's just your father's harmonicas."

"You saved them?"

"Of course," she'd said, like it had been a no-brainer. "Your

Uncle Louie's postcards?" She shrugged. "Well, I didn't care so much about them."

Annie and I stopped at the edge of the dock. We rolled the boat off our shoulders and set it into the water. The sky was a brilliant blue, and there was barely a breeze.

"Promise I won't fall in?" Annie said, looking out over the water.

There wasn't much traffic on the river. Only a few teams practicing in eights. If you're going to learn to row, noon is the time to do it. Early morning or late afternoon, we'd have wreaked chaos in the river crowded with varsity rowers.

"I can only promise that if you fall in, I'll fall in with you."

"Why don't I find that reassuring?" Annie distastefully eyed the brown, opaque liquid we call river water.

Annie held the boat while I went back for the oars.

I took off my sneakers. "Hold onto it now," I said. I put one foot in.

She watched in silence as I fastened the oars in place.

I stepped back on the dock. "Lesson one: getting into the boat," I said. Annie winced. "Take off your shoes and crouch."

Annie took off her shoes and squatted by the boat. "You're enjoying this, aren't you?"

I grinned. "Now grab both oar handles, step in, and sit."

I held the boat steady. Annie stepped in easily, as if she'd been doing this all her life. But once she was seated, she gripped the edges as the boat shimmied in the water, then steadied.

"Okay, now slip your feet into the shoes and fasten them."

"How come I get the front?" Annie asked as she worked on the shoes that were fastened to the cross stretchers.

"You don't. You're in the stern. Facing backward."

"Figures," she muttered. "Just like dancing."

"When you get used to this, Ginger, I'll let you lead," I said. "Promise."

I crouched, grabbed my oars, steadied myself. "Hold onto the dock," I said. "I'm getting in." I stepped into the boat.

"Holy shit," Annie said, exhaling as the boat sank lower, the edge now only three inches above the waterline.

I tied in, fastening the Velcro, then pushed away and took a few strokes so we'd be clear.

Just then, three racing eights came zooming down on us. Annie gave a yelp and I froze. The eights managed to maneuver around us, the last one brushing the tip of our oars.

"Sorry about that," the coxswain called out. "You okay?"

"Fine," I hollered back.

"Okay, that's it," Annie said as we bobbled on their wake. "You can let me out here. I'll walk."

"You can't wimp out on me now. Besides, it was his fault. We had the right of way."

"Said the sports car to the ten-wheeler," Annie muttered.

I ignored it. "Lesson two: taking a stroke."

I started her on the same drill she'd done in the tank. Annie steadied herself, evened her hands, pulled her knees to her chest, and took a smooth, clean stroke. Then another. I kept my oars flat on the water to provide a stable platform, training wheels.

I'd never seen anyone pick it up so fast. As the boat began to move, I joined in. We were gliding along more quickly now. I swiveled my head around after every stroke or two, keeping an eye over my shoulder to make sure we were going straight.

"Are we having fun yet?" Annie asked. "This feels like I'm doing all the work and you're giving all the orders."

"And I have the best view," I said as I watched Annie's back curve and straighten, her muscles rippling, her shoulders shining with sweat. Her stroke was equal to mine in duration, almost in strength. This was something I'd known would be true, without knowing I knew.

. . .

"It wasn't as awful as I thought it would be," Annie admitted when we got back to my place an hour later. Neither of us had eaten lunch.

We were in the kitchen, unpacking the bread and cheese and salad we'd picked up at Bread and Circus. Annie's hair was damp, and she smelled soapy from the shower. I uncorked a bottle of everyday red. Annie poured while I got out plates.

"How does someone get to be so paranoid that it colors his every experience?" Annie asked as she unscrewed the corkscrew from the cork.

"When one family member experiences a life-threatening blow, as Nick's grandmother did during the Armenian holocaust, it can result in a kind of psychiatric contagion. It gets passed from parent to offspring. Empathy serves as the vector for the disorder."

"Indeed, Herr Doc-tor," Annie intoned. "Meaning?"

We carried the plates and glasses out into the living room. Annie took the morris chair and I took the couch.

"Meaning that, in a sense, he may well have caught it from his grandmother. Certainly his mother, who never actually experienced the horrors, behaved as if she did.

"We had a patient a few weeks ago. A couple of weeks of sixty-milligrams of Prednisone made her delusional. For Nick, it was that steady diet of irrational fear that his grandmother and mother fed him." In turn, I'd almost caught a terminal dose of it from Nick.

"If he hated the Turks, then why did he act like one, killing his wife and then cutting her that way?" Annie asked.

"Identification with the aggressor," I said, putting the technical name to it. "His family had barely survived extermination. Nick was beaten up all the time growing up. Identifying with your aggressor is one way to maintain a sense of self when you're constantly being assaulted both physically and psychologically. As you experience more stress, you take on the characteristics of your aggressor, and in so doing borrow some of his perceived ego strength as a way of bolstering your own failing defenses.

"The stressor for Nick was his mother's illness. He was so enmeshed with her, and then her Alzheimer's pushed the paranoia that was already there into the semipsychotic realm. Psychotic defenses distort reality. He projected his own fears into the environment and then saw them come back on him.

"Then Nick discovers Lisa is leaving him. It's an assault on his ego that is incredibly damaging. To him, it means he's not a man. So who's the most powerful person he knows? The Turk. His response is to identify with what has been his lifelong aggressor."

"So he becomes his own worst enemy," Annie said.

"Literally."

Annie leaned back in the chair. She sat forward and adjusted the seat back. Then she settled again. I watched with my mouth open.

"You adjusted my chair!" I said.

Annie looked at me, surprised. "Now you *are* acting paranoid. See?" She pointed to the notches. "You're *supposed* to adjust it."

"Have you ever done that before?"

"I . . . I . . ." she sputtered, laughing. Then she saw I was serious. "I think so. Maybe."

I remembered. Annie had come over after my first special-delivery package. We'd opened a bottle of wine. Had she sat in the chair? I couldn't remember for sure. That was how it worked. Something bad happened, leaving you feeling vulnerable. Then you found yourself interpreting small, unexpected changes in your everyday environment as menacing.

I charged into the kitchen. The cork was on the kitchen counter, but the corkscrew wasn't. Annie came up behind me. "The corkscrew?" I said.

"I put it away," Annie said.

I reached for the drawer where I usually kept it. It wasn't there. Annie opened the silverware drawer. There it was.

"And I thought . . ." I said.

"What did you think?"

"After the break-in, my chair was adjusted too far back. And my corkscrew was in the wrong drawer."

"And you thought you had an intruder?" Annie asked. I nodded. "When all you had was me." Annie sauntered back into the living room. She settled back into the chair, adjusting it once more.

"Well, I guess in a sense you do. Have an intruder, that is," she said. "Don't you think it's about time you got used to it?"